THE GOLDEN AGE OF SCIENCE FICTION was considered to be a time when science fiction was a male domain. The reality, of course, was somewhat different. Women both wrote and read science fiction, but, at least in the case of those who wrote it, the fact that they were women was usually kept secret, hidden by a pseudonym or the use of initials.

Now sixteen creative talents, all of whom happen to be women, show us that they can not only write for men, but can write as if they were men. See how they met this entertaining challenge in such stories as :

"What Goes Around"—He'd been hired to do the unthinkable, to reap his employer's revenge on "good cops." And he'd found the perfect way to get away with it . . . or had he?

"Sweeps Week"—He finally had the proof he needed about the alien invaders, but sometimes finding out the truth can prove dangerous. . . .

"A Good Idea at the Time"—He'd learned to live in the past and the future, but whose past and future was it—and could he find the way back to his own?

More Imagination-Expanding Anthologies Brought to You by DAW:

Wondrous Beginnings *Edited by Steven H. Silver and Martin H. Greenberg.* The writers included in this volume are a real "who was and is who" in the field of science fiction, from such masters of science fiction's Golden Age as Murray Leinster, L. Sprague de Camp, Hal Clement, and Arthur C. Clarke; to a number of today's hottest-selling and award-winning authors such as Anne McCaffrey, Gene Wolfe, George R. R. Martin, Orson Scott Card, Lois McMaster Bujold, and Stephen Baxter. How and where did these writers get their start? Now you can find out by reading the stories that began their careers, along with an introduction by the author which offers insight into the genesis of both the particular story and the individual writer's career.

DAW 30th Anniversary Science Fiction Anthology *Edited by Elizabeth R. Wollheim and Sheila E. Gilbert.* In celebration of DAW Books' thirtieth anniversary, there are nineteen original stories by some of the authors who have helped to make DAW the landmark science fiction publishing house it is today. Includes stories by C. J. Cherryh, Tad Williams, Brian Aldiss, Frederik Pohl, C. S. Friedman, Kate Elliott, and many other top authors in the field.

Future Wars *Edited by Martin H. Greenberg and Larry Segriff.* Ten all-original tales of the many possible ways in which conflict may be carried out, resolved, or avoided in the future. Includes stories by Barry Longyear, Kristine Kathryn Rusch, William H. Keith, Jr., Bill Fawcett, Robert J. Sawyer, Robin Wayne Bailey, and more.

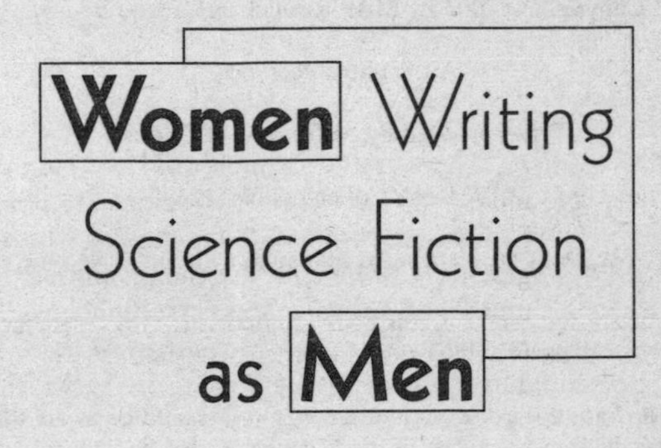

Edited by Mike Resnick

DAW BOOKS, INC.

DONALD A. WOLLHEIM, FOUNDER

375 Hudson Street, New York, NY 10014

ELIZABETH R. WOLLHEIM
SHEILA E. GILBERT
PUBLISHERS

http://www.dawbooks.com

Cover art used by permission of Corbis.

DAW Book Collectors No. 1259.

DAW Books are distributed by Penguin Group (USA) Inc.

First Printing, June 2003
1 2 3 4 5 6 7 8 9

DAW TRADEMARK REGISTERED
U.S. PAT. OFF. AND FOREIGN COUNTRIES
—MARCA REGISTRADA.
HECHO EN U.S.A.

PRINTED IN THE U.S.A.

ACKNOWLEDGMENTS

CONTENTS

Introduction

by Mike Resnick

WHEN we speak of the "opposite sex," most women will be happy to tell you that sexes can't get much more opposite than men.

And yet, at least partially due to the demands of the marketplace in the early days of science fiction, when all the heroes were men and the primary audience was adolescent boys, women have been writing about men since the field began.

(Yes, since it began. Mary Shelley's creation, Victor von Frankenstein, was a man—and his monster was, if not a man, at least a male monster.)

Back in the early 1930s C. L. Moore gave us Northwest Smith, one of my all-time favorites. Leigh Brackett followed in the 1940s with Eric John Stark. The most popular science fiction hero of the new millennium is almost certainly Lois MacMaster Bujold's Miles Vorkosigan. In between Northwest and Miles, hundreds of female writers have given us hundreds of male heroes and viewpoint characters.

But there is a difference between writing *about* a male and writing *as* a male.

It's a lot easier to describe a man's actions and reactions than to take us inside his head and convince us you *are* that man—and it's doubly difficult to do so if you're a woman to begin with.

So, since we hate to make things easy for science fictions writers, and since we had confidence that the ladies who practice the art were up to the challenge, we put forth the proposition to a handful of the best: write us a science fiction or fantasy story, not about a man's actions, not using him as a main character, but *as* a man.

There were only two rules: first, each story had to be told in the first person of a man; and second, if changing the narrator from Victor to Victoria didn't invalidate the story we didn't want it.

As usual, they did not disappoint.

Homecoming

by Kristine Kathryn Rusch

Kristine Kathryn Rusch is an award-winning author in three genres. In 2001, she won science fiction's Hugo for best novelette, her second—making her the first person in the history of science fiction to win the Hugo for editing and for her fiction. Under her pen name Kris Nelscott, she won the Best Historic Mystery award (and was nominated for an Edgar), and as Kristine Grayson, she won the Best Paranormal Romance award from *Romantic Times*. Even though she's published more than fifty novels, her first love is and always will be short fiction.

I'D been down maybe four hours, long enough to go through the newest version of decon—a ray of light that poked every part of the body with gentle warmth—not long enough to get a sense of this America one hundred years in my future.

Technology was different—that seemed obvious; laws were different—noticed that just a few minutes ago; but people seemed to be the same, preoccupied with their own agendas, too busy to hear let alone answer questions.

Not that there was anyone to ask. I was sitting in what passed for a police precinct interview room, a windowless square with blank white walls so clean I could almost see myself, and a table (also white) with tiny fingerprint-shaped indentations. No one sat across from me. I got a sense they all huddled outside the room, watching the hundred-plus-year-old man who looked like he was thirty-five—or, depending on your point of view, the thirty-five-year-old man who was actually well over a hundred.

My stomach was tied in loops—this certainly wasn't the homecoming I'd been expecting. Not that I'd been expecting a particularly good one. Hell, anything could have happened—an asteroid could've wiped out all life on Earth for all we knew—at least until we reached Earth Central (and managed to jury-rig our communications equipment so that we could unscramble their messages) somewhere around the Moon.

We'd been celebrating during our glide from the Moon to Earth, celebrating and trying to figure out how to land the damn ship, according to the parameters Earth Central had sent to us. Everything was different, which we had expected, but we hadn't expected our equipment to be so antique (by Earth's point of view) as to be nearly nonfunctional.

Someone slipped up and told us they thought we were dead. Seemed they never got our transmissions since we left the solar system. Or maybe they'd get them years from now, when it no longer mattered.

Comptin figured they'd upgraded their equipment, forgot all about us, and didn't set anything to receive. Worthy thought that we just didn't aim the communications equipment right after we'd left the solar system.

Me, I was beginning to figure the screwup was just one of many that was plaguing us in our relationship with Earth. Or my relationship, anyway. The others seemed just fine. They were heading off toward their grand homecoming parade, and media interviews (in whatever passed for media in the America of one hundred years in our future).

We'd even practiced those interviews during the long journey back. How would we describe the ALS drive to people who had either progressed beyond it or hadn't given spaceflight a thought at all during the time we were gone? I just hoped our trust funds still existed, that some EMP blast hadn't wiped out all banking records or something. We all got paid up front, and that money got stashed, untouchable until we returned.

To be honest, until I got arrested, the return had me the most nervous. I still wasn't sure I wanted to come back to the land of people. I liked the solitary nature of our journey. Sometimes I didn't interact with my fellow crew members for weeks on end. In fact, the thing that had me the most nervous about my return to Earth was dealing with large crowds of people. It simply wasn't something I liked.

We didn't know if anyone even cared we were coming back. No one had sounded enthusiastic, at least not the people we spoke to at Earth Central. We didn't even know if our parent company, *Dreamers*, still existed. They'd developed the first space drive that could go—as they termed it—"almost light speed" (hence ALS drive), and sent us on our merry way.

We knew the risks. Hell, I knew the risks. I just hadn't expected to be arrested the moment I got back.

The minute I stepped out of decon and figured out how to work the new clothes someone had thoughtfully provided, I met up with two official types who slapped the twenty-second century's version of handcuffs on me.

The official types muttered something about paternity suits and monetary provisos and skipping out on obligations, all of it in a legal mumbo jumbo that made no sense at all to me. Especially since I was twenty-five and single when I left, and only thirty-five and still single when I got back.

I just figured there was some kind of major screwup. Maybe officialdom didn't know their history. Maybe it got lost in the translation.

You see, our little team of six was chosen out of a field of more than a hundred qualified candidates because we had no surviving family members, and because we were single. Sure, we had attachments—friends, maybe a few ex-lovers—but nothing that would make us go bonkers should we discover that everyone precious to us had died in our absence.

We expected everyone precious to us to die. Or at least get older—like a hundred years older—and we all had the battery of psych tests to prove we could handle the changes.

Only I wasn't so sure, four hours into my return to America the Beautiful—which still existed, thank you very much, as a free and independent state, a reluctant signer (or so they told me) of the Treaty for Global Unification and, so far, the only major holdout from the Global Economic Union—that I could handle those changes.

I spent the first part of that conversation staring at the handcuffs which, in my day (feels strange to say "in my day" when you're only thirty-five) had been made of metal and unlocked with a key, just like they had for God, who knows, maybe a hundred years before that. These things they had on my wrists were made of a plastic so thin that it seemed sheer and so light to the touch that it felt like nothing held me at all.

Until I tried to move, of course. Then the damn things tightened, and caused shooting pains to course up my arms. The cuffs cut off circulation to my hands, making them swell, and finally one of the arresting officers (I guess that's what these folks are called) took pity on me and loosened the restraints.

"Better if you don't struggle," she said.

Thanks, I wanted to say to her. *Would've been nice of you to tell me that before you slapped the damn things on my wrists.*

But I was quiet. I figured justice in the twenty-second wasn't too different from justice in the late 2030s. After sitting alone in this all-white interview room for the last hour, I wasn't so sure I was right. But then—all of four hours ago—I had this confidence that I could figure out what mistake had been made, and could fix it.

They hauled me in here, after driving me across town (and I'm not even sure what town I'm in—we left from Cape Canaveral in Florida, but Earth Central told us to dock—Dock!—in a place called

CCNXY5. Tucker thought maybe there was so much spaceflight that landing areas had designations now, like airports did in our time. But that was a question we didn't even have time to ask).

Anyway, they drove me across town or what seemed like across town in something that resembled a cross between a car and a bullet train. It was sleek and sophisticated, and moved so fast that everything outside my grimy plastic window was a blur of light and sound and color.

We docked or landed or drove—at that point, I wasn't sure how to label anything—into some kind of parking structure, next to other car/bullet train hybrids, and I got hauled through a back elevator (yes, an elevator and I was glad to see it) to the interview room.

Alone. Despite my repeated requests for an attorney.

That was the other thing that differed, of course. It looked like they weren't going to let me have counsel even though I asked for it half a dozen times, until I finally got mad.

"Look," I said to the arresting officers, "I don't understand what you're charging me with. When I left Earth, I was a law-abiding citizen. Had to be or I wouldn't have gotten the mission. I never committed a crime. Hell, I don't think I even considered it, not once. I never married, had only a few girlfriends, and can guarantee that I don't have kids. Or didn't have kids. Or whatever. So throwing around the paternity, which in my day—" (and there it was, used in conversation for the first time, that awful phrase)

"—meant I had fathered a child. I haven't. Case closed. Let me go."

These two—Frick, Frack, whatever the hell their names were (they never told me)—stared at me like my head had exploded, then started talking about the charges all over again.

I kicked the table leg, causing everyone but me to jump (don't know if I activated something or alarmed something or if these folks just weren't used to sudden eruptions of anger), and Frickety-Frackety, the arresting officers, shut up. Finally.

"Look," I said. "We can go over this and over this, me saying you two really have the wrong guy, or you trying to explain, yet again, a hundred years of changes that I'm probably not going to understand. Or you can get me a lawyer, who'll figure all this out, talk to you nicely and in language you understand and who should, God willing, be able to talk to me in some sort of language I'll understand."

I looked at them, clean cut, athletic in a beefy way and humor-impaired just like generations of officials before them, and got the sense that no one had ever spoken like that to them.

They leaned together like parents figuring out how to discipline a recalcitrant child, and finally they left me alone.

For at least an hour, maybe more. I honestly couldn't tell. Time—the way it felt, the way it passed—was somehow not something I had a sense of any longer.

Finally—finally!—the stupid little white door that disappeared into the wall when closed burst open and this woman strode in. I gotta figure she's a lawyer, not just because of the businesslike don't-fuck-with-me attitude, but also because she wasn't wearing the green-and-gold clothes the other two had on, which, I was finally beginning to realize, was some kind of uniform.

She was wearing a variation on the business suit. It had a longer coat than I was used to, but the lapels were double-breasted. Underneath the coat, she wore a vest and a white shirt that looked like it was made of some hard unmalleable material. Her pants were creased and long, covering a pair of shiny black shoes that—in my day (dammit!)—would have been called men's shoes.

She didn't have a briefcase or even a Palm. Instead, she sat across from me, touched a button on her wrist and a small slightly see-through image appeared between us. It seemed to be some sort of legal document.

"You're in a lot of trouble," she said without a how-do-you-do.

I was tired of people telling me I was in trouble. I was tired of them treating me like a criminal. And I really hated the way they all looked at me, like I was pond scum instead of one of five people who took (at the time—note I avoided the dreaded "in my day"—) one of the riskiest jobs ever offered.

I leaned back in my chair, careful not to twist my handcuffed wrists. "How about an introduction before analyzing my life since I returned to Earth?"

She flushed, which I didn't expect, and then she gave me a sheepish smile. The flush highlighted her skin, which had some flaws beneath the surface, not readily noticeable.

"I'm Alison Yost," she said. "Sixth Star Media Incorporated hired me to be your attorney."

"Sixth Star Media?" I asked. "Who are they?"

She blinked twice, as if I'd asked who God was, then took a deep breath. "We have some catching up to do, Mr. Fortan."

"*I* have some catching up to do. A whole lot of it. That's why I had the cops send for you." I couldn't keep the irritation from my voice.

"The 'cops,' as you so quaintly call them, did not send for me." Yost touched her wrist again and the see-through slip of paper disappeared. "I came because of Sixth Star."

"Okay. Now we're back to my question. Who is Sixth Star?"

"They might be your salvation, Mr. Fortan. Or not. I suspect you'll see a whole battery of lawyers from a variety of different media outlets. You'll have to choose one."

I shook my head. "Don't people hire their own lawyers anymore?"

"Rich people do. And the poor still get the dregs from the court appointments. But people in your situation, Mr. Fortan, often get a media company's lawyer, for a price."

"So I still have to pay you," I said.

She shook her head, touched her wrist, and a document appeared in her hand. The document had the same see-through quality as the one before, only this one lay flat on the table. She pushed the document toward me.

"This is a standard agreement," Yost said. "In return for all your court costs, attorney's fees, and incidentals before, during, and in the days after the trial—"

"Trial?" My voice rose.

"—you agree to give Sixth Star Media Incorporated, which includes net-tech, downloads, airweb, TV, books, DVD, and any technology that has or will be developed, an exclusive right to the story of your legal entanglements, starting from this moment, and terminating no less than one week after your trial is completed."

"How can there be a trial?" I asked, still stuck on that point, "when I haven't been charged with anything?"

"You're charged and booked, Mr. Fortan. Didn't the officers explain that to you?"

"They tried to explain something, but it wasn't registering. Maybe no one's gotten the memo, but I've been *off the planet* for about a hundred years. Incommunicado. In deep fucking space. Or can't you people figure that out?"

She smiled at me. "I had forgotten how colorful our language was when I was a kid."

A kid? I frowned at her. There was no way she was over forty.

"We're a lot more polite now," she said. "Pendulum swings, I think, although it might simply be that there are more of us than ever. The Moon colony failed, you know."

No, I didn't know. I had no idea there had been a Moon colony and I certainly didn't care about its failure. "Maybe I'll be polite when this Kafkaesque nightmare ends."

She raised her eyebrows.

"You have no idea who Kafka is, do you?" I snapped, shaking my head. What else do you do for ten years besides read every classic in the database? Davidon learned four languages so he could reread books in the original.

"I read Kafka in college," she said. "I was a lit major."

"And now I know a lot more about you than I want to know, and still nothing about the so-called charges that I've been asking about."

Yost nodded once. "Let me put this in nonlegal terms, Mr. Fortan, something the police are no longer required to do. You've been charged with child abandonment, failure to provide for your family, and familial neglect. You have eighteen years of child support payments due, as well as one half of a college education—fortunately for you, completed roughly eighty years ago, so the cost was low—compounded by interest on all of that money—and, well, we're talking a substantial sum here, Mr. Fortan."

"It'll be easy to fight," I said. "I never married. I never had children. I was always careful. I used birth control and I made sure that no woman I ever slept with conceived. So there's no way this kid could be mine."

"This kid," she said, "is dead."

I let out a small sigh and stared at her, feeling even more confused.

"But he left a family—three children of his own, all of whom have children, and those children have children, and they have an attorney who is continuing the fight against your estate."

"My estate?" I said. "How can I have an estate? I'm not dead yet."

"Any living person with money has an estate, Mr. Fortan, or didn't they explain that to you in astronaut school?"

"There is—was–is–was–dammit—no such thing as astronaut school."

"I remember, Mr. Fortan. I even remember when the *Long Day's Journey* took off, and all the hopes for it. I was ten years old at the time."

"And what, they kept you in stasis?"

She smiled. "Very kind of you, Mr. Fortan. You've missed some developments while you were gone."

"No kidding," I muttered.

"We've managed to slow the aging process and now most people have a life expectancy of one hundred fifty years. By today's standards, I'm still in my late middle age."

"Oh," I said, because how else could you respond to something like that? We'd all known it was coming—all the breakthroughs before I left showed that. But I just hadn't expected it to be so soon.

Which, if I really thought about it, it wasn't.

Soon, that is.

"Okay," I said, shaking off the mind-numbing thoughts of all the changes that had occurred while I was gone. "If we've managed to retard aging and add years to normal life expectancy, then I figure it would be simple to prove that I'm not the dead kid's dad. Hell, DNA tests were so sophisticated when I left that you should be able to prove beyond a reasonable doubt—that is still the standard, right?—"

"In criminal cases," she said. "In civil—"

"—beyond a reasonable doubt that I am childless and that I am who I say I am. Besides, I've only been in the company of two women in the past ten years—one hundred years—whatever—and I know neither of them got pregnant. We'd have noticed if a kid were born on *The Long Day's Journey.*"

Yost threaded her fingers together and peered at me over them. Now that I was concentrating on her face, I did see a web of tiny lines near her eyes.

When she seemed certain that I was done, she said, "Do you remember a Janet Delancy, Mr. Fortan?"

Of course I remembered Jannie. We'd hooked up about a week before my quarantine in SpaceTech, a bar that catered to scientists and tech geeks. She'd been long-legged and pretty, with thick black hair that fell around her shoulders, and matching black eyes that snapped with intelligence. I bought her a drink, and she propositioned me, wanting—or so she said—to give me something to remember Earth by.

Which she did too, nearly a dozen times over the next six days, and I relived each of those times during my ten celibate years aboard *The Long Day's Journey.*

But I didn't tell Yost that. I didn't trust her. I didn't trust anyone I'd met since I'd come home.

"Why should I remember a Janet Delancy?" I asked.

"Because," Yost said, "she's the mother of your son."

I didn't have a son. I know that without a doubt. But I wasn't going to sit here and argue semantics with her. Not until I got a few things straight.

"You're *my* lawyer, right?" I asked.

"Hired by—"

"Yeah, I know. Some media company."

"My loyalties will be to them if you agree to their terms."

"Not to me?" I asked.

"Not entirely." She nodded toward the document before me, which I still hadn't read.

"So confidentiality—that's a thing of the past, too?"

"For the duration of the trial, no. But if you agree to my representation, then I may, when all charges are discharged, dropped, served or commuted, release my notes—audio, video, and written—to Sixth Star Media for use as they see fit."

"What if I hire you?"

"That would be irregular, Mr. Fortan."

"I don't care."

"I doubt you can afford me," she said. "Especially if we lose."

"Why especially if we lose?" I asked.

"Your funds will be dispersed to your family—"

"You people act like I have a family."

"You do, Mr. Fortan. That's been proven."

"Not to me," I said. "And not by any definition I know."

She stood, sighed, and said, "Look. I used to give free introductory consults. I'll do that now. You clearly need someone to explain what's going on here."

"You're taking pity on me?"

She tilted her head. "Yes." Then she paused. "I'm waiting for the lawyer joke."

"I figured they were out of fashion."

She shook her head. "Some things never change."

We smiled at each other then. I kinda liked her. She had a human side, which I hadn't expected and which I appreciated.

"After this first hour, though," she said, "we go back to the original arrangement. I'm going to be working for Sixth Star first, and you second. Agreed?"

"Agreed," I said. "I'd shake on it, but I'm a little tied up at the moment."

Yost didn't smile at that joke.

"So now we have confidentiality?" I asked.

"Yes," she said.

"For how long?"

"Until you waive it," she said.

"Okay," I said. I was ready to proceed. "I knew Janet Delancey. I even slept with her. Even though I wasn't allowed to have a birth control shot for more than six months before the mission, I used condoms, and I used them right. They didn't break. I never reused one, and we put them on long before they were necessary."

Yost sat down, her eyebrows raised. "You remember all that after one hundred years? That must have been some sex."

"I remember all that after ten years, and it wasn't some sex," I said. "It was the last sex I've had—at least with a partner—since I left Earth. Little things like that add some significance to a memory."

She touched her wrist, accessed another document, shoved the first one aside, and set the second one before me. "I don't expect you to read this," she said, "but you can if you want. It's a summary of all the DNA testing done in your case over all the years. There is no doubt that Charles Fortan Delancy was your son. So there is no doubt that all of his children are your grandchildren, and his grandchildren are your great grandchildren."

Great grandchildren, at thirty-five. That made my stomach hurt. "No doubt at all?"

"Stop the games, Mr. Fortan. DNA testing was accurate in 2039. Imagine how accurate it is now."

"Using what samples?" I asked. "From me, I mean."

"*Dreamers* released some of your records when it disbanded."

"It what?" I had wanted the company to remain. Not because I loved *Dreamers*—I didn't. It was a corporation—but because I hoped its institutional memory might give us a safe haven should there be trouble.

Like now.

"Long story." She smiled at me. "You've lost a lot of time."

I leaned back, beginning to feel all the losses. "What about Janet? What did she say?"

"That the child is yours." Yost studied me for a moment. "You know she's dead now, too."

I had expected that. Jannie and I knew we'd never see each other again, and I hadn't minded. I hadn't been in love with her. She'd been a good time, and, it seemed then, that was all she'd been offering.

"I don't understand," I said. "If everyone's dead—"

"Everyone but your grandchildren and great grandchildren."

"—why am I here? In handcuffs, no less."

"Let me see if I can untangle a hundred years of legal mess for you. First, Janet Delancy sued your estate in the name of her son Charles for child support payments. Then—"

"Wait a minute," I said. "I have a trust, not an estate. Everything I own was being managed for me inside of a trust until I returned. Nothing could be touched. All my bills were current, and all the trust was supposed to do was earn income so I had something to live on when I returned. My fee for this trip went into that trust."

"I know," Yost said.

"So it's not an estate. Even if they wanted to, the trust couldn't have paid out."

"We know that, too," Yost said.

"Then how could she sue?"

"You can sue for anything," Yost said, and the answer sounded reflexive. "However, you signed an agreement with *Dreamers* guaranteeing that you did not have family or spouse left behind who would have access to that trust. She tried to show that you signed the agreement in bad faith."

"Well, I didn't," I said.

"Apparently, the attorney for your trust figured that out, simply by using your son's birthdate. You would have had no way of knowing that Janet was pregnant because you were incommunicado when she took her pregnancy test."

"Off the planet," I said.

"Actually, you were still in quarantine, but the records show she didn't try to contact you."

I frowned. "Why not?"

"I suspect, she feared you would have asked her—on the record, one hopes—to get rid of the child. If you had done that, there would have been no case."

"So you can establish that I didn't know about the kid. Why should I be charged with all these things if I didn't even have a chance to do what the law demanded?"

Yost gave me a look filled with pity. "The fact that you didn't know is not an excuse, according to most of the case law I've seen. Apparently men are supposed to think about the consequences of their actions, and make sure—"

"I did think!" I stood up, jerking my wrists and the damn cuffs tightened again. "I used precautions. We were clear on the fact that this was fun only. And there was no way I could have made sure. I was gone for ten years. She knew I'd be gone. She knew that when she met me."

"One hundred years," Yost corrected me.

"Well, from her perspective, yeah."

"Which made you the perfect victim."

"What?" I sank back into my chair again. Then I raised my arms. "Can you get them to take these things off? Or at least loosen them?"

"They think you're a flight risk."

"Oh, really? Where am I going to go? Mars? I have no friends here. I don't even know what city I'm in."

"All fathers who've been charged with abandonment are assumed to be flight risks—"

"Well, I'm not all fathers and this is a weird case. Make them take the cuffs off."

To my surprise, her eyes twinkled. She touched one of the depressions on the table, and a little teeny person popped out of it. At least that's what it looked like to me. Actually, it was some kind of hologram.

"What?" the little teeny person—male from the depth of his voice—asked.

Yost made my request about the cuffs, got some disagreement from Tiny, then reiterated my argument, at which point Tiny disappeared and a different teeny tiny person, dressed in robes—whom, I soon realized was a teeny tiny judge—appeared, looking very annoyed. She was facing me, and Yost had to press a few more buttons to get that image turned around.

Yost spoke legalese for a good five minutes, the judge issued some kind of ruling—which appeared above another depression on the table—and my cuffs fell off. That simple.

I rubbed my hands together, wondering if the feeling would ever return to them. The little teeny judge disappeared, and Yost grinned at me, as if she'd performed some sort of magic trick.

It almost felt like she had.

"Okay," I said after a moment, "I was the perfect victim. What did you mean?"

Yost's grin faded. "You were being scammed, sweetie. Taken out and set up."

I shook my head. "All we did was have a fun week—"

"Maybe all you did was have a fun week. She had clearly done her research. You guys were the first to go to deep space, right?"

"Right," I said, thinking suddenly about my dreams of the triumphant return, the hopes I had for some kind of life when I got back.

"And she knew that."

"Everyone did, if you can truly recall the year I left. We were news."

"Testing a special drive for *Dreamers*, a private company, who helped you all set up your trusts, paid your fees, and wished you well."

"Yes," I said.

"No government involvement—"

"The government saw no percentage in deep space flight. It was private industry that stood to make a profit—"

"I know. I know. My grandkids are studying it in school." She smiled. "The questions they ask. You'd think I'm the relic."

The *instead of you* was implied.

"I'm guessing," Yost continued, "that your girlfriend—"

"She wasn't my girlfriend."

"—was gambling on the fact that the law said anyone who had not been heard from in seven years could be presumed dead. There was no guarantee you guys would ever come back. In fact, most people assumed you wouldn't. Your trust would then become an estate, and someone would get to inherit it."

"You're saying my trust is gone?" I actually felt a chill. This world was foreign to me and I hadn't even left the police station. I had no idea how I'd find work, what I'd do, what I'd live on—I hadn't planned on coming back just so that I could be destitute (although, I must confess, we all worried that we might come back to some kind of crisis).

"No," Yost said. "Your trust is intact. The *Dreamers* lawyers were good, and they drew up a solid document. You couldn't be expected to return until about last year. There was a window in there of years in which it would be likely that you returned. There's some sort of equation in the papers, but I just got them and I haven't had a chance to study them—"

"We figured our return would happen somewhere between ninety and a hundred years if all went well, one hundred and twenty or thirty if things didn't go as planned."

"Well," she said, "the upshot is that the courts decided you couldn't be declared dead until seven years after the last possible day you could possibly return. The trust was unbreakable, and so the family was waiting for your money whatever that date was."

"And then they got confirmation that we were

alive." Something sank in my stomach. I rubbed my wrists harder. The skin had turned red.

"They marshaled their lawyers, charged you with neglect, abandonment, and everything else they could think of, and are prepared to go after the sums I listed to you earlier—eighteen years of child support, plus interest and penalties accumulated over the time you were gone."

"I still don't get it," I said. "Why does this make me the perfect victim?"

"Because," she said, "your friend Janet didn't believe you'd survive the trip. She'd get the money to raise her son, and everything would be fine. Even if you had survived, by her reckoning, then you would return long after she got your funds. The money would be spent, she would be dead—as indeed she is—and going after her would be difficult to say the least."

"I don't see how I can be charged for things that weren't illegal when I left."

"Oh, but they were," Yost said. "You probably didn't notice, being a man who was determined not to have a family. A lot of the child protection laws went into effect in the late twentieth century, and so did many of the child support requirements. The modifications in the law occurred in the early parts of the twenty-first century, when women started using technology to conceive children years after their husband or partner died. First the laws said that if the woman could prove her spouse wanted a child but didn't have one before his death, then the child was entitled to part of the estate. Over the years, that rather sensible ruling got eroded until any child conceived with the father's permission—permission being in consensual sexual intercourse at the time of sperm collection—then that child was eligible for part of the dead father's estate."

"I'm not dead," I said, feeling odd each time I said it.

"And then came the modifications so that a man who participated in consensual sexual intercourse, and left sperm behind—either in a condom or a diaphragm or some other collection device—would be liable for child support."

I ran my fingers through my hair. "I'd remember that. Believe me I would. I'd've made certain that no one got me with that one."

"It looks like someone did," Yost said.

"Check the law," I said. "If it came into being after I left, how can I be charged under it?"

"I don't know," she said. "I'll have to check. Some laws concerning children have been applied retroactively, starting with the child's conception."

"Oh, for Chrissake." I paced around the small room. White on white, the only color being Yost. And me, of course. It was worse than the ship, worse than anything I'd experienced. "I'm trapped here. I'm an unwilling victim in a scheme that—"

"Yes, we'll have to prove all of that. Now you see why Sixth Star wants this case? Not only are you a minor celebrity—probably about to be major—but the case is salacious. It has human interest, sex, money, and could possible change the law down the road, if you win."

"If I win." I stopped pacing next to her. She smelled faintly of lilies, a scent I hadn't smelled for ten years.

"You know," she said, "you could just accept your family, pay them their fee, and then move on. In the end, it would probably be the cheaper course."

"It's not about money." And as I said that, I knew it was true. I had no idea how much money was in my trust. The people who represented my so-called family probably knew, and Yost probably knew, but I didn't. "It's the principle of the thing."

"Principles have changed since you left," she said. "Most people believe the child's welfare is paramount and that a child is entitled to care from both parents. The state's been mandating responsible parenting for decades now. This is just one of those cases. You can't ask the culture to go backward."

"So a woman can, at any time, assault a man, use him for procreation purposes without his permission, and then slap him with the responsibilities?"

Yost raised her eyebrows. "Sounds familiar."

"What?" I asked.

"What do you think men have been doing to women for centuries?" She stood. "And now, your consultation hour is up. I'm heading out of here, unless you decide to hire me."

"Answer something first," I said.

"All right." She tilted her head, waiting.

"Can you leave the information on my trust and exactly the amount that these people want to take from me?"

"Sure," She said. "I'll have to add fees and expenses for law firms who've been handling your cases up until now—"

"Who couldn't manage to show up once I'm home," I said, feeling slightly annoyed.

"They've shown up," she said.

I frowned at her. "I thought you worked for Sixth Star Media."

"I do," she said, "and several other conglomerates. The law firm who employs me handles hundreds of clients, and in this case, they just happen to intersect. When it became clear that you were alive, Sixth Star paid all your bills. They want to cover this case."

"If there is a case," I said.

It was her turn to frown. "What do you mean?"

"Well," I said slowly, "I can't help wondering why I'm liable for eighteen years of child support plus penalties and interest spread out over eighty-two years when I've only been gone ten years."

Her eyes lit up. It was as if I'd given her fifteen Christmas presents at once.

"I don't know," she said, "but it certainly would be fun to find out."

Fun. As if it weren't my future on the line. As if some woman—admittedly one very agile and interesting woman—hadn't targeted me and my money for her little schemes. As if I wanted, yet again, to be the risk taker, the point man, the first one into a bold new venture.

"Let's see what we can figure out," Yost said and started to sit down, but I caught her arm.

"Give me some time," I said. "I've got some thinking to do."

"But Sixth Star will cover this. It's hot, it's interesting, and it shouldn't be as embarrassing to you as the case initially was—"

"I know," I said, leading her to the door as if this interview room were mine, and not in the middle of some police precinct. "But why don't you research something, or something? I want a few moments to myself."

"Mr. Fortan, we have to get you out of here. I think, with this new argument, we can get all the criminal charges dropped, and let civil court handle the rest. It'll—"

"Fine," I said. "Get the criminal charges dropped. I'll wait here for you."

"I can call up the judge on the —"

"Somewhere else," I said, and the little white door opened as if I had made it do so (but apparently someone on the other side had been watching us—not listening, I hoped, but then what did I care? Everything was so different I couldn't keep track), and she left, still talking about how the time differential changed everything.

I guess it did, but not in the way she was thinking about. I sat down in my goofy white chair, in that pristine white room, with the depressed white table, and listened to the silence, like I'd been doing for years. Every room—even ones on a ship—had ambient noise, and this one was no different. The slight hum of some heating unit, the faint rustle of movement outside. Or maybe it was the rustle of my clothing as I breathed.

I didn't know and didn't care. I let the ambient

noise disappear into my subconscious like it was supposed to, and let my thoughts take me.

The psych tests conducted on me ten—or a hundred—years ago showed that I had a high tolerance for solitude. I had the ability to remain still and quiet for long stretches of time, yet I also enjoyed adventure.

One of the reasons I'd taken Jannie back to the apartment that final week before quarantine was that I didn't like the bar scene, and I had nowhere else to go, nothing else to do. I wanted to be doing something that I wouldn't be able to do in space, but I didn't want to surround myself with crowds of people.

I didn't like the choices. Hire a lawyer who represents a media company and let her steal my privacy as my reward. Hire my own attorney and I'd still lose my privacy. Of course, there was no guarantee of privacy. If human nature remained the way it had been in the two hundred years before my departure, I would become a celebrity no matter what and the privacy would be gone.

I slid the monetary information sheet that Yost left in front of me and studied the figures. If I gave the so-called family the money they were requesting, and paid off the attorneys who had fought on my behalf while I was gone, I would have maybe one percent of my assets left. I had no idea what modern prices were like, and I didn't know if that one percent would buy me groceries or an island off the coast of Florida.

Apparently, there were a few other questions I should have asked.

And there were a few other options that Yost should have mentioned. I could, theoretically, meet this so-called family of mine. If they reacted like people in the vids we took with us into space, they'd fall into my arms and we'd live happily ever after.

But faced with hard cold reality, I doubted that was possible. First of all, I didn't believe that we would like each other just because we shared some DNA. Secondly, I wasn't real fond of people who spend their entire lives grubbing for money they didn't earn. And thirdly, I wasn't the most social guy on the planet—or off, for that matter. I really didn't want to get involved.

And that, I realized, was the bottom line. If Yost had her way, the cases would drag on for years, she'd set a precedent for anyone who traveled in deep space, and every aspect of my life from the moment I returned to Earth until the moment I died, would be recorded, perused, sifted, and analyzed by people I didn't even know.

The risk in this case wasn't the obvious one. It was that I might get lost fighting someone else's battle for principles I didn't understand, let alone believe in.

It might have been different if Jannie were still alive—or maybe even my kid. Maybe I'd've been able to reason with him. But grandkids, great grandkids—hell, I'd been around long enough to know that family myth often became family destiny. So far as they knew, from time immemorial, Grandma or Great Grandma had been screwed over by this famous astronaut and they were only going after her share.

After all, she'd spent her life fighting for it.

I shook my head.

What I wanted was to get out of this little room. I wanted to go somewhere and look at the night sky, maybe talk to a few real scientists, see—perhaps—if someone would let me fly away again.

Some guys were made for home and hearth. Others for spending their lives fighting over principles in musty courtrooms. Me, I was made for solitary contemplation in tiny rooms with a view of the universe.

The stupid white door opened and Yost came back in. "Criminal charges dropped," she said. "And I've got the first leg of my argument for the civil trial."

"There won't be one," I said, standing, knowing I was now free.

"What?"

"We're giving them what they want."

"But you can't," she said.

"I can."

She took a deep breath. I could see her lawyer brain preparing the arguments for me now, and I didn't want to hear them.

"I hired you to get me out of here," I said. "You did that. And now I'm going to pay off these people, and then I'm going back to my life. You can help me, or not, up to you. But I'm not signing your little agreement and I'm not giving up my privacy."

She studied me for a moment, then smiled. "I don't remember guys like you from a hundred years ago."

I smiled back. "It was only ten years."

Yost laughed and held the door open for me.

"How about you let me fight this one anyway. You won't have to sign the agreement for Sixth Star, and I promise I won't spend more than the money you have in the trust defending your honor."

"Nope," I said. "My honor doesn't need defending. I slept with her. I'll pay the consequences."

"It shouldn't have to work this way," Yost said.

"That's right," I said, "but you've told me that's what the law says."

"I told you that so you'd fight it."

The hallway was a muted blue and gold with lights that seemed to flicker inside the walls. The floor, which looked like some kind of tile, was actually soft to my feet. And the place smelled like good, fresh mountain air.

We were inside a building with no windows. Hallways shouldn't smell like this.

"Look." I pointed at the lights flickering in and out. "I have no idea what this stuff is, and it's just part of an everyday wall inside some police precinct."

Yost turned toward me, obviously fascinated in spite of herself.

"I have a whole world to discover," I said. "The last thing I need to do is tilt at windmills."

"You wouldn't be tilting—"

"Case closed, counselor. Now," I said, putting a hand collegially on her shoulder. "How about you help me figure out how to leave this building and get some lunch?"

She looked at my hand as if she were going to ask me to remove it. "You're crazy, you know."

"No," I said as she led me through a silver-lined gap in the wall. "I'm just someone who knows a bad risk when he sees one."

After a moment, she smiled and shook her head. "I think I might grow to like you, Mr. Fortan."

I doubted she'd have enough time. I was going to be out of her life as quickly as I entered it. But I didn't tell her that.

I wanted to stay on her good side, at least until she paid for lunch.

Big

by Leah A. Zeldes

Leah A. Zeldes is a longtime journalist who spends most of her time—between rare bouts of short fiction—editing newspapers and writing truth and opinion about current affairs, food, and entertainment in Chicago. She has been enjoying science fiction since she could read and has played an active role in the international SF community for more years than she cares to admit. Zeldes notes that this story is something of a "found" piece, based largely on real e-mail she received.

IT all started with the spam.

I mean, I always had been just a little embarrassed about the size of my penis. I wasn't tiny, but I felt like I was smaller than average. It made me shy in locker rooms, so I didn't go out much for sports as a teenager, and it helped to undermine my confidence with women.

Not that I ever got into too many situations where a woman might actually look at my penis. But I was always afraid that if I did, she might laugh.

I didn't figure there was anything I could do about it, though. I was just, you know, born that way and that was how it was. It was genetics, or something.

Then I started getting e-mail messages. You know the kind:

```
> > Ever wonder why some people are
> always surrounded by members of
> the opposite sex?
> Now YOU can. . . .
>    * Attract Members of the Opposite
>      Sex Instantly
>    * Enhance Your Present
>      Relationship
>    * Meet New People Easily
>    * Give yourself that additional
>      edge
>    * Have people drawn to you, they
>      won't even know why
> A BIG PENIS is yours for the asking!
> Curious? YOU SHOULD BE!
> Get the FACTS NOW!
```

I ignored it at first. I mean, I figured if there was something like that out there that really worked, I'd have heard about it somewhere else than in my e-mail.

But the messages kept coming. . . .

```
>   Why Have a Bigger Penis?
>
> All other organs on a man's body
> are nondescript. The penis is
> the one that stands out.
>
> Nearly everyone would acknowledge
```

> that cock size is not the
> measure of manhood. But in the
> Real World, men with short cocks
> are humiliated and made fun of – by
> other men especially, but also by
> some women. Men with big dicks feel
> more manly than other guys. No matter
> how much a man some guy might be,
> being humiliated, embarrassed and
> told "you don't have enough" leaves
> a mark on a guy's sense of self worth.
>
> A man with a larger, harder penis will
> be more confident and experience
> greater pleasure from sex. Most women,
> when asked, say they are not satisfied
> with an average-sized penis.
>
> We can not only increase the size of
> your penis and give greater pleasure
> to you and your partner, but also give
> you the ability to experience harder
> and more frequent erections with only
> a simple effort on your part.
>
> Give yourself and your partner the
> ultimate sexual present. . . . When she
> says "Wow!" you'll know it makes a
> difference!

I started wondering if there might be something to these things after all.

I thought about myself with a bigger penis. I saw myself standing taller. All of my life, I've felt inadequate, like nothing I ever achieved made me good enough. Was it because of my penis? I needed something. Maybe a bigger penis was it.

> This message IS NOT an ADULT Website
> Solicitation nor an Invitation to View
> Pornographic Material.
>
> YOU CAN Increase Your PENIS SIZE
> Naturally! It's Guaranteed!
> It's time you discovered what has
> been kept SECRET for so long!
>
> * The Silence Has Been Broken – the
>   Secrets ARE OUT
> * No Pills, Creams, Pumps Or Surgery!
> * No more EMBARRASSMENT
> * No More SHAME
> * AMAZING Results . . . FAST!
> * Adds LENGTH & WIDTH!
> * Develops a STRONG – MUSCULAR penis!
> * Works on ANY SIZE PENIS!
> * Your Lover Will Thank You!
>
> The Size-UP Program for Penis
> Enlargement not only shows you exactly
> what to do to get the penis you may
> have always wanted, but it also
> combines modern scientific discoveries

> for greater sexual and physical
> health, and secrets for being a better
> lover. Increase your self-confidence!
> Life's too short to be unhappy.
>   Get the FACTS NOW!

It couldn't hurt, I thought, to get more information. I clicked the link. The web page told me about an ancient Middle Eastern technique called "jelqing." Desert fathers would prepare their sons for marriage by teaching them these exercises to enlarge their penises' length and girth.

It worked, the web site said, because the *corpora cavernosa* and *corpus spongiosum*, the erectile tissues of the penis, are spongelike and full of spaces. These fill with blood when the penis is erect. With exercise, the spaces would become larger, and the body would generate more erectile tissue.

> Penis enlargement is very similar to
> bodybuilding in nature. This is
> because the penile tissue is in fact
> smooth muscle. By making your penis
> (or the heart) work harder, it will
> grow. And because the actual mass of
> your penis increases, instead of just
> inflating, as with penis pumps, your
> gains are permanent!
>
> The more blood that you push into the

> chambers of your penis, the larger you
> can become. Jelqing helps force more
> blood flow so these chambers stretch,
> creating substantial growth in both
> length and width. In just a few
> months, your penis can lengthen up
> to 27%. Substantial increase in
> circumference can also be easily
> achieved. Desire and concentration by
> the client can also enlarge the size
> of the penis glans (head). Moreover,
> exercising your penis just feels good!
>
> Whatever you desire, you can achieve.
> Your penis is made of soft tissue. We
> are not growing muscle or bone. We
> have found that all men can grow an
> inch. Most men can do better. But
> growing 6 inches is unrealistic. (We
> hope someday someone will prove us
> wrong!)
>
> You can have a LARGER more VIBRANT
> penis! Get DETAILS Now!

Complete directions were only $29.95. What the hell . . . I typed in my Amex number and downloaded the file.

The exercises were quite rigorous and time-consuming, taking at least forty-five minutes at a stretch—which is more or less what they consisted of: a kind of stretching or milking maneuver. After warming my phallus with a hot towel and coating it with baby oil, I clamped one hand at the base of my shaft, and, gripping it with the other, applied pressure while sliding and stretching down the length.

Then I switched hands and did it again. The direction said to do it 500 times, two or three times a day, at least five times a week. It was hard to fit this much exercise in.

I also had to shave to keep from pulling the hairs as I pulled on my schlong. Getting the pressure right was difficult, too.

```
> The key to achieving real gains is to
> consistently fatigue the penis with a
> thorough workout and then allow full
> recovery. At no point during the
> exercises should your penis feel
> completely numb. If this should
> happen, gently slap your penis against
> your leg a few times. This should get
> the blood flowing again. By the time
> you are done, you will know that your
> penis received a first-class workout
> because it should tingle and feel
> quite tired.
```

At first all of this exercise made me sore. I had bruises and little red and blue spots all up and down my shaft. But the literature said this was normal, so I kept at it. Like the directions said, I focused on my end goal, the exceptional penis I hoped to achieve.

```
> Really focus on your penis while you
> exercise. Close your eyes and get a
> good picture in your mind. Every time
> you milk and stretch, imagine your
> penis growing a little bit, becoming
> the size that you desire. Focus on
> every stroke you take. Doing this
> every day not only forms a better
> habit, but also makes you feel more
> fit and potent.
```

After a while, I really started to enjoy it. I began to look forward to my sessions. I'd started out doing it in the mornings and after work and then just before bedtime. Now I began to sneak in a few jelqs in the men's room at work, when things were slow. (I'm a database migration support specialist for an actuarial firm. Things are often slow.)

These exercises really made me feel I was accomplishing something. And they worked! When I measured after three weeks, I had grown almost a quarter inch! My penis seemed firmer. It felt like it was hanging really well. I was amazed. I was fascinated.

I set to with a will and did the exercises even more faithfully. No Guernsey was ever milked with the vigor I applied to my johnson. I cut back on going to my war-gaming and fantasy-baseball clubs, so I'd have more time to exercise.

After three months, I could see real results. My fully erect phallus measured nearly three-quarters of an inch longer and a quarter-inch bigger around. I was thrilled, and determined to keep on going. How massive could I get?

I was now "average," anyway, at least according to a web site that purported to survey such things. I felt pretty good about that. I had achieved penile fitness. I thought maybe I should celebrate this by sharing my newly fit penis with a female.

If only I knew any that seemed likely. The Size-UP program didn't address this problem. Somehow, the literature implied, once your penis got big enough, the women would come to you . . . as if they could see it through your pants. I resolved to buy tighter trousers. And I kept up with my exercises.

But I soon plateaued. After a while, no matter how much effort I applied, my willy would just not get any bigger. Worse, I was starting to get carpal-tunnel symptoms from all the handwork I was doing.

I imagined myself describing what I'd been doing with my hands to my family doctor, a kindly old Marcus Welby type who played canasta with my mom and dad every other Friday night. Somehow my gains didn't seem worth bragging about anymore.

I tried to taper off my exercises, but I missed them. I didn't feel right when I didn't do them.

But my wrists were really starting to hurt, and my fingers were getting numb. I had more trouble controlling the pressure, so sometimes my pecker was numb, too.

So when I got this message, I was really intrigued:

> NO Gimmick – REAL SCIENCE!
>
> With today's technical advancements in
> medicine, there is no reason for a man
> not to have a larger, healthier penis.
> In this age of constant self-
> improvement, where men may purchase
> pills that grow hair and women can buy
> bigger breasts, it stands to reason
> that there are simple, effective ways
> of improving the penis. Our safe and
> effective blood-flow stimulator makes
> the most of your natural potential.
> Even if you have tried other exercise
> regimens with limited success, with
> our simple device, you'll achieve
> results you never dreamed of!
>
> INCREASE YOUR PENIS SIZE BY 1 INCH . . .
> 2 INCHES . . . 3 INCHES . . . OR MORE IN
> JUST A FEW SHORT WEEKS! Get:
>   Faster results
>   Fantastic length

```
>    Immense girth
>    Increased Sex drive
>    Stronger Erections
>    Thundering ejaculations!
>    Longer Lasting orgasms!
>
> With Supr-Jelqr, you can achieve an
> advanced penile workout in a much
> shorter time than with old-fashioned
> hand exercises. This product can give
> you that extra little "push" you need
> to move up to the next level. The
> synergistic effect produces maximum
> results in the least amount of time.
>
> Over 95% of men who try our product
> say it works wonders in only 15
> minutes a day! It's entirely Natural!
>
>    Send for your today!
```

For $39.99, I received a device that resembled the gizmo my mom used to lift hot mason jars out of her canning kettle, a sort of tonglike thing with foam-coated rollers at one end and handles at the other. You slide this thing on at the pelvis, and clamp the handles tight. (You can tell when you've got it on right, because your penis gives a little jump.) Then you roll it out toward the glans.

You only have to do it half as many times as the hand exercises to get the same workout, and it's a lot faster and easier on the hands. I had no more worries and loss of sensation; my dick looked thicker and longer and my erections were harder and firmer. I did exercises every chance I got, focusing hard on my penile goals.

Oh, how I focused on my penis! I loved my penis. By this time, my erections were as hard as a length of pipe, and my cock was much larger and thicker. For comfort, I had quit wearing jockey shorts and switched to boxers.

My penis hung lower even while flaccid. Erect, it was a kosher salami. Well, a chub, anyway. A pity I couldn't find some *maidel* to share it with.

I thought maybe I should go to a singles club or something to meet women. But those places are always so smoky, and with my asthma. . . . Besides, who had time?

I wondered whether I could do the exercises even faster. Maybe there was some way to rig the Supr-Jelqr on pulleys? Make it electric?

Then I got this e-mail:

```
> Now Offering for your "Sensitive"
> Delight . . . NEW & IMPROVED . . . a
> viripotent alternative for puissant
> penile strength, colossal size,
> adamantine hardness, blissful orgasms.
>
> Thanks to recent dramatic advances in
> the laboratorial processes, we are now
> able to offer the most incredibly
```

```
> potent jelq alternative available on
> the planet. . . .It is NEW, IMPROVED and
> 20 times more potent in its function.
> The benefits of this product go way
> past the ordinary "strong penis," and
> give new definition to penile ability.
>
> Our new medical breakthrough has
> created a system guaranteed to
>    * Give you a MASSIVE penis
>    * Make your ERECTIONS Iron-HARD
>    * Increase your Semen and EJACULATION
>      by almost 600%!
>
> You will:
>    * THRUST HARDER!
>    * PENETRATE DEEPER!
>    * TASTE SWEETER!
>
> This amazing new product works by
> simply taking 2 capsules every day
> for a month.
>
> Experience the incredible confidence
> boost that comes with a HUGE penis!
> There is nothing like it for relief of
> vexatious depressions.
>
>      Click HERE for Details!!!!
```

I was a little dubious about this. Pills? I was reluctant to try anything that wasn't all-natural. But I'd come so far. It couldn't hurt to find out more. I clicked the link.

> Nano-Thrust Enhancement Program
>
> New science has now created
> revolutionary nanotechnology
> guaranteed to increase your penis size
> by 4" . . . 5" . . . 6" . . . or more in
> just a few short weeks!
>
> Nano-Thrust drastically improves
> blood circulation, massively boosts
> ejaculation volume, intensity and
> staying power. You will be able to
> last for HOURS, have ROCK HARD
> erections of steel, and climax like a
> fountain. Nano-Thrust enhanced penis
> also inspires and heightens Penile
> sensitivity. You will know what it is
> for a penis to come truly ALIVE.
> Achieve
>   * Extreme penetrations
>   * More Intense Orgasms
>   * Shoot up to 13 feet!
>
> This amazing new product works by
> simply taking two nano-capsules
> every day for a month. You need do
> no exercising – nanobots do it all
> for you!

It seemed too good to be true. But there was a convincing technical explanation:

> This principle of nanotechnological
> interactiveness and precursorship
> which in essence is a molecular
> equation of the relevant organic
> alkaloids and glycosides interacting
> with Nano-Thrust to prolificate
> molecular communion and thereby to
> achieve demonstrative efficaciousness
> without negative implication to any
> aspect of human composition. This
> Product is incredulously and
> thoroughly effective. Enjoy!

There were also compelling testimonials from satisfied users:

> "Thank you so much for the
> Nano-Thrust! It is everything you guys
> claim, and then some! I was a bit
> skeptical when I read your description
> of its effects, but there is literally
> no exaggeration in your
> advertisements. It feels great too!
> The increased sensation is the best
> part, incredible feeling to touch now.
> I am so glad I took a chance and
> ordered. Blessings to all of you."
> —Andy H.
>

> "You can't imagine how my life has
> changed since using your techniques.
> I never realized what effect one's
> penis has on your life. The confidence
> that I have now is amazing, and, I
> feel shallow in saying this, but it is
> all because of the growth in my penis
> size. I have gone from 4-1/2″ in the
> erect state to 15-1/4″. I've quit my
> job at a marketing firm and am working
> on opening my own PR business. I've
> also left a dead-end relationship with
> a woman that I was never really
> attracted to, and am happy to be a
> bachelor again. Even people on the
> street seem to treat me differently.
> I have never been happier. I can't
> thank you enough."
> —Steve S.
>
> "It's like having my own steel pipe on
> call 24/7. My Cock is so big, I'm
> already screwing a girl tomorrow!"
> —Joe F.

It was costly—$499.95—but the guarantee seemed reassuring.

> Simply try this Amazing Product for 30
> days and if after 30 days you do not
> experience a minimum of 2″ gain in
> length, simply send the empty package

> back and we'll refund you 100% of
> the cost including shipping. With this
> guarantee, our product must work for
> you . . . or we will lose money on every
> sale!

I could afford the money. Nothing was too expensive if it would give me a bigger, better penis. I typed in my Amex number and address. The site promised delivery within a week in a "plain brown wrapper," and was true to its word.

The box that showed up didn't even have a return address on it. Inside were two bottles of large gel caps—round red ones and oblong blue ones. The directions said to take one of each every night at bedtime, and to expect feelings of warmth and tingling.

I took the first two pills and went to bed. After about half an hour, I could feel my gonads start to heat up. There was a kind of crawling sensation. All of a sudden, I felt my penis become erect, and then it gave a little jump. . . . It was, I realized, as if ghostly hands were milking my member—from the inside out!

This gave me an eerie feeling, at first, but then I got used to it. In fact, the similarity to the sensation of exercising was reassuring, compared to what I'd imagined the nanobots might be doing, crawling around in my *corpora cavernosa* and *corpus spongiosum*. I began to concentrate on my penile goals, just like when I did the exercises on my own, but after a while, I drifted off to sleep.

In the morning, I awoke feeling refreshed . . . and with a tremendous woody. Measuring, for my log, I discovered I'd grown an eighth of an inch overnight!

It was a bit awkward, though, because the sensations continued throughout the day, as well. I began to have difficulty concentrating on my work. But the results were amazing! As I continued to take the capsules, I experienced almost exponential growth. Taking my measurements, I felt like Priapus.

After two weeks, I had to give up wearing tight pants. My erections were so strong, I could do push-ups without using my hands. What a penis!

I was so excited by my penile progress, I kept feeling compelled to go into the men's room so I could drop my pants and gaze at it. My boss started to make pointed inquiries about my health.

But one day, I was at the urinal when Ralph, this goon from Facilities, came in. His eyes bulged. *That* was extremely gratifying.

I was really going to have to take it out and show it to some female soon.

No need to hurry, though. I decided I might as well wait until my course of capsules was over with, and I was full-size, so to speak. Besides, I wasn't sure what too much stimulation would do while the Nano-Thrust 'bots were doing their thing.

I was already experiencing increased sensitivity, as promised.

I took the last two capsules with a feeling of regret . . . and of anticipation. Now, at last, my real life could begin. My shaft was truly splendid. I was seriously well hung and ready for anything. And yet, I couldn't deny that I would miss the pleasurable outlook of watching my penis evolve. Could there be anywhere to go from this peak of perfection but down?

Therefore, I was surprised, but also delighted, when the familiar sensations continued after I'd run out of capsules. The directions that came with the Nano-Thrust capsules had said nothing about how long they kept working, but clearly the 'bots stayed active in the body longer than the thirty days one consumed the product. Outstanding! My staff continued to swell and strengthen at a tangential rate.

When I had to buy larger, baggier trousers, I began to get just a little alarmed. When was this going to stop? I continued to feel the nanobots working. Was there something I'd neglected to do that would arrest the process?

I combed the literature that had come with the capsules. Nothing. Only now did I notice that there was no company contact information on the packaging. I called Amex and they said the company was no longer authorized to accept their card. They didn't have a current mailing address.

I tried to go back to the Nano-Thrust web site, but I hadn't bookmarked it, or saved the original e-mail, and when I tried what I thought was the right address, all I got was "Socket Error: Host name lookup for 'nano-thrust.com' failed." Search engines didn't find it, either. Nor any similar products.

My penis kept growing. It was gorgeous . . . but I started having trouble walking, because my third leg kept getting in the way.

I combed the web. Searching on "big penis" turned up mostly porn sites. (It was kind of satisfying that none of theirs were as big as mine.) "Penis too big" got me mainly not-very-funny humor, and a few sex-advice sites that counseled using extra lubrication and careful positioning when having sex.

Small chance of that, unless I met an Amazon with cavernous capacity. . . . When I thought about it rationally, I realized I was now well beyond what any normal woman could encompass.

Such a shame, though, it was superb . . . and still growing. And strong as a tree trunk. If I'd asked some girl to sit on me, she could—literally, like on a bench.

I finally called in sick and went to the doctor. Under my health plan, I had to see my G.P. to get a referral to a specialist. I didn't tell him how I'd got that way—just showed the results. His jaw dropped.

Then he asked me if I'd been in Africa. I was

thinking he knew about the desert tribesmen and their exercises, but when he started talking about parasites, I realized he thought I had something like elephantiasis. I managed to reassure him that I hadn't been anywhere exotic and steer him away from tropical-medicine specialists to a urologist. And I got him to promise not to say anything to my folks, and to write me a letter so I could take a medical leave from work.

With the urologist, Dr. Epstein, I was more candid. By the time I got to see him, I could no longer wear trousers. My flaccid penis was as big around as my leg and dragged on the floor. I rigged myself a kind of gigantic jock strap, and wore a long, loose-fitting overcoat. I could no longer drive—I had to take a taxi.

Dr. Epstein was just as visibly shocked as my G.P. But when I started talking about the nanobots, he clearly thought I was nuts. Even when I showed him the empty bottles, he was skeptical. And he pissed me off, talking about my "deformity."

So I tuned him out for a few minutes, just long enough to indulge in my favorite fantasy, and got a hard-on. It bowled him over—literally. I hadn't noticed where he was standing.

"My God!" Dr. Epstein cried out, as he toppled. A nurse came running in, took one look at me, and screamed.

Fully erect, my rod was a sight to behold! As tall as I was, and nearly as big around, it slanted ceilingward, muscular, glistening, pulsating slightly. It might have been a little awkward, but it was majestic.

"Let us," I said, "have no more talk of deformity."

Epstein recovered himself. He sent the wide-eyed nurse from the room. He would, he told me, have to consult, do tests.

Well, I told him, I hoped they could schedule them soon, because at the rate I was growing, I was going have to get a larger apartment.

Epstein looked stunned. "Still growing? Perhaps," he said, "we should admit you for observation."

So that's how I came to be a resident of the Tucker Institute for Male Health. Epstein leads a fresh round of interns in every day to see me. If I'm feeling frisky, sometimes I put on a real show—he's learned to provide them with rain gear. They always leave the room looking shaken, the men anyway. The women look . . . thoughtful.

That's something I like to think about.

I don't have much else to do nowadays. I can't move around very much, and I had to give up my job. I tried to telecommute for a while, but it became too difficult, what with all the distraction. The nanobots seem to be more active than ever, and the sensations are stronger. I do some exercises—of my back and legs, so I can still stand up. Sometimes, I walk around the hospital a bit, pushing my penis in front of me on a gurney, but mostly I spend my days in contemplation of my magnificent member.

In consultation with the world's experts in

nanobiology, Epstein thinks they'll soon understand what happened and be able to halt the growth.

"I'm afraid, though," he says "that we haven't a clue as to how to reverse the process."

I just smile.

Prayerville

by Janis Ian

Janis Ian has been a published songwriter since the age of twelve. Her work as a recording artist has garnered her nine Grammy nominations as well as platinum and gold albums from the USA, Japan, Holland, the United Kingdom, South Africa, and numerous other countries. In addition to her international touring and recording schedule, she is a monthly columnist for Performing Songwriter magazine. Her website, http://www.janisian.com, contains a plethora of information about her work and life. She resides in Nashville with her partner of fourteen years and their dogs. She does not consider her life very interesting.

I TOOK the Lone Star from base down Hope Highway, where I switched to a local. After a couple of transfers I managed to catch the last bus toward Prayerville. It was midmorning by then, the orange sun just beginning to cast long shadows on the grass. I had a million things to do before we mustered out the next morning, but I'd put this off about as long as I could.

The kit bag lay lighter in my lap than a week before; my stops had seen to that. This would be the last.

It didn't hold much anymore; a couple of peanut butter and jelly sandwiches to tide me over, a razor to keep me from scaring the natives, and Joe's effects. Didn't seem like enough to warrant crossing half a light-year, but there you have it. A job's a job, and the Army tries to pick the best man for it. Namely, me.

Things have gone a lot easier for us since the Joes joined the war effort. They were built for combat—immune to most bacterials, and strong enough to scare everyone silly. Their Joe-to-Joe Code was the best we've had since the Navajo Talkers, and damn near unbreakable. The glottal stops that came so naturally to their race were impossible for us to pronounce, let alone understand. Half the noises they make are too low for human ears to follow, anyway. That's why they're all called Joe in the service; we can't hear most of their names, and what we catch usually sounds like "Jooooeeeee."

Damn fine soldiers, though their local customs are a bit peculiar. That's why I had the gun with me.

Lord, but I hate this job.

I've spent a lot of time thinking about balance since the Joes joined my unit. How to balance my life with my job. How to balance the job with my heart. How much of my heart lies in the balance, each time I make one of these calls. Most of all, I try to balance the young recruits' stupid sense of invincibility with the reality of war. Sometimes it works.

Sometimes it doesn't.

The bus creaked to a halt outside a run-down barn. Paint was peeling around the edges, but the fencing looked well-maintained. I got up too fast, and my heart sounded in my ears. At least, I think that's why.

Half a dozen hatchlings came running up to me as I stood in the doorway, all from the same brood by the looks of it. They clustered around me as I dismounted, chattering furiously at me and each other. "Me! Me! Me!" they signed, jumping up and down. "Me be soldier! Me be soldier!" I grinned and pulled a chocolate bar out of the kit, dividing it carefully among them. Three females, three males.

I made a mental note to mention that in my report. We don't know much about the Joes' breeding habits at this point. Maybe understanding that the birth ratios stayed even would help our PR.

They fell into step behind me as I headed toward the house, giggling and saluting one another in mock seriousness. This bunch couldn't be anywhere near adolescence; that didn't bode well for their survival. I hoped there were a few older ones to balance them out. After today, they'd need all the help they could get. It's a peaceful enough planet, but any society that evolves their kind of religion has to be.

I waited with a sinking heart as the door announced me. Maybe the rest of them wouldn't be around this time of day. Maybe I could put it off.

No such luck. It sprang open and I quickly pulled off my cap. The young Joe's eyes widened as he took in my uniform and the bag I carried. He looked a little shook for a moment, but then he squared his shoulders and gestured me in, the younger ones melting away at his scowl.

We walked into a pretty, sunlit kitchen where three more Joes were busy preparing some kind of food. At the sight of me, one dropped the knife she'd been holding, and it clattered to the floor. The male went over and put a hand on her shoulder, saying something under his breath. She ducked her head and left the room.

"I am here," I signed to them.

"You are welcome here," the second male signed back. He looked to be a slightly older version of the first. That was good, three generations under the one roof. I don't know why, but it made it easier on me.

"I have news for your parent—" I wanted to say more, but waited. There's a formality to these things. God knows, after the last three I should be expert at it.

"She comes," he signed, motioning to a chair. I sat down, gratitude in every weary bone, and accepted a cup of hot tea from one of the females.

There was no chitchat. The Joes don't seem to believe in small talk. Even in the barracks, the younger ones keep to themselves most of the time. There's a rumor that most of them feel incomplete until they find their mate, and if you tried to engage a bachelor in conversation you halfway believed it. The older ones, the married ones, they seem to get along okay, but the single Joes aren't very quick on the uptake, if you know what I mean. It's one of the reasons we've been promoting enlistment for married men. The bachelors need to be told everything twice.

The Joes sat around me in silence, waiting for balance to be achieved. I admired their stoicism. Then again, if you really believe in that kind of afterlife, with eternal marriage part of it, maybe they weren't stoics at all. Maybe it was just acceptance. Either way was okay with me; I didn't have to live with it.

They rose before I heard anything, and I hastily got up to greet their mother. She came in slowly, followed by the other male. Her eyes searched my face, but I have special expression I've cultivated for these moments—blank, with just a hint of pity around the eyes. I couldn't afford to get involved. That would make it harder to send my men out, the next time.

"You are welcome here," Her signs were fluid, more economical than the children's. A sign of age and maturity, that sparseness.

"I have news," I indicated. "Gather your family, please."

She sent one of the females to bring the rest of the children. They came bouncing in, still giggling, but the oldest boy barked something at them and the noise subsided. In a few minutes I had a captive audience ready for my presentation.

I put my kit bag on the table and pulled out Joe's effects. The first time I had to do that, I almost dropped the container. I'd forgotten how heavy ashes can be, packed so densely into a small space. By now I was used to it. The weight, anyhow.

I laid the box on the table in front of me, straightened the corners, and nodded toward the mother. She inclined her head. Part one of the ritual was completed.

Next I took out a small scroll. At the sight of it, one

of the little ones gasped. A harsh look from his sister froze him back into silence. I opened it to lay flat on the table, then turned it so it was facing the mother. I couldn't read it, but I knew it contained the Joe's name, his wife's name, their marriage announcement and their intent to remain together throughout eternity. It's a pretty piece of poetry, even in translation.

Then I pulled out the folded flag and arranged it to cover both box and parchment. I smoothed it out with fingers that had begun to shake slightly, and wished I were anywhere but here, in this cozy kitchen, light streaming through the open windows and nothing but quiet fields beyond. I tried hard not to look up yet, particularly at the littlest ones. They were completely still now, the kind of immobility you hope never to see in a child.

My heart began to ache. I hate this job.

My eyes strayed to the countertop as I waited for her response. Maybe this time would be different. Maybe this time I could go home feeling clean. Then I noticed the icon hanging over the sink, and I knew nothing would change.

The mother sighed, one of those drawn-out sighs that speaks volumes. Smoothing her dress, she leaned forward slightly and said in heavily-accented Terran, *"A soul has been cleaved from this rock."*

I started at her choice of language. She must have been practicing the ritual for months, learning the sounds phonetically, pitching her voice high enough for me to hear. It was an elegant gesture on her part.

Then I remembered my job, and answered, "A soul has been cleaved from this rock." The formal response to acknowledge that I understood, which I didn't.

She smiled slightly, looked around at the children, and continued in sign. *"The rock we stand upon is called a marriage."* Yes. Without the marriage, there could be no rock. When a Joe ties the knot, it means together forever, with all that implies.

"The marriage, too, is cleaved in half." I've never understood that either. Where I come from, so long as you hold someone's memory in your heart, they're still with you. And you with them. I've got a couple like that myself, unbelievable as it would seem to my troops.

I thought of breaking tradition to argue the point, but I knew it wouldn't work. It hadn't done any good the first three times I tried. I'd only ruined the ceremony.

"The soul wanders alone." Whoever came up with the idea that uniting two souls in a marriage means each soul is somehow halved by it? I'm sure it wasn't a woman. And somehow, it's always the women who are left behind.

"Two must be joined." There's that damnable balance again. All things even. A Joe can spend decades searching for his other half, but once found, they're joined forever. One of my Joes tried to explain it once, saying, "What if you spent three lifetimes searching for your other half? Feeling empty and only part-man the whole time? When you finally found her, you'd be whole. It follows that without her, you'd be half." I understood the words, but it made no sense.

"In life eternal, so be it."

She'd finished her part of the ritual, face composed, and sat waiting for me to continue. Instead there was only silence—long, stuttering silence. I was supposed to make the response, but I couldn't get the words past my lips. My heart began banging again, insisting I pay attention. I told it to get lost.

How could I condemn this woman?

She waited, head bowed, and I noticed the muscles of her arms tensing as her hands tried to sit quietly in her lap. No weakling, this. A farm girl, born and bred to labor. She'd borne three litters, kept the place going without a man at her side, all so he could go off and get slaughtered in a war that left her nothing but a box of burned bones and a scrap of cloth to remember him by. A good-looking woman, by any standard. An open, honest face. A mother's face.

"In life eternal, so be it," I muttered, looking down at my own twisting hands. One of the kids began to cry, big silent tears that made me think of melting ice. Another hid his face in his hands, but none of them left the room.

I rose, tucking the cap under my arm, and saluted them all. "I'll wait for you outside," I told her. "Take your time."

I couldn't wait to get out of there.

Back in the open again, I heaved a sigh of relief and tore open a packet of Lights. I know they're bad for me, but at times like this a little self-punishment goes a long way. I'm not used to houses anymore. Maybe they grow on you.

After a while, she came out. "We'll walk, yes?" she signed.

I shrugged my shoulders. "Where?"

"Past that hill, I think. Away from the house."

She stood there patiently while I GI'd the cigarette and stuffed the butt in my pocket. No point in rushing things now. At least I wouldn't have to face the kids again.

As we walked, I tried to think of something to say. Something to show that, while I didn't agree, I understood. But there was really nothing to say, and whenever I'd tried before, I'd been ignored. So we walked in silence, breathing in the scent of trees and clean air. The sunlight against her hair reminded me of someone, a girl I'd dated years ago, before duty called.

"You don't understand, do you?" she asked. No, I didn't understand. I didn't understand leaving those kids with nothing more than a regular veteran's check from the Service. I didn't understand why we had to abide by their customs. I didn't understand any of it, least of all why I had to be the one to carry them out. But I understood orders.

Of course, I didn't say any of that, just shrugged. But she looked at my face, and something must have showed, because our eyes met for a long time before she started off again.

When we reached the top of the hill, she paused, then turned to face me.

"All this," she gestured, pointing to the peaceful fields, "comes from this." She touched her heart. "From our prayers. From our faith. From our belief that we are destined to be one. Surely you can feel that?"

I felt nothing but a slight breeze and a strong sense of guilt, so I paid her no mind and kept on going. For a few minutes we strolled in silence, but then she stopped again. She looked back at the house and sighed.

"I'll miss them," she said. "I'll miss this," throwing her arms out to encompass the soil and sky. "But there is no choice.

I'd had just about enough, so I grabbed her hands in midair and brought them together, wrist against wrist, holding them as tightly as I could. Hoping it hurt.

"What do you mean, *no choice?*" I hissed. "There is *always* a choice."

She pulled away, rubbing her wrists. I was furious with myself for getting involved. I still had a job to do, and this would only make harder.

"Do you know what happens to those of us who stray from this path?" She was signing slowly now, thinking her way through to the right words. "To those who are prevented from taking it?"

Her gestures were speeding up, and she began to tremble slightly. "Have you ever seen one who has refused The Ritual? Have your travels taken you that far?" The trembling was becoming obvious, but I just looked at her noncommittally. Goes with the territory, that ability to show no interest when someone begins drowning before your eyes.

She mistook my silence for concentration, and continued.

"They lose themselves. They go away somewhere and they never come back. It can take weeks, or sometimes months, but in the end, they are gone. They live on with half a heart, half a soul, half a mind, unable to fend for themselves."

I tried to keep the mask on my face, but I could feel it slipping now. What HQ would give for this information! A promotion, at the least. Maybe even a transfer. My eyes met hers, and I attempted to look understanding. But she wasn't buying.

"You have no idea!" she exclaimed. "They live with no self. . . . They are more dead than the dead, for their bodies still demand nourishment, warmth, shelter, though they can give nothing back!" Her eyes flashed, whether in anger or indignation I don't know.

"*That* is why we have The Ritual! *That* is why duty is so important! *That* is why I go with you now!" She came to a screeching halt, staring back at the house, then began waving her arms again. "You think all this means nothing to me? My home? *My family?* I would not burden them so!"

I was stunned. So those who refused to participate in the ritual slowly faded away? Who else knew about this? And why hadn't anyone warned me?

The shock must have shown, because she looked concerned all of a sudden. She took a half step toward me, closer than I'd ever been to a female Joe. There was a long pause while she searched my face.

"You did not know this?" If it was possible for a signer to speak softly, she was managing well. I didn't need her pity.

"No. I didn't know . . . I had no idea." It all started to make horrible sense now—why I'd been volunteered, why no one would give me any information beyond the most basic directions. There's a reason they named my ship *The Hardened Heart*. My non-coms don't need me to spout philosophy; they just need orders they can follow.

"But . . . you must know! You must understand. Otherwise, The Ritual is meaningless. They would never have sent you . . ."

She kept talking, but I tuned it out. I didn't like the way this conversation was going—not at all. The others hadn't bothered trying to explain, they'd just walked docilely out of the house and into my arms. After that it was only a matter of logistics.

I was starting to get a little edgy now, and my heart was beating in my ears again, threatening to drown out everything around me.

No, I didn't like it at all because, above the hammering of my heart, I could see her *looking* at me, *really* looking, the way you look at an old friend you haven't seen in a while and try to explain why you're in the Service now. Or a lover who suddenly confesses they dreamed of someone else last night, only they think it might have been you in disguise.

But part of my job was seeing this through, so I told my heart to cut it out, and tried to tune her back in.

"You see, even the dead make their contribution to our lives. We memorialize them in song. We weep over their loss, each tear carving a deeper niche into our capacity for joy. And most of all," she said, turning to face me head-on again, "they allow us to keep our memories intact, of their beauty, of our wholeness together."

She finally stopped talking, and waited for me to say something. There was nothing to say. Only the sound of my heart in ears, and the silence of her voice.

"Why didn't any of the others explain this to me?" I finally asked. It might have helped if they had.

"They must have thought you knew." She pressed a hand against my chest, and her eyes widened as she felt the triphammer going.

"But if you did not know about The Ritual . . . then all this time, you have felt like a–a—what is the word?"

I winced and removed her hand. She was way too close for comfort now, and it reminded me of something I'd been trying to forget. I was fast losing what little patience I had.

"The word is murderer," I said, and turned toward the field below. There was a wooded copse about half a mile away; that would do nicely.

She hurried up to catch up, smiling. "But no, of course you are no murderer! How could anyone with anger in his heart perform The Ritual?"

That stopped me cold. What the hell did anger have to do with it? I was just doing my job. I shoved the thought away for later inspection, and continued walking. After a few minutes, though, she began making noises and waving her arms around again, so I heaved a sigh and turned to face her. I'd already spent most of the day on this, and it was time to go back. The last thing I needed was to miss that bus.

I caught her attention in mid-sentence and said

"Look. I don't know what you mean by 'The Ritual.' As far as I'm concerned, it's a bunch of gestures we both go through to make the family feel better, that end—" I waved at the trees, then pointed to my holster "—in this."

"Oh, no!" She looked aghast. "No, no, no! The Ritual is our redemption. It is a thing of beauty. It is everlasting."

Now, how can anything but death be everlasting? And how could this kind of death be a redemption? I slowly shook my head.

"You mean you're redeemed when you die?"

"No, silly." She laughed out loud, a lovely cadence in sharp contrast to the subject matter. "*You* are redeemed when I die."

That made even less sense, and I said so.

"But how can it be otherwise?" she asked.

God, I hated this conversation. But she showed no inclination to move forward, and I wasn't about to drag her, so we continued.

"Still doesn't make sense to me," I said. "And what about the children? How can you leave them behind like this?"

She smiled. "What about them? They will be fine with you. You're strong—the farm and fields will prosper under your care, as they will."

I felt my jaw muscles sag as her words sank in. How many children had I left behind by now? Twenty? Thirty? All still sitting in their kitchens, waiting patiently for me to return?

It was too much. I couldn't stand it. My heart felt like it was about to jump through those medals on my chest and flee for its life. The noise was everywhere, like the fluttering of thousands of tiny wings, beating against my eardrums, covering up all thought and response.

She moved closer still, and I felt myself backing away. This wasn't how it was supposed to go! She edged up to my face and smiled, the sure, beatific smile of someone without a care in the world. The smile of a saint, about to be set on fire.

And then she kissed me, and I saw stars.

No, I mean literally. Stars. The universe, expanding and contracting. The planets, spinning around in orbit, each one bound by the actions of the other. The deep connection of each particle of dust to every other thing in creation.

And time. Time as one long, magical fulcrum, moving each separate star and planet and the people within it in one dizzying, perfect order. Time, just waiting for the right second to link up two people and a moment like this.

I broke first, gasping for air and trying to stay on my feet. I've never felt that kind of connection before, a bond with everything and everyone, and it made me dizzy. Almost nauseous, in fact.

She smiled again, eyes tender. "Now you understand, yes?"

Yes, I understand. That's why they picked me for this job, I guess. I've always been able to understand both sides of a situation. I motioned her towards the woods, and she walked into the copse with a smile on her face.

* * *

I caught the last bus back to base. It seemed quicker going back than it had been coming, but it's always that way. The kit bag was empty, stuffed in a spare pocket until I needed it again.

My heart was hardly hammering now. In fact, I could barely hear it at all.

Kingdom Come

by Kay Kenyon

Kay Kenyon is the author of five science fiction novels. Her most recent, *Maximum Ice*, was a finalist for the 2002 Philip K. Dick award. It is the tale of a ship of gypsies who return to Earth to find it dreadfully altered by an icelike ecology of information. Kay believes in character-driven science fiction with strong world-building. She was written about the collapse of terraforming (*Rift*); a galactic search for biodiversity (*The Seed of Time*); and a world where seasonal change transfigures the ecology and life forms (*Tropic of Creation*). "Kingdom Come" takes place loosely in the universe of her novel, *The Seeds of Time*.

MY name's Jacob. Never mind Jacob *who*. I don't fill out forms—not anymore. So you can take your creamed corn, your Muzak, and your forms in triplicate, and stuff 'em.

Now, where was I? Oh, about leaving the door open. At Fairhaven Home, doors are closed and locked at 8:00 PM, that's the rule. *Was* the rule. Can't you get it straight, there aren't rules anymore? So, you say, all those soft-headed loonies got out and ran across the lawn, nightgowns fluttering open, and scaring the neighbors half to death? Hell, those neighbors been scared to death their whole lives. A few crazy people running around naked in the grass is nothing.

Besides, Fairhaven's out of time. No more meals on wheels, boys and girls. No more 6:00 o'clock news in the holo alcove. We're goners if we stay.

Jungle's comin'.

Oh, it's *been* comin'. You can hear it at night when the refugee traffic quiets down. Distant crashes, muffled thuds. Those spindly trees fall over in the front lines and advance the jungle another fifteen meters. Or sometimes, it just sounds like soap bubbles fizzing down to scum.

Gets on your nerves. That's why I gotta be on my way. Well, maybe not the only reason.

Crissy, now. Crissy was all skittery about it. I told her to get the hell out of here, now that the doors aren't locked, and the food's running out.

She came into my room as I was packing, her eyes big as bagels. "Jacob," she said, "you're not leaving?" Crissy looks up to me like a dad, so I guess she hated to see me go.

"'Course I'm leaving," I said. "Jungle's comin'." I crammed another pair of socks into my duffel, stamped "Space Recon," in bright green letters. The doc told me I wouldn't be needing the duffel, my spacer years were long past. Good thing I don't listen to twenty-years-olds.

Crissy eyed my bright yellow jogging shoes. You're supposed to wear slippers. Slippers! Bet those nurses were wearing their combat boots when they high-tailed it this morning.

"They're gone," Crissy said, practically reading my mind. "The staff is all gone."

"'Course they're gone! Those geese don't know what to do with the new world. They're running just like everybody. Flew past my window about five AM, honking and crapping. Circled once and flew north."

Tears came into Crissy's eyes. I paused, sunscreen in hand. Then I tossed it on the bed and sat next to her. "None of that now, Crissy. If you're gonna cry, let 'er rip, none of that snuffling business. Makes it look like you got a dose of spacer's crotch."

I got a smile out of her, but it wobbled.

"You want to come along?" I didn't look forward to a greenhorn slowing me down, but if Crissy got up the nerve, I wouldn't leave her behind.

From where we sat, the window looked out on the weedy monotone of Westphal County. The world these days was the same everywhere, just one big monoculture of weeds and grasses and junk shrubs. Except that, hovering on the edge, just half a kilometer away, was a looming wall of jungle. That day, more than ever, it looked like a turquoise tidal wave humping along the horizon as far as you could see. If you listened hard, you could hear it coming: vines plowing toward the light, buds erupting. The kingdom coming, I guess, and not the kingdom most folks had in mind either.

"It's done three kilometers since yesterday," I told her. "It's the heat, see. Whole thing's got a new head of steam, since summer."

Crissy was looking doubtful about the jungle. About leaving. I didn't blame her, but I wasn't going to sit in my rocking chair and let it kill me. I can still walk faster than the jungle grows—I ain't *that* old—and I'll be headed to the mountains, same as everybody. I turned back to my duffel, picking up a length of bamboo. "See this? Know why I'm taking this?" Crissy looked blank. "'Cause it lets *live* things be. Or things that used to be alive." I played a few notes on the hollow cane. "See? A flute. Ever think, Crissy, that the jungle might be *boring* instead of scary? Just like space. Nothing to be afraid of, you just play a little music when you get to feeling wacky." I knew what I was talking about. Down in the boiler room of those big starships, sometimes there's not much to do. You kinda hope there won't be. I blew some notes of "When the Saints," then tossed the flute into the duffel.

"See this?" I patted the duffel. "Cotton. Anything synthetic or metal or plastic or transmetal, it just eats it up."

I could see that part scared her. But she was always one for scary stories, coming and asking me about other worlds, and Space Recon, and the sights I had seen. Sometimes, to tell the truth, all I saw of alien ground was through the porthole. Other times we got ground time, though, and stood outside the tub, smoking cigarettes and taking it all in: remnants of old cities, not shaped right, the wrong colors. Trees growing upside down, their roots sticking out like frizzled hair. Stuff like that. I seen some sights, in my twenty years of service.

The way it worked, those Recon ships were more than spaceships. They were also time ships. Time travel was the missing link in getting to the stars, because stardrive—faster-than-light—never came true, just like they said it wouldn't. But then they figured out how to use time as a back door to the stars, and they called it a time sling, because time can sling you to different places, if you really think about it. The whole galaxy, see, is moving at a fast clip, round and round, so at any given moment, the Earth's on or near a point in the universe where another solar system might have been, millions of years ago. And where a planet like ours might have been. If it looked like a water planet, they'd send out a Recon ship. To mine the biota. Though we'd bring home thousands of plants, most of them weren't keepers, weren't going to help us out for that good ol' bio-di-versity, that we needed so bad.

Never mind whose fault it all was.

Blame the corporate farms, the genomic engineering—hell, blame Nostradamus if you want to, but old *terra firma* was becoming *terra the sama,* and it was killing us, what with susceptibility to diseases, and maybe downright boredom.

That was before Niang's Planet. The greenest world we'd ever seen, the most earthlike. Maybe that was why the biota, or seeds, or whatever they were, escaped quarantine. You couldn't keep Niang biota down, not even with all the poisons they tried.

Out in the hallway we heard shrieks. I peeked out. "All clear," I told Crissy. "It's just a food fight." I paused. "Second thought, you oughta tell them to save what's left. If you're going to try to run for it, you'll need provisions."

I couldn't put it off any longer. We walked down the hall together, stepping over food trays and bed pans and hairbrushes.

Out on the porch, I hoisted my duffel. "I gotta go, Crissy." I hugged her, hard. "You can still come with, Crissy. You're the daughter I never had, see?"

She nodded. She believed me, but she didn't see. Not the way I saw. None of them saw that this was the kingdom to be. Did they want to be knights or drudges? Heather, Janie, Kev, they all stood there in their pink and blue nightgowns.

Nope, not knights. I shook my head. "Watch out for yourself, Crissy!"

She waved. Big phony smile, but I blessed her for it. Then I was on my way.

I been on the road a while now. Feeling good, except that I forgot to pack food. The wind brings a fruity smell, putting me in mind of breakfast. The home took my edge off, that's for sure. How long was I there, anyhow?

This two-lane highway parallels the blue forest wall. By tomorrow, I figure this road will be gone. I can hear the tall, frondy stalks breaking in the distance, falling, reaching for the road: a big tasty strip of asphalt. Roadway to us, licorice to them.

An occasional car speeds by. Sometimes they honk, I wave. They see me muttering as I walk, and they're scared to give me a lift. They don't know how a lot of spacers talk to themselves, and count it damn good company. Besides, they got no room in their cars for an old geezer, stuffed like they are with holo-

Vs, lamps, rocking chairs, microwaves, baby buggies, and that one right there, a patio grill, roped to the roof. The plastic and metal are refugees, same as their owners. We're all heading to the mountains, the pass, where it's too cold for the jungle. Only thing I worry about is, how long will it take before the spores blow on the wind, and come at us from the other side?

But that's the glory of it. You don't know. Back with Crissy, we had everything on time, knew the drill: meals, baths, social hour, bed. But here, outside . . . it's a new game. Don't know the rules, maybe make a few of 'em up, by God.

It snuck up on me, getting old. Used to be heating /ventilation chief, I climbed that high in Recon. Worked on the big machines, and calibrated, tinkered, jury-rigged, made do, and made up what I didn't know. Then one day I saw that my hair was the same color as the metal I worked on: gray. I still felt twenty-five, but nope, I was fifty-five. Then pretty soon, that young fellow, he took my spot. It didn't go over too good, and what with words being said that the geese didn't like, I found myself with a slip of paper saying thanks for the twenty years. From the grandstand I watched that big ship blast off, yanking my heart out of me like a bad tooth. Then, groundside, nothing seemed right. People with their patio grills and leather sofas, watching sports, watching life. 'Course, folks thought *I* wasn't quite right. Guess I lost that argument.

Tell you one thing, though. If I had it to do over, I wouldn't be in the boiler room—we called it a boiler room, why get fancy—I'd be getting an eyeful outside, with those field teams that saw all the sights. Still, Crissy thinks I've had a big life, and maybe I have, at that.

This here's a telephone pole. It's all wrong, festooned with turquoise vines. The front line's still a kilometer away, but some advance scout's claimed this pole. The metal conduit running up the side is a braided blue vine. And no, I don't mean *covered* with vine, I mean it *is* a vine. And the transformer barrels are friggin' flower baskets, with orange, egglike flowers. The transformer transformed. Now that's a thought.

Along the fence here, the barbed wire's got a fleshy yellow star at each barb. Couple of crows eating those stars . . .

Okay, I ate a few myself. Can't be squeamish if you're in the wild. Got to be wily, got to take the plunge. Like I told Crissy.

The cars hum by, electric motors groaning under the strain of their big loads. They're heading to the mountains, and maybe over the mountain, if that side is still the old world. Funny thing is, what they're looking for is just what they had. That's why they're bringing their holo-V sets and leaf blowers, so they can set up all their stuff and carry on. But, see, maybe we *can't* carry on what's past. Even if we could, what place is there for an old Recon recruit like me with his head full of bolts?

I got to admit those yellow stars sit just fine in my gut. Long as I don't see no dead birds.

Moving on, I can see there's a town over there.

Don't even remember what town it is, but it's right at the foot of the big turquoise wall.

If you already figured out that I'd be leaving the road, then you been paying attention. The mountains ain't for me. Can't see myself fitting in, can you?

Okay, here's the local Stop and Shop, deserted like everything else. Still got its old gas pumps like they stopped using in the 'teens. Water nozzle still works, though, and I drank my share, and hosed down my face. Comes a sweet burst of wind, picking up the smells of a fruity kingdom. The street's a thick, woven mat, and those giant staples are the hoods of sunken cars. I sit on the bowed roof of what might have been a Volkswagen, and eat some of the antenna, jerky-flavored.

Nobody here to share the meal with. They all ran away, scared to death. Folks think the jungle destroys what it touches, but when you look close, you can see that things aren't destroyed . . . only revised. Maybe for some folks it amounts to the same thing.

I go on. The closer you get to the jungle wall, the odder the town gets. For instance, that house there, near the outskirts. You got your gables on the roof, but they're like ladies' bonnets, all leafy. Under that, those windows, with their alien glaze—and gaze. Garage door's still open, from when they made their run.

Looking inside the house, I'm expecting a mess. But, no sir, it's all regular. The flowered doorknobs work when you turn 'em, and the matted door opens. In the parlor, the flowered upholstery's got some strange new flowers, like a five-year-old's coloring book. Lots of it's outside the lines.

The picture window looks out to the tidal wave, frozen in the upswing. The more I stare, the more I can imagine all the stuff of the town mixed in there: knickknacks, footstools, shoe horns, bookends, deck chairs, blenders, coat hangers, silverware, rakes, and what not, all jumbled up into a froth. I'm thinking maybe the wave'll just pass over my head, like I'm a swimmer near the bottom. All the fuss is on the surface. If that's where you live your life, well, son, you're gonna get thrashed.

It's a new order of things, I figure. Things ripe and strange—full of the sap of life. If I told Crissy one thing wrong, it was that the jungle might be boring. No such thing. 'Course, I ain't *in* the jungle yet.

That's next.

I should have known, calling it the kingdom, and all. I was thinking back to knights and kings, and riding out. But an old spacer like me should know the new stuff when he sees it. It's getting revised, like I said. It's all getting a second chance. I feel those gold stars swimming in my blood, lighting a fire.

Just as I close the front door, I hear it. A rattle like a toolbox, only in pulses. Turning back, I follow the sound into the parlor. Next to the couch, I see the mossy outline of a telephone. Somehow its circuitry—though revised—still works. The notion hits me that Crissy is calling. I pick up the fuzzy receiver and press it to my ear. A woman's voice comes from far away, a woody remnant of a voice, maybe not even a language I know anymore.

I'm thinking, maybe somebody's selling magazine subscriptions. Then, on impulse, I speak into the receiver. "If that's you, Crissy, you should come on down. The kingdom's come, see? The big wave won't hurt you, it'll just pass on over, coloring things."

There was a gargle of electrons from the other side. I nodded to her. "Tell the folks at Fairhaven old Jacob went first."

Licensed to Reclaim

by Laura Resnick

Laura Resnick is the Campbell Award-winning author of forty science fiction and fantasy short stories, several fantasy novels, numerous articles, and one nonfiction book. In addition, she's the award-winning author of more than a dozen romance novels written under the pseudonym Laura Leone. In her copious spare time, she writes two regular opinion columns. You can find her on the web at www.sff.net/people/laresnick.

IT was the threat of imminent castration which really distressed me. Up until then, I had maintained a stoic air of manly calm, and even made a few deft puns about my seemingly hopeless predicament. But the prospect of being emasculated, I confess, briefly unnerved me.

Only briefly, of course. *Very* briefly. So briefly that I doubt my evil captor noticed it. Only my admirably modern yet somehow classic masculine sensitivity compels me to admit, in retrospect, that I was—*briefly*, as I say—anxious about the prospect I suddenly found myself facing.

Mine is a steely courage which does not readily succumb to external pressure or tolerate internal wavering. Naturally, I bore with fortitude the discovery that I had been drugged and captured by the minions of my fiendish foe, Professor Phosphor. Of course, I behaved with grim courage as that villain laughed maniacally while I tested the strength of the chains which bound me. It goes without saying that I was mentally prepared to face any torture he devised for me, and physically prepared to endure any privation.

Except, of course, for being castrated. I really hadn't taken that possibility into consideration when I accepted this mission, and I was now reviewing my options.

"You *have* no options," Professor Phosphor advised me with a demonic sneer while his minions set up the menacing-looking apparatus which was about to force a whole new lifestyle on me.

"What do you want?" I demanded.

"I want to get away with my diabolical scheme, of course," he replied. "Tax free."

I glanced over to where his minions were testing the laser which would, in just moments, forever end my need to tell my tailor to make sure the crotch wasn't too tight.

"Do you think you can make me talk?" I sneered.

"Actually, I was hoping I could make you *shut up* for a change, but Nemesis informs me that it will take more than a little maiming to do that."

"Nemesis?" I narrowed my eyes. "So you've taken her captive, too, you fiend!"

"You're really very slow, aren't you?" Phosphor said, shaking his head. "Dear boy, my lovely Nemesis captured *you*."

"Captured me? But . . ."

Of course!

It was starting to come back to me now. The last thing I remembered before waking up enchained in Phosphor's subterranean lair was . . . yes! I was in a five-star hotel, skillfully seducing the beautiful and mysterious Nemesis Coquette. My mission was to stop Professor Phosphor's evil plan, and I thought Nemesis might be able to lead me to the scoundrel. Phosphor had financed her education at Princeton and her postgraduate work at the Sorbonne, and he now paid for her apartment in London and held the deed on her villa outside of Cannes. So I had shrewdly deduced that it was possible she knew him well. It was only a short step from this realization to recognizing that she was in an ideal position to betray him for me and thereby ensure the success of my mission.

Yes, I admit, I knew there was a chance that my ruthlessly using her as a pawn could get her killed; but a man in my line of work has to keep his mind on the mission. And I certainly kept my mind on the mission as I wooed Nemesis Coquette—who was at least half my age—in gourmet restaurants and first class hotels at my employer's expense. No thought but my duty was on my mind as I cruised on yachts with her, drove along sunset-streaked cliffside roads with her in my red Ferrari, and continually replenished my wardrobe with new tailored suits in an effort to win her blind devotion. Then, finally, as I held Nemesis in my arms that night and kissed her with consummate mastery . . . she had suggested we have a drink.

"My martini . . ." I said aloud now, while Phosphor's minions rolled the castration apparatus toward me.

"Yes," purred a sultry feminine voice. "Your martini."

"Nemesis," I hissed as I saw her emerge from the shadows. She crossed the polished floor of this strange hideout to slip her arm through Phosphor's and stand by his side.

She smiled snidely at me. "I put the drug in your martini while I was shaking it."

"How many times do I have to tell you?" I felt a sudden burst of exasperation. "I like my martinis stirred, not shaken!"

"He was so busy trying to get into my pants," Nemesis told Phosphor, "he didn't even notice what I was doing. I could have put a kilo of paprika in there, and he probably wouldn't have noticed. The man's libido really rules his life."

"Not for much longer." Phosphor cast a significant look at the machine which his minions were now ready to use.

"So," I said, stalling for time. "You two were in cahoots the whole time, eh?"

"Cahoots?" Nemesis sneered. "I'm in love with him, you fool!"

"How can you possibly be in love with this fiend, Nemesis?"

"He's smarter than you, richer than you, better-looking than you—"

"Is not!"

"Am so!"

"And he doesn't subject me to tedious sexual come-ons, double entendres about my body, and bad puns every time he commits an act of violence. He is a real man."

"A real man? Would a 'real man' pay your tuition at two major universities, buy you a villa, buy you a London flat . . ." I stopped, realizing that I probably wasn't marshaling the most effective possible argument to win her away from Phosphor at this juncture.

"And *he*," Nemesis said to me, "doesn't need a red sports car to compensate for subconscious fears of masculine inadequacy."

"Those fears won't be merely subconscious after this," Phosphor said gleefully.

"They weren't," Nemesis said, "merely subconscious fears in the first place. Trust me on this."

Phosphor made an imperious gesture to his minions. They immediately seized my legs and began tearing off my trousers.

"Stop! Stop!" I commanded. "Get your hands off me! Phosphor! What are these minions of your doing?"

"Removing your pants, of course. Those are exquisite trousers, and I don't want them ruined. I don't suppose you'd care to share the name of your tailor?"

"Why, in God's name, are you doing this?" I shouted, now wearing only my socks and shirt.

"Frankly, dear boy, if it were up to me," Phosphor said, "I'd just kill you. Castration was Nemesis' idea."

"What?" I cried.

"If you had spent the past few days in his constant company," Nemesis said to Phosphor, "fighting of his unwelcome advances and listening to his boorish jokes, you'd want to castrate him, too. I promise you."

"Phosphor," I said, breaking into a cold sweat as the laser beam was fired up and started slowly moving toward my loins, "you can't do this, man! It's inhuman! It's unthinkable!"

"Sorry, dear boy. I'm an absolute slave to the wishes of the woman I love. By the way, we want you to be the first to know—we're getting married."

The laser beam was leaving a charred swath on the marble floor as it made its way toward my vulnerable flesh. "Phosphor, we can make a deal! Stop this! Stop it now!"

"My darling Nemesis was uncertain about committing to me . . . until she met you," Phosphor explained. "After delivering your unconscious carcass to me, the first thing she said was, 'If this is an example of what's out there in the dating world, then I know I was a fool to hesitate even for a moment. Let's get married.' Sort of touching, don't you think?"

"Phosphor, stop this infernal machine!"

"So, in a way, I owe you," he said to me.

"So stop this, then!"

"Can't. Promised Nemesis. But I will see that you get the finest medical care after it's done, dear boy."

"No!"

"All right, then, if you insist—no doctors. We'll just leave you chained to the floor until you die."

"Phosphor, you cad!"

"Can I ask your advice about something, man to man, as long as we're killing some time here? That laser is *slow,* isn't it?"

"Damn you!"

"Where was I? Oh, yes. You see, I have an enormous family," Phosphor continued, "and many colleagues and acquaintances, so I really had my heart set on a big wedding. Nemesis, however, wants a small, intimate affair. Just immediate family, maybe a few of our most loyal minions. Her position—and, I confess, it's a sensible one, Nemesis being so much less sentimental than I am—is that we're international criminals and therefore need to keep a low profile, even on the happiest day of our lives." He kissed Nemesis' hand, then said, "Tell me, as a man of the world, what do you think?"

"I think you're a diabolical fiend who will never get away with this!" I cried as the laser beam burned the floor within millimeters of my—

There was a sudden, deafening explosion. The halogen lamps flickered, the ground shook, the laser machine ceased functioning as it exploded in flames, Nemesis shrieked, and the minions started babbling in panic. Black smoke poured out of the laser machine, obscuring my vision and searing my lungs.

Then a woman's smooth voice said, "We both know who the *real* diabolical fiend is, don't we, Nemesis? But your prisoner's right about one thing. You'll never get away with this."

I heard something whine through the air, and then Phosphor gasped, clutched his chest, and fell on top of me—still holding the trousers which his minions had handed to him after stripping me.

"Get off me, you oaf!"

Nemesis screeched and fell on top of both of us.

"Get *off* me!" I repeated.

"Phosphor!" Nemesis cried. "Speak to me!"

Phosphor's only reply was to shudder briefly in his death throes.

"Good God!" I said, realizing the truth. "There's an arrow in his chest! Straight to the heart!"

"That's not an arrow, you dolt," Nemesis said, ducking her head as another arrow whined past us. "It's the bolt of a crossbow."

"*Looks* like an arrow."

"Only one person would be foolish enough to come here armed only with a crossbow." Nemesis fumbled in her ample cleavage—and then pulled out a pistol.

"How do you do that?" I asked, momentarily distracted.

Nemesis shrieked and tried to crawl between Phosphor's body and mine—which still lay beneath Phosphor's—as gunshots exploded all around us.

"I didn't come here armed *only* with a crossbow," the mystery woman said from the depths of the smoke.

"Damn!" Nemesis chewed briefly on her lush lower lip. "Time for a new plan."

"While you're thinking . . ." I ventured. "Phosphor's getting awfully heavy. If you wouldn't mind . . ."

She shoved Phosphor's corpse off me.

"Thanks," I said.

"You useless idiot!" she said to Phosphor's body, then she kicked it away from us.

"He was right," I observed. "You're not exactly sentimental."

"He served his purpose," she said. "And now you'll serve yours."

She pulled an enormous key out of her ample cleavage—

"How *do* you do that?"

—and then unlocked the manacles which held me prisoner.

"Thanks again." I sat up and gave her a seductive smile, though the smoke was making my eyes water. "Does this mean you're having a change of heart?"

She punched me. A good solid roundhouse to the jaw. I saw stars. Also burning baby fish swimming in the air, which puzzles me even now.

Next thing I knew, she yanked me off the floor by my hair—

"Ow!"

—and held me against her, as a human shield, by applying an excruciatingly painful grip to my jaw.

"Urrnnnngh!"

"Xenophobia!" Nemesis shouted. "If you don't put down your weapons, I'll kill the prisoner!"

The gun she held against my temple lent veracity to her claim.

"Then I suppose," said the mysterious Xenophobia, "that it's a good thing I haven't had time to become emotionally attached to your prisoner."

Nemesis ducked barely in time to avoid a bullet in

the brain as Xenophobia fired on us. Nemesis returned fire—but, as the smoke suddenly cleared, we saw that Xenophobia had already abandoned her position. Nemesis spun in a circle, dragging me with her by the jaw, as she searched for her opponent.

The last of the panicking minions fell to the floor with an agonized cry as a crossbow bolt caught him through the neck.

"Unnnngggghh!" I gurgled as another bolt flew directly at my crotch. My flinch shifted my position enough to escape castration once again, and the bolt instead buried itself in Nemesis' thigh. She shrieked, let go of me, and fell to the floor clutching her leg. I was reaching for the gun she had dropped when a black leather boot kicked it up into the air and a gloved hand captured it in mid-flight.

"Good reflexes," Xenophobia said to me with a devil-may-care grin. "You'd be singing soprano otherwise. Sorry about that."

She was . . .

"You're Xenophobia?" I asked, gaping at her.

"Damn you!" the beautiful Nemesis cried.

Xenophobia stomped on Nemesis' thigh wound, effectively distracting her.

"*You're* the one who . . ." I made a gesture encompassing Phosphor, the dead minions, and the destroyed laser machine.

Xenophobia looked me over. "You're a little underdressed for the occasion, aren't you?"

"They, um . . . took my trousers."

"You want to find them. Right away. Trust me on this."

She was a short, sturdy, middle-aged woman with brown hair cut in a sensible style. Her brown eyes were not highlighted by even the faintest hint of makeup, and her sensible khaki clothing ensured that the details of her figure were largely a mystery. Her black leather boots, I now recognized, were Doc Martens—the only thing even less sexy than Birkenstocks.

She saw my disappointed gaze lingering on her feet and said, "You were thinking I would single-handedly attack the well-guarded lair of an international mastermind in stiletto heels and a skintight latex jumpsuit, right?"

"Well, I . . ."

"And I probably should have put on makeup before blowing up that machine, killing eight people, and—incidentally—saving your life."

"I didn't actually say . . ."

"Of *course* that's what he thought," Nemesis muttered. "Good God, why do you suppose I'm wearing this absurd slinky outfit?"

"I was wondering about that," Xenophobia said, looking down at Nemesis, who was clad in an alluring black evening gown. "It's two o'clock in the afternoon and we're in the suburbs of Rabat, for goodness sake. What were you thinking? You look ridiculous."

"We're in Rabat?" I said.

"Phosphor told me Bind would expect me to dress this way." Nemesis lashed out at me with her good leg. "Phosphor was right."

"Rabat, Morocco?" I said.

"Bind?" Xenophobia repeated.

"Morocco, North Africa?" I said. "That Rabat?"

"Yes, that Rabat. You were thinking, what—Rabat, Indiana?"

"But we were in Monte Carlo last night . . ."

Nemesis made sure I saw her roll her eyes. "And after I drugged you, I brought you to Rabat. Well, to the suburbs, really. Real estate was too expensive in the city for us to build our lair there." She added, "By the way, Bind, you could stand to lose a few pounds. *Man*, were you hard to haul aboard the aircraft."

"Bind?" Xenophobia repeated.

I smiled seductively and held out my hand. "Bind," I said. "James Bind."

"How do you d . . ." Xenophobia paused and frowned. "Do you hear something?"

"It's just my theme music," I explained. "It'll fade in a moment."

"Right. How do you do, Bind? I'm Dr. Xenophobia Smith, Professor of European Folklore and Literature. I'm also an archaeologist and explorer, and I play the sax in a semi-pro band downtown, but that's not important right now."

"Charming. And it was nice of you to stop by, Doctor," I said, "but I'll take things from here."

"Excuse me?"

"I'll wrap things up here and report back to London," I said, speaking more loudly, in case a woman of her years—forty-five at *least*—was a little hard of hearing.

"No need to shout, Bind. Unless you're already a

little hard of hearing? Damn shame. You can't be more than—what? Fifty?"

"Forty-seven!" I said, stung.

"You're still shouting, Bind."

"Sorry. Where was I?"

"I really couldn't say."

"Oh, yes. As I was saying, I'll take it from here. You can go back to your classroom now."

She snorted. Very unladylike. "Sorry, Bind. I have business of my own to wrap up here. Why don't you go pay a visit to your tailor?" She glanced pointedly as my muscular legs. Or maybe she was glancing a little higher up.

Realizing that my dishabille was a distraction, I pulled my trousers out of Phosphor's death-stiffened grip and started putting them on.

"I've got to interrogate Nemesis," I explained. "She may know where Phosphor hid . . . what I've been sent to find."

Xenophobia frowned and looked at Nemesis. Nemesis gave a weary sigh.

"You're at least one step behind this parade, Bind," Xenophobia said to me. "Nemesis is the evil mastermind of this operation. Phosphor was just her love slave and decoy."

"Impossible!" I said. "The money trail led straight to Phosphor. He paid for everything Nemesis had."

Nemesis sighed again.

"Of course the money trail led to Phosphor, Bind," Xenophobia said. "Do you really think she'd be stupid enough to have it lead straight to her?"

"Look, what you're saying is absurd. Nemesis is just . . . just . . ."

"Yes?" Xenophobia prodded gently.

"Yes?" Nemesis prodded less gently.

"Um . . ."

"Were you, by any chance," Xenophobia asked me, fingering her crossbow, "going to say . . . just a *woman*?"

"Phosphor was right about the slinky black dress," Nemesis said from her prone position. "Even now, this guy can't believe I'm anything more than a sex kitten."

"You've operated successfully for years behind that camouflage, Nemesis," Xenophobia said, "but those days are over. You're going to tell me where the lost Tolkien manuscript is if I have to drag the information out of you one dismembered digit at a time."

"Good God!" I exclaimed. "You're after the lost Tolkien manuscript, too?"

"That's what you're here for?" Xenophobia said. "I thought you were just some dumb schmuck who'd put the moves on the wrong woman."

Nemesis said, "He *is* some dumb schmuck who—"

"What's your interest in the Tolkien manuscript?" I demanded.

"You first," Xenophobia said.

"No, you," I said.

"Let's remember which one of us has all the weapons," she said.

"Right, then. I work for Her Majesty's Booksellers. When the lost Tolkien manuscript was stolen from our offices, we realized that an international mastermind of monumental daring and skill must have taken it."

"How did you realize that?"

"Well . . . the manuscript was kept in a locked office."

"Go on."

"It was imperative that we get it back. Perhaps I needn't explain to you the cultural importance and economic magnitude of the discovery of the lost Tolkien manuscript?"

"No, since *I'm* the one who discovered it in the first place, you really needn't."

"Good God!" I exclaimed. "You're *that* Xenophobia Smith?"

"How many did you think there were?"

"I didn't make the connection when you told me your name today. I had naturally assumed that the great Dr. Smith, internationally renowned scholar and discoverer of the lost Tolkien manuscript was . . . um . . . never mind."

Nemesis sighed. "He was, of course, going to say that he assumed Dr. Smith was a m—"

"Yeah, I figured that out for myself, thanks," Xenophobia said, fingering her crossbow again.

"Anyhow," I continued, eager to move past the awkward moment, "once the manuscript was discovered missing, Π recalled me from my assignment in Las Vegas—"

"Pie?" Nemesis said.

"Π" I said.

"Pie?" Xenophobia said.

"Π!" I repeated impatiently. "Π! It's his code name."

"Pie? Why not Cake? Or Muffin?"

"Ooh," said Nemesis, "I like Muffin."

"I sighed. "Let's skip it. My *boss* assigned me to the case. I am licensed to reclaim."

"Licensed to reclaim? That sounds a little . . . limp."

"I really dislike that word," I told Xenophobia.

"My mistake, Bind."

"I was assigned to find and reclaim the lost Tolkien manuscript."

"So you tracked down Nemesis."

"No," Nemesis said, "he tracked down Phosphor."

Xenophobia looked disgusted. "Of course."

I said, "Now tell me what *you're* doing here."

"When the lost Tolkien manuscript disappeared without a trace, I knew that the thief had to be the most brilliant student I've ever had. A student who, alas, was also a rebel."

"A rebel?" I prodded.

"She hated—"

"*She?* You're saying that your most brilliant student ever was a . . . Never mind."

"Yes, let's skip over your slack-jawed incredulity and get to the point," Xenophobia said tersely. "Nemesis hated the printed page, the cracked bindings, the smeared ink of real books. Her allergy to dust made her loathe the way it collects on shelf after shelf of books, year after year. She came to have an almost pathological horror of how easily the alphabetical order of any book collection is disturbed by careless browsers, even in a prestigious English department."

"And then," I guessed insightfully, "she met Phosphor."

"He was a visiting professor in computer technology." Xenophobia made a despairing little gesture. "I was fond of Nemesis. I wanted to believe it was Phosphor who was corrupting her, not the other way around."

"He took over financing her education."

"Yes, and bought her a computer. Soon he was exposing her to computerized catalogs and databases, electronic text, and on-line archives."

"But it didn't stop there, did it?" I guessed.

"No. Before long, Nemesis surpassed her mentor. She got involved in virtual storytelling, hyperlinks, and multiuser dungeons. Looking back now, I realize there was nothing I could have done."

"And Phosphor paid for it all," I said. "Did you know his wealth came from hacking into political accounts used to bribe pizza delivery services to arrive at the Capitol Building in under twenty minutes? That's why no one could ever convict him."

"Wake up, Bind! Did you seriously believe that a man whose greatest criminal achievement was ripping off Congress really had the vision to understand what the lost Tolkien manuscript means to the world?"

"You're saying Phosphor was her pawn, her tool."

"Even in her undergrad days, Nemesis knew *The Lord of the Rings* the way you know the swimsuit edition of *Sports Illustrated*. I realized that, over the years, her obsession with it could only have grown, ripened, deepened."

"Wait a minute!" The full weight of everything Xenophobia had told me suddenly sank in. "You're saying she stole the lost Tolkien manuscript so she could . . . *No*. Surely not!"

"Yes!" she cried.

"*Diabolical*," I said.

I'm a man who has seen great evil and faced terrible enemies. But even I had never foreseen anything as gruesome as this.

"You disrespectful fiend!" I said to Nemesis.

"Actually," she said, "I'm sort of bleeding to death from this thigh wound, so could we—"

"I thought she and Phosphor just wanted to scan the manuscript," I said to Xenophobia. "Turn it into an e-book. Distribute it worldwide over the internet." Phosphor's webcraft was sophisticated enough for him to sell pirated copies of the lost Tolkien manuscript all over the world, getting millions of Tolkien fans to deposit the exorbitant purchase price into Phosphor's offshore accounts, without our being able to trace his physical location. "It was a brilliant scheme . . . but now you're telling me that wasn't the end of Nemesis' plan."

"In fairness to Phosphor," Xenophobia said, "I think he had not idea just how far Nemesis intended to go. I think he thought they were just going to pirate Tolkien. Not . . ." She couldn't bring herself to say it.

"*Rewrite* Tolkien." God, it was obscene! "With hyperlinks, interactive visuals, even . . ."

"Yes," Xenophobia said, her revulsion plainly written on her face. "Even alternate endings."

"Excuse me," Nemesis said, "I'm still sort of bleeding to death here, so if you—"

"You deserve to bleed to death!" I snarled.

"Er, actually . . . Bind?" Xenophobia said.

"No!" I insisted. "I will not give in to your tender feminine sentimentality! She deserves to die! To bleed to death right here like an unwanted cockroach!"

"An unwanted cockroach?"

"To die in utter desolation and—"

"Bind! If she dies, we may never find that manuscript!"

"Yes!" Nemesis hissed. "That's right! And if *you* die, I can still go through with my plan, make millions of dollars, and finally give Tolkien's work multiple endings!"

"You monster!"

"Bind! Watch out!"

In a brilliant display of bravado, Nemesis pulled the arrow out of her own thigh and lunged at me. Xenophobia shot her. It was all over in a split second.

Nemesis lay dead on the floor.

"It's a pity," Xenophobia said, staring down at the body.

"Yes."

"To die in a dress like that. Tragic. She had much better taste in clothing than this outfit would suggest to the casual observer."

"Um, you saved my life," I said to Xenophobia. "Thanks."

"Sheer reflex, Bind, nothing personal. Damn! Now we'll never find that manuscript."

I looked at her expectantly.

"What?" she said.

"Well . . . don't you want to make a clever pun now? I usually do, after I kill someone."

"You really are a sick bastard, aren't you?" She sighed wearily. "All that matters now, Bind, is finding that manuscript. And I don't see how we're going to do that."

"We'll ransack the place," I suggested.

"Useless. She'd have thought of that."

"If you knew her so well, surely you must know where . . . Hang on! I think I may know!"

"My God, you ghoulish pig, what do you think you're doing?"

"It's not what you think," I insisted as I investigated Nemesis' ample cleavage. "Ah-hah! Here it is!"

"You found the manuscript in *there?*"

"No, her cleavage isn't *that* ample. But I found the next best thing." I held up my discovery. "A diskette containing Nemesis' scan of the manuscript!" I gave it a graceful little flip and then pocketed it.

"But what about the manuscript itself?"

"Destroyed, obviously."

She gasped. "Yes, of course! Once Nemesis had the scan, she'd have wanted to destroy the original as soon as possible."

"All that dust. All that smeared ink."

"Indeed!"

"So, the villains are dead, and the intellectual

property is recovered and safe from . . ." I grimaced ". . . rewriting."

"Thank God. That was a close call." Xenophobia gazed down at Nemesis' corpse for a moment. "So sad."

"The dress?"

"No, Bind, I've moved on. I was thinking about what a gifted student she was. One of the few people who could read James Joyce without getting a migraine."

"Waste is always such a tragedy. But it's time we got this diskette back to Her Majesty's Booksellers."

"Of course."

As we turned to leave, I confessed, "Although you're too old for me . . ."

"Bind, I'm two years younger than you."

"Yes, my point exactly. Anyhow, I nonetheless find myself strangely attracted to you."

She went rigid for a moment, then started fingering her crossbow. "If you ever touch me there again, Bind, your next assignment will be singing for a girls choir."

Yes, she was definitely starting to fall for me.

Better Than Ants

by Barbara Galler-Smith

Barbara Galler-Smith lives in Edmonton, Alberta, Canada, with her fabulously supportive husband, two white dogs, a dwarf hamster, and a zebra danio named Johnny Deep Diver. She also teaches junior high school science and dabbles in the mystical arts of gardening, blacksmithing, and home renovation when not writing.

I LOVED killing ants best. As a kid, I'd watch in fascination whenever my dad sprayed ant powder into their holes. Learning the habits of my quarry helped make me the most successful exterminator in the province. Like my father before me, I'd never found anything I couldn't outwit, and in the end, kill.

The phone rang, insistent and loud, and I reached for it, remembering to put some pride in my voice.

"Boyd speaking."

A smoke-husky voice answered. "Boyd Brown, the exterminator?"

"Yes, ma'am," I said, letting the smile into my words so my customer would know I was on her side.

"This is Miss Ellen Owens here. Your ad in the Drumheller Gazette is very impressive, Mr. Brown."

I felt a prideful grin creeping over my face. Pride is a dangerous thing, but knowing you're the best makes it hard to keep the satisfaction from showing. The grin eased into my voice. I stood a little taller, resting one hand on the reproduction Jim Bowie knife Dad had brought back from San Antonio. "Satisfaction guaranteed, and I'm listed with the Better Business Bureau." Being the best also meant I'd always have work to do. No matter what, people always had something that needed killing. "Now, what's the problem?"

"I hope you can get rid of some pests in my back yard."

"What kind of pest are we talking about? Skunks? Slugs?"

"No, Mr. Brown. Nothing *usual*. I can't say over the phone what they are, except they're about the size of my St. Bernard and they're . . ." She paused, cleared her throat, and her voice dropped to a whisper. "They're carnivorous."

I perked up. Ants and mice paid the bills, but larger pests always offered a challenge. "Carnivorous? Those are my favorite kind. You sure they aren't cats?"

"Mr. Brown," she said slowly, "they're eating my cats."

Most likely renegade coyotes, I thought. Coyotes, nature's best pest exterminators, could sometimes get too good. "Cat eaters. I can handle 'em. How about next Thursday?"

"Impossible," she said. "Heavy rains are forecast. You've got to come now."

Something in her quiet urgency appealed to me. I

checked my bookings. I had two calls to investigate: something getting into the bins and eating garbage down at the Badlands Hotel, and a family of skunks living under a porch. "I'll have to cancel my appointments, Miss Owens. That'll cost you extra."

"No problem, Mr. Brown. I'm prepared to pay for your immediate response. Get here quickly."

I nodded and smiled even though I knew she couldn't see me. She seemed like a take-charge, no frills kind of woman and I looked forward to helping her. "I'll be there in an hour."

I poured an extra-large serving of coffee into my oversized wide-bottom travel mug, stowed my trusty 12-gauge shotgun, Sophie, and a box of shells in the back of my truck, then headed toward Drumheller.

I lived on the prairie flat above a valley carved out by the Red Deer River. By the time I reached the spot where the road snaked down into Drumheller, it was hotter than hell and black thunderheads loomed all the way to the horizon. Dust kicked up a warning that the approaching storm wouldn't be long in coming. A narrow strip of greenery bordered the river as it cut through town, and canyons and rain-washed gullies etched the valley. On the steep northern slopes stood the wind-and water-carved *hoodoos*. An old local legend said the eroded sand formations were really Rock People buried long ago, and one day they'd return from the clay like they'd never been gone.

I crossed the river and smiled at the landmark

stegosaur with its spiked tail dragging, at the corner where the ice cream parlor used to be. The *T. rex* in the center of town, old and weatherworn, had been replaced. I figured those museum people had pressured the town to put up something more "real," as if anyone knew what dinos really looked like. I knew they'd all died out a couple million years ago—probably killed off by saber-toothed tigers. I wished I could have seen that. Stalking and taking out those big beasts appealed to me.

Miss Owens lived on a little spread just outside of town on the old highway. As I pulled into the gravel driveway and parked, a wiry and tight-muscled woman emerged from the house and waited on the wide porch, standing like a queen and carrying a shotgun with both hammers pulled back. I raised an eyebrow in appreciation. Her eyes, lively and canny, looked me up and down and I had to stop myself from doing the same. I wouldn't have said I noticed her full figure first off, but I'd be lying. Best of all, she didn't look the type to yip and cower at a spider or a mouse nest.

I eyed her weapon warily and decided not to get out. Instead, I rolled down the truck window and stuck out my head. "If there's one thing my dad taught me, it's never step out of your truck when a lady has both barrels of her shotgun cocked."

She nodded curtly and lowered the firearm. "This way," she said without smiling.

No *Hello Mr. Brown, nice of you to drive over here on short notice to kill something for me.* Not even a civilized *Would you like a nice cold glass of beer before step-*

ping into the hot sun? Just a simple command. I followed her, and my eyes wandered from the swing of her honey-brown ponytail sticking out the back of her baseball cap to the swing of her hips as she sauntered away from me.

Summer thunder rumbled as we walked into the shade behind the house. I wiped my sweaty forehead on my sleeve. A little rain would cool things off nicely, but too much rain would turn the backyard into a mud pit.

That's when I saw the torn-to-bits remains of two dead cats.

I toed the carcasses. Definitely no coyote did that, but I didn't want to worry her. "Most likely coyotes, ma'am."

She licked her lips, squinted her blue eyes at me, then pointed to the nearby steep embankment.

I followed her gaze to the hillside, expecting another dead cat. Instead, I saw something embedded in the hard-packed clay. Around here I'd expect a fossil. Or maybe some old burial ground eroding away to expose relic bones.

"What the . . . ?"

Movement caught my eye.

It looked to be about dog-sized. One leathery shoulder stuck out. Half of the face was exposed, and I caught the glint of stiletto-sharp teeth, gleaming in the afternoon sun.

The grape-green eye blinked.

I jumped back, moving faster than a striking rattlesnake. "It's alive!"

"Yes, it is," she said from behind me, "and I want you to kill it."

"Damn!" I said. This was better than ant-kills any day. "It's some kind of alligator!"

"No, it's a young dinosaur, Mr. Brown. I haven't told anyone else about it," she added as if to anticipate my question. "If folks knew about this, there'd be a terrible panic." Her eyes flashed. "These creatures are coming out of the clay by the dozen, Mr. Brown, and I don't doubt there are even more in there."

I studied the thing's eye. It stared back at me and for a brief moment I understood what it must feel like to be prey. I shuddered. "It can't get out, can it?"

Clouds obliterated the sun.

"Not yet, but in a hard rain, enough mud will slide away and it'll be able to pull itself free. We have to kill it and the others that are popping out all over the place."

I swallowed hard. She had the shotgun. "Why haven't you blasted them all yourself?"

A little avalanche of sand fell, and another reptilian head the size of my fist poked up, shook itself free and struggled upward. It had a wide mouth equipped with two rows of sharp little teeth. A long tail balanced the scrawny two-legged creature, and it waved two tiny arms. Then it sniffed the air like a dog.

"Too many of them," she said.

At the sound of more scratching I turned and saw more avalanches. Six dirt slides accompanied the appearance of six more little dinosaurs. Once free, they made straight for the cats' scattered remains.

Miss Owens traced the little herd with her shotgun, squeezed the trigger, and sent a blast of buckshot toward the creatures. The noise and the dust cloud raised startled them, and they disappeared into the dense sagebrush.

I raised an eyebrow. Her aim was lousy.

She pulled the eyeglasses from her nose and wiped the grimy lenses on her Tyrrell Museum souvenir T-shirt. "And my aim's not too good. I can't handle them alone, which is why I called you. If we don't do something soon, the whole valley will be overrun with them. No cat, dog, or child will be safe. And they grow very fast. When they're adults, none of us will be safe."

Not to mention the press, the movie people, and the collectors, I thought. "Where are they coming from ?" I asked.

"I don't know. The *hoodoos* are full of ancient mysteries."

I nodded, remembering the legend. "Did you ever see anything like this before?"

"When I was a girl, my dad and I were caught in a rainstorm in the Badlands. He shot something. Said it was a rabid coyote. He wouldn't let me see it up close."

I felt like the luckiest pest-control man alive. This was the opportunity of a lifetime.

Miss Owens loaded two more shells into the double-barreled shotgun.

I squinted at the watchful eye of another reptile

waiting to escape the clay and rubbed my hands together. I'd solve this problem because I was a professional. When Boyd Brown killed something, it stayed dead.

I rushed back to my truck to get my strongest poison, Boyd's Kill All. A sprayer full of good old BKA should do the trick. I preferred the quiet methods, and besides, too much gunfire would bring the Mounties.

One of the little meat-eaters leaped up on the tailgate and wagged its tail. Bright intelligent eyes looked from me to the interior of the truck and then back again. I was about to spray it when it hopped down and ran behind the house.

Thunder cracked behind me loud enough to make me jump and the hairs on my arms rose from the static electricity. A fat glob of rain hit me in the middle of my forehead. Then the sky opened up.

A blast from Miss Owen's shotgun hurried me. I scooped up the BKA sprayer and rushed to rejoin her.

She stood with her back to the building with the shotgun at her hip and six dinos moving cautiously in a semicircle around her. She'd already killed one. She fired both barrels at the three on her right. She got the center one. The other two retreated amidst the splatter of mud and blood. They turned around twenty feet away, paused, before returning to fall on their dead comrade with a hungry vengeance.

I dusted three full in the face with BKA. Undiluted, it was strong enough to kill a horse. The closest dinosaur coughed. Miss Owens took aim, fired, and disintegrated it.

Lightning flashed directly above us, followed immediately by a thunderous crackling. The little herd scurried under the bushes where they peered at us, tails flicking. I hadn't taken any out and my pride started working on me. I ran to the truck and retrieved old Sophie. That 12-gauge had worked on a rogue grizzly up in the Yukon and would work now on a bunch of overgrown lizards. Miss Owens kept the remaining dinos under cover of her shotgun, and I approached with all the confidence I'd approach any vermin. No matter how many or how plentiful, the little pests would be no match for Boyd Brown.

The deluge continued. In the cold, sharp wind gusts of the storm, I stumbled and fell to one knee in the slick, wet clay. As one, the dinosaurs turned their attention to me. Miss Owens ran toward me, but tripped and tumbled in the mire.

The dinosaurs charged her instead.

"Mr. Brown!" she shouted. The first one clamped its jaws around her forearm. She screamed and hit at it with the muzzle of her shotgun. The dino did not let go.

I aimed at the beast, blinked against the rain spiking into my face, but waited. I could take off her whole arm at this distance.

I struggled to regain my footing against the rising gale. Staggering toward her, I forced the muzzle flush against the dino's midsection, pointed away from Miss Owens and myself, and squeezed the trigger. The shotgun roared and jammed into my hip where I'd braced it. The dino was reduced to a smear from the chest down.

One, no taller than my knee, ran past me and nipped a chunk from my jeans. I stumbled, jerked the trigger, and blasted a sagebrush to smithereens. Now I was angry.

"Try that again!" I yelled.

The second one rushed at me. I sidestepped but slipped on the wet muck. I struggled to my knees, and two of the critters lunged at my feet, gouging my cowhide boots. I twisted and kicked at them, pumped another shell into the chamber, and fired. The closest one's bloody remains lay at the bottom of a smoking crater.

The other joined the attack on Miss Owens. I half crawled and half staggered to her, and with the butt of my shotgun battered at the beasts. They snarled and gnashed their teeth at us, tails twitching, but backed away.

I had just enough time to reload. One of them chomped on my calf. I howled in pain, stumbled, and fell again, dropping the shotgun into the mud. It landed just out of my reach. I squirmed, stretched, and clawed at it, but it slid away. A second dino bit my thigh.

Propelled by the pain, anger roared through me. No pest was gong to get the better of Boyd Brown! I flopped through the mud to retrieve the shotgun, dragging both dinos with me. My fingers closed on the butt, and I twisted around, pulling the shotgun into position. With the muzzle flush against the dino's leathery skin, I fired. The blast sent it sailing in three directions and tumbled the other one away, bleeding and missing one forearm.

Miss Owens, her breath quick and jagged, tugged me to my feet. She stood beside me, cradling her bloody torn arm. We struggled to catch our breath as the remaining two dinosaurs circled warily. I slipped my last two shells into the shotgun and slammed it closed.

With her one good hand, Miss Owens patted at her pockets, then looked up at me in dismay. "Damn! I'm out of shells."

I gave her a little smile. "We'll make do. Two of them. Two of us." She nodded and gripped the barrel like a club.

The last two dinos chattered at each other. The taller one edged away as if to draw around us. It faked a lunge and when we backed up, the other one ran behind Miss Owens and bit her leg. She fell, screaming and pummeling the beast with her bare fist.

Unable to get a clear shot, I grabbed its tail and yanked. The dino let go in a snarling rage that ended abruptly when I blasted it with both barrels. The second one leaped on my back and bit hard into my shoulder, its sharp claws like curved ice picks on either side of my spine. Unable to reach it, I threw myself down and backward, like a pro wrestler. The take-down worked, and the dino released its hold.

I rolled to meet the dino head on. This was hand-to-claw combat now, and I needed to equalize the odds. I fumbled at my hip for the Bowie knife, but the dino's rush surprised me. It knocked me backward, and the knife splashed in a mud puddle a half dozen feet away.

I scrambled toward the knife and just as the dino again landed on my back, my fingers closed on the hilt. I tried to twist and turn, but the dinosaur grabbed my shoulder.

Desperate, I struck out with the knife.

It found a target—the sensitive skin around the dino's eye. I stabbed again and the dino let go. I lunged, and plunged the knife deep into the creature's chest. The dino sagged and kicked once, shuddering to stillness.

Fighting for breath, I crawled to miss Owens through the blood-darkened mud and cradled her head on my good hip. I'd been looking all my life for a fearless woman, and now I dreaded what I might find. I gingerly touched the pulse point in her throat and was rewarded with a strong beat. She was alive! We were bloodied, but not beaten.

"I think we got 'em all, Miss Owens," I said.

She moaned and struggled to sit up, but finally just let me hold her. "Call me Ellen," she whispered and smiled for the first time.

We made our way to the back porch where we collapsed on the steps, finally sheltered from the pounding rain.

"We did it, Ellen," I said, but my gaze drifted to the water cascading down the steep clay slope behind the house.

I watched in fascination as rivulets of mud streamed from the cliff and exposed a small bit of lizard skin. "We better get more shells, Ellen. There's at least one more."

A little avalanche of sticky mud fell. Then another.

I felt a tingle of deeper fear as the little landslides merged into a larger one. I took Ellen's hand and gently pulled her to her feet.

In the midst of a rapidly diminishing layer of clay, an eye the size of a bowling ball blinked at us. We were going to need a lot more than a few shotgun shells for this one.

The phone rang, loud as always. As I picked up the receiver I smiled at my bride, who was busy making a new batch of Boyd's New and Improved Kill All and Dino Bait.

"Brown and Owens, Exterminators. Boyd speaking. How can we help you?"

"It's the museum again, Mr. Brown. Do you think you could bag us another adult?"

Blackbird, Fly!

by Linda J. Dunn

Linda J. Dunn has been writing professionally since 1991 and has sold about fifty short stories to various magazines and e-zines in addition to print anthologies. She is a graduate of Indiana University and has been a civilian DoD employee for almost twenty years. Linda is a computer specialist whose background includes VAX, Macintosh, and Unix operating systems as well as Windows. Until its closure, she worked for the Naval Air Warfare Center in Indianapolis and, for a short time, she was a member of an avionics simulations software team. Her website is at http://www.lindajdunn.com. She and her husband, Greg, share a home that includes networked offices and at least six functional computers running various operating systems. Her hobbies include knitting, gardening, and fitness training.

BLACKBIRDS don't sing; they rumble with thunder in the dead of the cold desert night when only those with the need to know are around to hear them. Add a few rattlesnakes, coyotes, and jack rabbits, and you've got your typical audience for a take-off that includes the best damn light show you can find anywhere: a shock wave of flaming diamonds that's a Fourth of July rocket ride through the dark, black sky into the light of the sun.

Marysville residents never quite got used to those booming afterburners back when I was a kid spending summers with my grandparents; but I thought that was the sweetest sound I'd ever heard, and I loved those window-shaking sonic booms. When I caught a glimpse of one in flight, I set my heart on becoming a Blackbird pilot.

That dream kept me going while cancer slowly ate its way through my mother's body; and keeping my eyes fixed on that goal helped me cope with my father's attempts to drink himself to death while I struggled through college.

I put a Blackbird poster in my dorm and I called Jack Chain an "SR-71" hater along with everyone else when he slashed Blackbird funding in favor of converting B-52s to conventional bombers. After that, the Blackbirds were flying on borrowed time and I was flying a B-47, logging flight hours toward the 1,500 minimum required to qualify for Blackbird piloting. Seven hundred and fifty of those had to be as aircraft commander.

On March 6, 1990, I made aircraft commander in an F-16 and Ed Yielding and JT Vida flew a Blackbird to Washington DC, where the aircraft would become just another museum display. My dreams of becoming a Blackbird pilot crashed and burned that day, knowing that this delivery was the beginning of the end. I met Teresa at a bar that night, where everyone was talking about the threat of war in the Middle East. She said, "I can't bear the thought of a world without you," and I got a little stupid.

I came back from being king of the night sky, kicking ass and taking names, to being my wife's Lamaze coach. When Teresa held John Wagner, Junior, in her arms and said, "Please, John. If you won't do it for me, do it for your son," I quit the Air Force and went to work for TWA.

I might as well have become a bus driver.

Boeing 757s are fine commercial aircraft; but it was like trading Seattle Slew for a Clydesdale. Different size. Different handling. Different temperament. Worse, it meant admitting I'd never sit in a Blackbird cockpit except maybe in some museum.

For Christmas, Teresa gave me a computer and a flight simulation program. "I thought we should finish the basement. You could move all your aircraft memorabilia down there and have a separate room for the computer where you can fly your military aircraft to your heart's content."

What she really meant was that she wanted all my junk out of her way so she could redecorate the house to look like something out of a magazine: ugly and impractical. But she did give me an idea.

What I couldn't buy off-the-shelf from a company like Thrustmaster and modify, I could probably find through one of the companies that bought excess government equipment. For that matter, I could build a few things myself. After all, I did earn an engineering degree and you don't become a fighter pilot without learning something about how they're put together.

Before long, I was flying a Blackbird simulation that I told myself was probably better than the one Lockheed originally used. The ceiling in the basement was low and the carpet I tacked up and down the walls was insufficient insulation; so I only hooked up the speakers, the vibration equipment under the seat, and the heaters when Teresa was out of the house. When John was old enough, I showed him how to work the controls and he enjoyed the setup so much that he wanted to take flying lessons.

Teresa squashed that interest like a bug under her spike-heeled shoes. "You're not turning my son into a pilot."

"He's my son, too."

"Not when it comes to this, he isn't." I guess that was when I realized that whatever we had a few years ago was gone.

I promised John that we'd find a way to do this anyway, but disaster struck. I was in the air on September 11, 2001, the day four planes were hijacked. Two were flown into the World Trade Center towers, one hit the Pentagon, and the other crashed in Pennsylvania. I landed my plane in Canada, as instructed, and stayed four days before we could fly back. John told me later, "Mom went nuts."

Nuts doesn't begin to describe it.

"You can't keep doing this, John. It's too dangerous. I'd be worried sick the whole time. You've got an engineering degree. You could get a job somewhere else that pays just as well."

I guess it was that last bit that got me. What she was really saying was, "Change jobs, but don't take a pay cut because I don't want to change my lifestyle." We fought for days and she had the locks changed before my next flight left the runway. In the end, we came to an amiable agreement. Teresa took the house, both cars, and John. I got the payments and my electronic gear.

Teresa wasn't the only person who swore she'd never fly again, and the airlines industry was going through rocky times. Eddie called to tell me that Lockheed won the contract to build the F-35. Lockheed was working with several contractors, but the job I wanted was at Falcon AFS in Colorado. The avionics integration designs were tested, simulated, and finalized for the last few aircraft at Falcon and I was betting the F-35 would follow that same pattern. I wanted to be involved in those tests. The only problem was that it would mean leaving John. I'd left the Air Force for him long ago and the selfish part of me wanted a piece of the action back at any price. I still dreamed of Lockheed's Blackbird and while I knew this wouldn't be the same, it was as close as I'd ever get. I got a job offer from Lockheed on October 1, 2003.

"You're leaving me?" was John's response when I broke the news to him.

"It's not working out here. Your mom and I are fighting constantly over my visitation schedule and last summer was . . . well . . . if I move to Colorado, you can spend summers with me full-time and half the school holidays."

"That's bullshit." Sometimes, John was too much like me. "You'll get out there and forget all about me."

"I'll never do that. I couldn't do that." John looked at me and his eyes were tearing. I balled my hands into fists and said, "You don't trust your own dad? Hey! Those are fighting words." I punched him in the arm and he didn't move. I dropped my hands and took a deep breath. Time for a different approach.

"Look . . . what do I have to do to prove you mean more to me than anything or anyone else in the world . . . and still take this job I'd give my right arm to have?" I gave him the old great dad grin. "Want me to cut off my arm and leave it with your for safe-keeping until you can fly out and give it back to me?"

The look he gave me told me more than words could ever convey just how much he'd grown up since the divorce.

"Give me you cigarettes."

I would have preferred my right arm. "What?"

"Give me your cigarettes. If you want to prove that you're serious, give me your cigarettes and tell me you won't smoke again until I hand you this pack when I see you again."

I hesitated, wondering if I was up to this. The look on his face told me I didn't have much choice. If I wanted my son to believe me, I had to give up cigarettes. "You've got a deal."

"You know Mom will never let me fly."

"She won't have a choice. The court will order it."

The court let her put him on a bus or a train. He looked half-asleep when he handed me the pack of cigarettes. I tossed them in the trash, and he was suddenly wide awake.

"You really did it?"

"I've never lied to you, John, and I'm not gong to start now. I quit cold turkey."

He grinned. "Mom said you couldn't do it."

"Your mom and I have some serious issues with one another—sort of like Israel and the Palestinians have serious issues with one another. How about you stay out of our war and let's make this the best damn time together that a father and son ever had?" He nodded and I paused for dramatic effect. "Guess what I've lined up for you?"

"Flying lessons?"

"How did you guess?" I squished my face into my best impression of dismay. "And here I'd hoped it would be a surprise."

He pounded me on my arm. I dropped the bag and pounded him on the back. He got me in the chest. I messed up his hair. We fell into a big hug and it was like old times, only better because Teresa wasn't there to tell us to stop roughhousing.

Damn! It felt good to be with my boy. I took a deep breath and picked up his bags. "Pizza?"

"Again?"

"How long has it been?"

"Since the last time we got together."

"Has it been that long since I smoked?"

He hit me and we went through the whole routine all over again. I finally dropped into bed that night about 0200 hours, full of heartburn from the pepperoni and green peppers on the pizza and more hyped up than I've been since the Gulf War. Half of me was basking in the glow of knowing I had a good kid and everything was going to be all right and the old half of me was shaking in my shoes, scared that tomorrow he'd be hit by a car or something.

Outside the window, I could hear a blackbird—not a jet, but a feathered blackbird—singing in the dead of the night. It was the closest I'd felt in all those years to being back at Grandpa's and Grandma's again, listening to metal Blackbirds.

That's when I finally lay back, closed my eyes, and drifted off to sleep. Everything was going to be all right. I still wanted to fly a Blackbird . . . but that impossible dream was going to have to go on standby status while I took care of more pressing business.

John's grades improved when he returned to school that year. I arranged for a tutor and groveled until Teresa agreed to it. She didn't really object . . . it's just that fighting anything I suggested had become a habit with her. A habit I was determined to break.

I made a date with her for dinner and flew out.

"You look beautiful," I told Teresa, and didn't have to lie. With the alimony I was paying, she could afford to look good.

"You usually complain when I order the most expensive meal on the menu."

I bit my tongue before I said, "That's all right, I know you're just doing it to annoy me." Instead, I said, "Obviously, you wouldn't have ordered it if you didn't want it and I want this dinner to be a special one because I want to declare a truce."

"We're not at war, John."

"Aren't we?" I gave her my best, good morning passengers smile and took her hands in mine. "We had some wonderful times together and I'll always cherish those memories, but we've reached the point where it's almost impossible to even have dinner together without bringing up all the old issues and anger."

"You chose flying over me."

She had always been jealous of my first love. "Yes. And I regret that, but flying is a part of me that I can't give up and still be me."

"I don't ever want John in a plane. It's too dangerous."

I bit my tongue so hard that I could taste blood. It was 2004 and it seemed everyone felt safe flying again, except Teresa. A moment later, I could finally speak without my voice being tinged with anger. "Can we sidestep this argument and discuss those issues we can agree upon? For John? You know I want the best possible education for him and I want to see him—"

"So that's what this is all about." She stood up and threw down her napkin. "You're going to try to take custody from me."

I stared and wondered what she was smoking in her cigarettes. She glanced around to see everyone watching her and sat down quickly. I think my mouth was still hanging open.

She leaned forward and whispered. "That's why you invited me here, isn't it?"

I shook my head. "I—"

"Good! Because I'll never give up custody."

"I wouldn't ask—"

"I couldn't possibly live on less."

Any love I had left for Teresa crashed and burned with those words. It was all about money. It had always been all about money. Even now, she couldn't hold down a job for more than a few months because they either expected too much for her—meaning they expected her to work while she was there—or she decided that wasn't the career she wanted after all. Oh, she loved John, all right . . . but he had a mind of his own now and was pushing for independence. She couldn't deal with that.

I cleared my throat and said, "I wouldn't ask you to." I smiled and watched her eyes carefully. She couldn't meet my gaze.

"Oh, John! He's turning into such a handful. Last week he slipped out the window and it was almost midnight before he came home again."

"Where was he?"

"He said he went to a wrestling match. He looked like he was the loser." She shook her head and when she looked up, her eyes were full of tears. "I've always been a good mother. You know that."

Yes, she had. Past tense. Teresa was the kind of woman who was wonderful with babies and toddlers and fine with cookie baking and soccer teams. Once those children started going their own way—and not the way she wanted—she didn't know what to do anymore. I felt relieved we'd decided John should be an only child. Maybe I sensed it back then, when she criticized everything I did, that it would come to this someday. Or maybe I was just damn lucky.

"Why don't you have him move up with me after

Christmas? When summer arrives, we can decide what to do next. You both need a short vacation from one another."

"Thank you, John."

The waiter arrived with our salads and I spent the rest of the meal wondering how I got so lucky and found out when the dessert arrived. "By the way, I may be moving."

"Moving?"

"Yes. I met someone."

Alimony stops with remarriage. I held my breath for a moment before asking, "Is this serious?"

"I hope so. We'll see."

"Well, then . . . congratulations."

She leaned forward and for the first time, I didn't see hate or animosity in those clear, green eyes. "And what about you, John? Are you happy with your life?"

"I'd be happier if I were making General about now," slipped out before I could stop myself.

She pulled back. "I'm sorry."

"No. It's all right." *No, it isn't, damn you.* "I made my choice."

"I just . . . couldn't . . . deal with the risks." She shook her head. "You and your John both! You're risk takers. You frighten me to death."

"Flying is safer than driving a car."

I thought about those words fifteen years later, when John and I stood beside her coffin. Teresa had turned off the auto-navigation system on her 2015 Chevy Corsair and disabled the safety features. She always did have to be in control.

Funny how you think about things like that at funerals and not the bitter words and the court fights. We had peace for about six months, until her special friend proved he wasn't quite as special as she thought. Then it was all-out war and the battle was both ugly and expensive. After I won custody, she married again . . . a police officer, of all things.

I glanced over at him, looking as uncomfortable as I felt. Flying was too high risk, but dodging bullets was perfectly acceptable.

I'll never understand women!

John flew home with me so we could spend a week hanging out together before going back to work. It had been far too long since we'd had more than a day together here and there, and talking online—even with all the latest features—just wasn't as good as being together. Besides, we couldn't beat up on one another online.

The next morning I woke up to the sound of a dumpster being deposited next to the driveway. "What the hell—?"

"Morning, Dad." John stuck his head inside the door. "I'm cleaning your house. You can't possibly build a Blackbird out of all these parts. Besides, I think it would probably be a violation of the local zoning ordinances."

"What are you talking about?"

"This . . . junk . . . scattered all over your house. There is memorabilia and there is trash. Dad, you've got too much trash." He took a deep breath and his smile faltered. "Besides . . . I know."

"Know what?" I stood up and nearly tripped over

the shoes I didn't see on the floor. Damn it! They build hearts on an assembly line and they gave Eddie pills that eliminated his lung cancer; why can't they do anything to stop me from going blind?

"Leber's Hereditary Optic Neuropathy." His smile was gone. "You should have told me."

I sat back on the bed. "I was going to . . . later. . . . You don't have to worry—"

"I know. Children of men with LHON don't inherit the disease. I made an appointment with a specialist—"

"How would you know a specialist?"

"My fiancée and business partner has a double degree: medicine and engineering." His grin was a little lopsided. "She made a few calls."

"Fiancée?"

"Her name's Gloria, she's two years older than me and she has six patents pending. She specializes in neurosensory problems. Dad, they're doing great things with neuro implants today that—"

"Halt! Stop the sales pitch. You're getting married? To a girl genius?"

"And business partner. She started as a consultant, but we worked well together and . . ." He spread his arms. "I didn't want your first meeting to be at Mom's funeral. Besides, I thought you might need some time to get used to the idea."

I looked around at the electronics scattered across the floor. "I guess I do need to clean up before I trip over something and break my neck. But . . ."

"No buts. Glory's flying out in three days to meet you. This house will be clean before she arrives." He winked and added, "Pretend to be normal, will you?"

Glory wasn't at all what I expected. Her hair was dishwater blonde and she needed to eat less and exercise more. But at least their kids would be smart. Persuasive, too, if they were anything like their mother. Before I knew what hit me, she had me flying east to meet some kid who talked in polysyllables. He said I was an excellent candidate for some experimental, optical nerve implant once my eyesight deteriorated to the degree that it became necessary. I hoped for years; I got weeks.

I had to relearn how to see after that surgery and what I saw didn't match the world I remembered. Still, it beat being blind; and especially so given the current job market.

When times are good and everyone feels safe, bean counters target defense spending as unnecessary. Then you get another Pearl Harbor or suicidal hijackers and the pendulum swings back again. The 2018 multinational manned mission to Mars gave the public a perception of peace and goodwill that I didn't trust. The bean counters seized that as an excuse to slash the defense budget to the core and I, along with about 200,000 other aerospace workers, became unemployed.

I did some beta testing for John's company—not nearly enough for what he paid me—and sent a bitterly brief report.

I saw better in arcades at shopping malls back in the nineties. The public is going to go for this the same day hell freezes over and I fly a Blackbird. The sim suit feels like I'm wearing chickenwire two sizes too small and you've only got sight, sound, and feel. Give me smell and taste and you might have something you can't already buy off the shelf. In the meantime, I resign. I don't trust companies that overpay their consultants.

John's response was, *Hell is a small town twenty-one point four miles northwest of Ann Arbor, Michigan. It freezes over every winter. You gave up too easily on the damn Blackbird. Quitters never achieve their dreams. Test the damn simulation. Do something to make your dream a reality even if everyone says it's impossible.*

He sent another package. The suit was larger and the payment smaller. This time, I could feel the dryness in the air and I could smell my own sweat. This simulation felt real . . . better than real. I didn't have the stuffy head and irritated throat that should follow breathing 100% oxygen in flight.

John's company retrofit my implant with their new 20/20 vision enhancement software—a nice play on the date and the software's capabilities—and I beta tested it. He tried to explain how the device translated the implant's signals for me, but I wasn't paying attention. Who can listen to technobabble when you're getting your first real look at your grandkids? Ellie had all the best parts from both, and Glory's nose looked much better on Trey—John, III—than it did on her.

John's company couldn't compete with the major gaming companies, but they were landing big contracts with medical firms and the federal government. We could deliver a simulation that was cheap, fast, and good, where the punchline before had always been "pick two." The government loved us and they rewarded us with a contract to write the mother of all aircraft simulations—one that allowed ground control to take over while virtually in the pilot's seat. The industry had possessed this capability for years and it was about damn time we got around to doing it. The moon shuttles were already remote-piloted.

My job was mostly PR at this point. Here I was, a legally blind man who wasn't quite as old as Glenn was when he went back into space but still old enough to scare hell out of the young punks; and I was sitting at the pilot controls on the ground, controlling aircraft overhead. My participation marketed the modified implant and the simulation at the same time.

I don't know what kind of strings John pulled, or if it cost him a great deal of money, but one day they put me on a plane to fly out to a base that didn't exist and rolled out an SR-71. Skeet Jackson would fly, ready to take over if anything went wrong and her RSO was hanging around because they were shaking the bugs out before the 2026 parade of Planes to celebrate the nation's 250th birthday. This was only one of a few flight tests prior to its planned surprise appearance in the air show.

I hadn't had a chance to look up Skeet's bio, so I wasn't expecting to hear a woman shout, "Hey Wag! Over here."

A fighter pilot. A general. A woman who looked a good thirty years younger than me and probably met the minimum height requirements by a fraction of an inch. Skeet must have asked a thousand questions about John's company during lunch and I don't remember anything except that stupid grin on her RSO's face.

We got the same meal they used to give in the old days—a high protein, low residue meal of steak and eggs—followed by the usual brief medical exams. Only Skeet was flying this time, so she got into the PSD van and security escorted me into a small room with a sim suit, props, and a neural connection, that held a wall-length window where people could watch me in action . . . like there'd be anything worth seeing.

The moment I hooked up, I felt I was in that cockpit. It wasn't what I'd envisioned all those years ago and yet, here I was, preparing for flight.

The engine-power hydraulics and flying controls checked out. Second engine started. Fifteen more minutes of checklist items. I tested the brakes and began to follow a yellow guideline down the taxiway to the ramp adjacent to the active runway entry point. The ground crew chocked the wheels. I fired up each engine to full military power while I watched the EGT. Temperatures stabilized. Another five-to-ten minute wait; and cleared to lineup, they unchocked the wheels.

I pushed throttles to full military power, checked the engine instruments, and released the brakes while engaging the reheat power. We surged forward and it was a freight train rolling downhill. Damn, but this was great! At two hundred and fifteen knots, I pulled back and the nose lifted. Three hundred knots and then four hundred and an easy left turn and up into the sky.

The silver sow was waiting up there for us and the boom lowered and connected just like it had in all the simulations I'd run during the last quarter century . . . only better because this one was for real.

I knew I was grinning like an idiot, but I didn't care. I disconnected after fueling, cleared the tanker, and climbed to an operational altitude. Skeet's finger was right on the manual override the whole time. I could feel the instrument panel and sense it was there. She may have talked big during lunch, but she didn't trust this anymore than any other pilot would trust sitting in the cockpit while someone else did the flying. It was demeaning, and I couldn't help wondering how she was dealing with that up there. By this point I was feeling pretty confident. That's when both engines rumbled slightly in compression stall and flamed out.

Shit!

I had to get the craft down to denser air, so I pushed the nose down hard. Skeet's finger was still on that button and if I'd been her, I would have rammed it through the panel and taken control. Instead, she was letting me take it down and trusting me to do an air-start. I needed 450 knots KEAS and 7 PSI on the compressor face or it wouldn't turn and burn again. AT 39,000 feet, I gave the throttles a nudge, giving both engines positive fuel flow, and a shot of TEB. No response.

Skeet still didn't hit that button.

Down to 30,000 feet and I tried again. No go. No

panic manual override from Skeet. Shit, but I loved this woman! What nerve!

I felt the aircraft shake around me and for a moment, I forgot I wasn't there. One of the engines was going. A moment later, the second kicked in. Skeet's finger relaxed pressure slightly and I breathed a sigh of relief.

The rest of the flight was pretty uneventful and when I pulled off the gear, I saw everyone applauding behind the window. It was a test. Whatever it was that had happened up there, it had been arranged in advance and no one had told me. While they thumped me on the back and shook my hand, I resisted the impulse to wrap my hands around someone's throat and squeeze.

Skeet and I had dinner together that night and I asked her. "It was all staged, wasn't it?"

"Mostly." She looked beautiful when she grinned like that. "I wasn't supposed to let it go that low. I played it a little close."

"So why did you?"

"Because you were doing all the things I would have done if I'd been doing it. I'm going to rip someone a new orifice when I talk to them later for making that test a little too realistic." She smiled, and I drowned in that smile.

"You're a damn good pilot, Wag. You should never have left the service."

"I know." I grinned and felt about thirty years younger. Young enough to do something stupid. "My wife hated the military. Funny how she married a policeman after the divorce."

"I married the force. It's easier that way."

"I wish I'd done that. My biggest regret is that I've never flown a Blackbird."

"But you just—"

"I never left the ground."

She leaned forward and smiled enticingly. "I've got an evening flight coming up next week. Final shakedown. I bet I can talk them into putting you into the RSO seat."

John couldn't understand why I had to stay over and why he had to send someone else out there to man the simulation. I told him I had a hot date.

I wore a David Clark suit this time, and that was real oxygen going into my lungs. I was going to be sniffing and clearing my throat for hours afterward and it was going to be worth every damn sniffle and cough.

"Ready?" Skeet asked after going through all the usual checks.

"All my life. Or at least the last sixty years."

We roared down the runway and lifted into the dark, black sky, heading into the light of the evening sun.

Call for Submissions

by Severna Park

Severna Park won a 2001 Nebula Award with her short story "The Cure For Everything," which also appeared in Gardner Dozois' annual anthology *The Year's Best Science Fiction 18*. Her stories, including "The Golem,"a Nebula finalist, have been published in a number of magazines and anthologies. She is the author of three novels; *Speaking Dreams; Hand of Prophecy*; and *The Annunciate*. Both *Speaking Dreams* and *The Annunciate* were finalists for the Lambda Literary Award.

EVEN if you've never actually picked up a copy of Ed Plummer's famous, or more accurately infamous, *Destiny* magazine, you've certainly seen it in the dealers' rooms at SF cons. It's usually piled in with dog-eared issues of *Analog* and *Amazing* even though *Destiny* wasn't technically science fiction. Ed loved aliens and could spin government conspiracies that make *The X-Files* look like amateur video, but his real interest was in the Hollow Earth theory. That's not news, of course; everyone has at least a nodding knowledge of Ed's primary obsession. What most people don't know is that *Destiny* wasn't Ed's first magazine. I met Ed in college and helped him publish his first effort in the years just before World War

Two. It was what you might call nowadays a fanzine, what we called a mimeo, back in the day, down in the beer-scented depths of the Ratskeller at University of Northern Indiana. We called it *Universe*.

UNI-verse was what I thought he meant, a play on words with the "University of Northern Indiana," or UNI. It was supposed to be a student mag of scienti-fiction, and in the beginning that's all it was, but Ed always had a bigger vision. That's why things turned out the way they did, for him, and for me, and most likely for PatPhang.

Ed and I met at UNI in Professor Thorsen's Physics 201 class in the fall of 1938. I was the first girl admitted into the science program there, and before I left home in Durham, my mother handed me a pair of thick, black-rimmed glasses. They didn't fit and they made my head ache when I wore them for too long, but Mother had a strategy, and she explained it to me in the simple terms of those pre-feminist days.

She said, "Boys don't make passes at girls who wear glasses."

It was more original back then, trust me, and I suppose it was good advice. Mother's theory was that it would pay to be homely and as unnoticed as possible, to keep my head down and study until my eyes burned. When I had the degree, then the job, I could throw away my disguise and burst upon the world in my true form of an Educated Woman with Tremendous Potential. Then I could have the husband and the kids and the dog, and all that traditional sort of thing, but in the meantime, in order to seize the education normally reserved for boys, I had to be stealthy, or someone—some*thing* would stop me. Romance, I thought, but in retrospect, I'm sure she meant men in general. As I got on the Greyhound in early September, I was thinking of my college career as a sort of spy movie. No one would notice the ugly girl in the science lab, undermining the foundations of male professions until the deed of graduation was done. But enough about me. Let's talk about Ed.

Even from the back of Prof. Thorsen's physics classroom, I could see that Ed was different. The rest of the boys sat up straight in their seats, hair slicked down with Brylcreme, taking copious notes. I'd known boys just like them in high school and none of them were a mystery. The one who leaned back in his chair, arms crossed over his chest, hair tousled like he'd just rolled out of bed—*he* was the mystery. He sat there, head tilted as Thorsen shouted from the podium, as though he was speculating on possibilities far beyond the molecules drawn in chalk on the dusty board. Thorsen was a little deaf and more than a little blind. He called us all by our last names and I know for a fact that he never noticed that I was a girl. In his class, I was *Mister Cassidy*, which didn't hurt my spy movie approach to college, but made the rest of the class snicker. When I raised my hand with a question on the first day of class, everyone turned and stared like I was an alien from outer space. Not Ed. When I said, "What about the differences in molecular weight, Professor?", Ed nodded and cocked his head for the answer. I liked Ed from the very beginning.

I tried to stay away from him. I had my whole future to consider, my entire super-secret college career. I was scared to death when he caught up with me after class just before midterms, and I tried hard to fend him off with my glasses and my mouse-colored hair, bad posture, and really terrible shoes.

"Say, Mister Cassidy," he said. "Some of us are getting together for a study session at the library. Want to come?"

I looked at the ground, at the books in my arms, at the blurry world my glasses showed me. I felt my cheeks burning instead of my eyes. "Nah," I said, meaning to sound certain, but it came out in a cough.

"You sound like you're getting a cold," he said.

"I'm fine."

"I think you should come."

I finally got the courage to look up and see what his face was like closer than six rows away. He had a square kind of face, brown eyes, brown hair cut short and practical without much in the way of style, and a little stubble where he'd missed with the razor that morning. He was suddenly very human and approachable. Not that realizing that made me any less shy or nervous. It made me start sweating under my jacket. "Why?" I said.

"Because." He grinned with straight white teeth. "You're the smartest guy in class, Mister Cassidy." He gave me a slip of paper with the time and study room on it. "Show us a thing or two," he said and walked away across the quad through autumn trees and crisp afternoon air.

I knew I shouldn't. I knew what my mother would

have said, but wild horses couldn't have kept me away.

Half a dozen students from Thorsen's class showed up and we did actually study, but by a quarter to eleven, when the library was about to close, Ed and I were the only ones left.

"Let's go get a beer," said Ed.

I'd never had a beer in my life. "Sure," I said, bleary from way too much physics and so charged up from sitting next to him for the last four hours, that I could hardly think. It was what my mother would have called a "compromising situation."

We walked across campus in the chilly October night. The stars were out. The air was sharp and full of dry autumn energy. It was the kind of night that makes you feel like you could run around, kicking up the piles of leaves and rolling in them, free and happy in the dark. I held these feelings in because they would have further unraveled my steadily disintegrating stealth. Instead, I watched the steamy puff of breath that came out of Ed's mouth every time he said something. I had no idea what he was saying until he caught my arm and pulled me to the right.

"Where're you going?" he said. "It's this way."

The Ratskeller was down in a dark, smelly little basement room lined with a old, ragged carpet. The carpet, Ed informed me, was infested by a microbial mass that sustained itself entirely on a diet of spilled beer.

I studied the carpet, my first beer just about to touch my lips. And then I studied Ed over my frosty, sweating mug. He seemed pretty darn serious. "Really?" I said politely.

"No," said Ed, "not really." He leaned toward me over the bar on his elbows. "But what if there was such a thing? And what if it got loose from a place like this and evolved into something more complex, or dangerous, or even something useful?"

I tried to think of some reply that wouldn't sound judgmental of his sanity. "Maybe you should be taking biology classes."

He grinned. "I have. Biology, chemistry, astronomy, you name it. If they teach it here, I've taken it."

"But shouldn't you be, um, declaring a major?"

"Oh," he said, "I have."

I raised an eyebrow. "In?"

"Publishing. I want to start a magazine."

"A science magazine," I said, relieved. Mother would love it.

He shook his head. "Scienti-fiction."

I took a swallow of beer. It was watery, bitter, and flat. I'd heard of "Scienti-fiction," even read some. Back in Durham, the drugstore clerks shelved stacks of those magazines beside the comic books. My mother put her nose in the air and told me it was all trash, so when she wasn't watching, I read it furtively and discovered that, frankly, she was right. Scienti-fiction hadn't impressed me any more than "Superman."

"With space monsters." I couldn't keep the disappointment out of my voice, but he shook his head.

"Maybe one or two of those, just for sales, but I want it to be more about the future of science, and civilization, and the way people might live when they're traveling between planets. And," he said, leaning closer, "the future of love."

I nearly dropped the mug. Beer sloshed on my skirt and splashed on the rug, where scienti-fictional microscopic organisms rushed to soak it up. I grabbed at my glasses and pushed them onto my nose. "I have to go now."

"Hang on." He opened his satchel, pulled out a sheaf of papers and handed them to me. "Read these tonight and tell me what you think."

I squinted at the scrawl of pencil on lined notebook paper. "What's this?"

"Our first submission," said Ed. "I want you to be my coeditor."

"Coeditor?" I echoed. "Of your magazine? But what's it called?"

He took a long swallow of beer. "That'll be a joint editorial decision, Mister Cassidy."

I was too overwhelmed to refuse. I couldn't just leave the manuscript on the bar to get soaked with the beer I'd spilled. So I took it back to my dorm room, crawled under the covers without undressing or brushing my teeth and started to read.

To be fair, the story wasn't bad. Instead of some pointlessly horrific yarn, it was a thinly veiled tirade against Prof. Thorsen. In the story, an out-of-control physics experiment ended his tenure for good. Some of it was gripping, but the plot was trite and the ending predictable. It occurred to me that I might have done a better job of writing it myself.

* * *

In Thorsen's class the next day, I found myself drifting off into scienti-fictional fantasies about molecular structures as tiny solar systems, and who might be living on them. I began to wonder how the beer-drinking microbes might look at those levels of reality. I glanced over at Ed, leaning back in his seat, head tilted to an angle of thoughtful speculation as Prof. Thorsen bellowed about atomic bonds and I realized that Ed might very well be thinking the exact same thing. That was the day my entire life changed. My stealthy education, my plans for the future, and those awful glasses, all took a sharp left turn, and I became, heart and soul, the coeditor of UNI's UNI-verse.

We had a number of student contributors whose names you'll probably recognize. Asa Ikamov, who was working toward a degree in cosmetology at the time, Bobby Silver, who had just declared his major in Accounting, and Sheldon Raccoon, who was a freshman using an obvious nom de plume. It was only years later that we discovered Sheldon was really a woman writing as a man. All of them got their start with Ed in *UNI-verse*.

We received some truly amazing submissions. One was a novel-length manuscript concerning a certain individual's psychological experiments on water. He would play music to water in a drinking glass, or say nasty things to it, and then freeze it to see if the resulting crystals showed any emotional response. We read chapter four, where the ice crystals appeared to form organized stanzas of self-doubting poetry, searching for the grain of story hidden in the idea. But, fascinating as it all was, there wasn't a plot to speak of, and the manuscript really belonged in some kind of science journal. I spent hours on the rejection slip, trying to keep it from being too discouraging.

One freezing afternoon in early December, Ed came pounding up the stairs to my room on the top floor of the women's dorm with his satchel in one hand and a big manila envelope tucked under his arm. He was windblown and pink in the cheeks like he'd run all the way across the campus.

"You have *got* to see this." He dropped onto my unmade bed, pulled a thick sheaf of handwritten pages out of the envelope and slapped them down over Prof. Thorsen's physics textbook. "Go on," he said, glowing with the cold. "Read *that*."

I picked up the manuscript doubtfully. The handwriting slanted weirdly to the left at a forty-five degree angle and the letters were tightly packed. It looked like one of those flowing south Asian scripts, but compressed. The only thing I could make out was the title and the author: *TheHollowEarth, byPatPhang*.

"PatPhang?" I said. "Is that his last name?"

"Pat Phang," said Ed. "Chinese. I think."

"Does he go to school here?" There was a Chinese restaurant in town, but the owners were Mexican. I couldn't think of any Oriental students at all. In those days, of course, we were much more isolated than we are now.

"He's not a student," said Ed. "See the address? It's a Post Office box in Lake Okichobi. That's way north of here, in Michigan."

I frowned at the envelope. Stamps were plastered all over the top right corner, as though PatPhang had guessed at the weight of his great work instead of taking it to the post office. "Why is he sending it to us?"

"You'll see." Ed snatched the manuscript away, grabbed a pillow and made himself comfortable. "Listen. I'll read it to you."

I made a helpless gesture at the physics book. He ignored me.

" 'I have traveled in a dark and silent place neither your children nor your ancestors have ever, or will ever see. I am the single survivor returned from a great city a thousand miles below the surface of the Earth. This is my story.' "

" 'Dark and silent,' " I said. "Nice imagery. But wouldn't it be awfully hot in a great city a thousand miles below the surface of the Earth?"

Ed grinned. *" 'Twelve thousand years ago, the Atlerians ruled the Earth. They were a giant race, made up of giants, both in their bodies and minds and the scope of their thinking. Atleria was their continent and from them flowed all the future myths of humanity, every god and goddess and every evil. All this, all our history has sprung from them.' "*

"A little repetitive," I said. "Giant this, giant that."

"Just listen," said Ed, and kept reading.

" 'The Atlerians came from throughout the galaxy, but settled here on this planet until a solar disaster occurred.

The positive, healing light from the Sun turned to a dark, malevolent emanation of night . . .' "

" 'Emanation of night?' " I said, thinking of what Professor Thorsen might have to say about that.

" '*. . . and thus,*' " Ed continued, " '*the Atlerians were corrupted and driven underground, mutating from the disaster, and all their good went with them. Some returned to the surface as human beings, forgetting their true past. Some stayed below and became the evil overlords of the cities built by their elders. They became corrupted and evil in the dark, no matter how many artificial sources of illumination they devised. The longer they stayed in the caverns, the more corrupt and despicable they became.*' "

"Corrupted this and corrupted that."

"We're editors," said Ed. "Editors edit what needs to be edited. Now, listen."

" '*I have lived with a twisted spine for most of my life. The Atlerians are responsible for this. When they realized that, even as a child, I could hear their conversations under the floorboards of my house, they began to send corrupting beams of negative energy to silence me. The negative energy has polarized my body in two directions, and so, as the years go by, my spine and body spiral, each year to a more excruciating degree. I am crippled, with the ability only to listen and to write down what I hear. I have had the strength to take up a few of my floorboards and crouch there in the hole I have made to hear more clearly what is going on in the caverns beneath my home.*' "

"Oh, I see," I said. "This is all supposed to be true."

Ed just raised an eyebrow.

" '*They are evil. I have heard them saying how they*

have created a 'master race' to defeat and exterminate the mud people and their ilk. I have heard them speaking in great detail about mechanical weapons and missiles with the ability to fly enormous distances. I have heard them talking about a bomb that can wipe out a city with a single flash of light. I don't understand the language they use, but as I said before, I understand their thoughts, and though I am trapped here, I will relay them to you, incoherently perhaps, but this warning, this record must be relayed at all costs.'"

"He's read a lot of H.G. Wells," I said. "Some of that sounds like it's taken straight out of *The Time Machine*."

"I checked," said Ed. "It's not."

"*'Before my crippling was complete, since I knew the source of my corruption, I went, many years ago, to see the faces of my tormentors. One, who I had befriended, took me to the edge of their despicable city, but first we traveled through the wilds of the subterranean world. We killed a huge and malevolent worm with pickaxes, and its blood was black, and as thick as asphalt.'*"

"It sounds like Burroughs' *Pelucidar*."

Ed shook his head. "All original."

"But it's terrible, Ed. It's immature. It's barely original, and the writing's . . ."

"Awful," said Ed, "I know." He flipped through the rest of the manuscript, about ten more pages. "But it has everything—a mysterious main character threatened by evil from an unknown world for unknown purposes. It has adventure. It has atmosphere." He looked up at me. "And there's a lot more than just this. PatPhang's been mailing in thirty pages every week for the last three weeks. Either it's already written, or he's pumping it out as we speak."

I had to laugh. "This is going to be a *novel*?"

"More than a novel," said Ed. "It's an epic." He tapped the pages together into a neat pile and gave me a funny, almost guilty look. "Remember what I told you about the beer-eating microbes in the Rat?"

"What—the part about 'one day they may become something useful?' Sure, I remember."

He tucked the pages back into his satchel. "Mister Cassidy, I think people might just pay to read this."

I didn't see much of Ed for the next few days. I had my own pile of editorial slush to pick through, and I applied myself deliberately to the task. By the end of the week, I'd decided on a short-short by Bobby Silver—beautifully written, tightly plotted, with a wonderful twist to the end—which needed a minimum of tweaking. I also chose a longer piece by Asa Ikamov, which, though a little flat in the narrative, had some fascinating ideas about robots. I chose a rip-roaring spaceship battle-piece by Clem Halmont as well. I was happy with the way the stories balanced each other—a little speculation for the intellectual, a nod to the more demanding literary reader, and something for the boys in search of a "shoot 'em up" adventure.

I met Ed at the Rat that night and laid my choices triumphantly on the bar. He leafed through them with fingers blued by mimeo ink. "It'll be a little thick," he said, "but it'll be our best issue."

I thought this praise was intended for me. I

beamed and prepared myself to kiss him. But Ed opened his satchel, pulled out a mimeo master, and gave it to me gingerly. It was the cover drawing for our next issue. (Collectors know that Ed drew all the covers—he'd taken an art course at UNI along with everything else.) It showed a cartoonishly buxom young woman screaming as she was attacked by a huge, furry gorilla-type creature emerging from a dark blot, which I could sort of imagine was a cave. The headline, drawn with an italic lettering stencil read; *UNI-verse! The New Magazine of Scienti-Fiction.* And, at the bottom of the page, *"A Warning from Atleria," by Patrick Fang.*

"You changed his name?" I said. "And I don't remember a gorilla. Was there a screaming girl? I don't remember that either."

"Artistic license," he said and pressed his lips together like he was waiting for me to notice something else. I peered at the cover again. Up in the left-hand corner was something I hadn't seen before. A price tag.

"I hope you're not planning to print a lot of these," I said. "And I hope you have a place in your room to put them when nobody wants to shell out a quarter. I mean, you can get a comic book for less."

Ed took the cover back and snapped the satchel shut. "We're not selling comic books, Mister Cassidy," he said. "We're selling the future.

To my amazement, every single copy was gone by the end of the week. We usually set piles of *UNI-verse* out in the student union, the Rat, of course, and this time in the local drugstore at the end of the soda fountain (suggestively close to the comics). We put a coffee can next to each pile with a slit in the top for the quarters and checked them every two hours. At the end of the first day, we'd made fifty dollars, which was absolutely unheard of, and for students like us, a small fortune. By Friday, we were completely sold out, and it fell to me to dig the old mimeos out of the trash and print a hundred more copies.

"What're you going to do?" I said to Ed as he prepared to leave me in the basement of the library with the mimeo machine.

"I'll be putting together the next issue," he said and patted his satchel. "We'll release it on Friday next week. Strike while the iron is hot."

"You mean I have to do all this stapling by *myself*?" I demanded, but he was already gone.

So I spent the night in the copy room, alone with the stink of duplicating fluid. And as I waited to collate what the machine spit out, I began to read what we had published, and was selling so well. I was just a little surprised at what I had coedited.

A Warning From Atleria did indeed contain a scene with a gorilla. It did indeed have a screaming woman—Petra was her name. Only the very barest bones of PatPhang's original story were left.

Around midnight, I went up to Ed's room and found him hunched over a typewriter. PatPhang's manuscript, all two hundred pages of it now, was stacked on the right. An open box of mimeo masters spilled out onto the desk. What Ed had already transferred to mimeo was scattered on the floor like a complex carpet, patterned in blue ink. He didn't look up when I came in.

"You rewrote his entire story," I said, and read from the page I'd brought with me. "*'Before I could enter the unholy city of the Atlerians, there was, of necessity, a sacrifice.*" I stopped and eyed him. He just rolled another mimeo into the typewriter and poised his fingers over the keys. I continued in a louder voice; "*'Near to where those high, shining walls nestled in the embrace of the Earth, were wilder places, untouched by civilization or the wonders of their evil technology. These places retained their original inhabitants, creatures nearer to the dawn of time than even their masters, surviving from an era even before reptiles walked the upper reaches of our world-in-light.'*" I came over and rattled the paper in front of him. "PatPhang never called it '*World-in-light.*'"

He made a dismissive gesture and started typing. "I fixed it."

"You rewrote it," I said.

"I thought it needed more texture—more *oomph.*"

"You can't just rewrite his entire manuscript—not without telling him. It isn't ethical."

Ed stopped typing and rocked back in his chair. "You think it's a great masterpiece the way it is, Mister Cassidy?"

"Well, no. The guy's obviously an amateur and clearly some kind of nut, but that doesn't mean you can just—"

"What do you think the editorial staff does at

Amazing, Mister Cassidy?" said Ed. "Sit around and drink coffee all day?"

"No," I said, "but I don't think they rewrite an entire novel."

"They don't have the time." Ed leaned forward, and the chair's front legs hit the floor with a defining *thunk.* "I have all the time in the world."

I was so woozy from mimeo fumes and lack of sleep, and such a long way from understanding what was going on, I started to laugh. "If you rewrote that nutty crap a million times, you still wouldn't be able to make it into a masterpiece."

"Fortunately," said Ed, with a distinct frost to his tone, "that's not what we're after."

"Well, then," I said stupidly, "what are we after?"

"Sales, Mister Cassidy," said Ed, as though it should have been obvious. "Now, if you don't mind . . ." He pointed at our slush pile of brown envelopes by the closet. "You can go through those. Try to pick stuff that'll complement *The Hollow Earth* series. You know. Nothing that'll outshine it."

"Series?" I said.

"Like the *Saturday Evening Post,*" said Ed, "Like *McCall's.* Like *Amazing,* Mister Cassidy. We have two hundred pages to publish and more coming." He eyed me. "Have you finished stapling?"

"Well, no, but that wasn't—"

"Then you're *wasting my time,* Mister Cassidy."

I felt my mouth fall open. I didn't know what to say. This wasn't an "equal partnership" kind of conversation. But then I was an equal partner of a mimeographed school magazine. What did I (a girl) know about the real world of publishing? I closed my mouth, scooped up an armload of envelopes, and left without another word. When I'd finished the stapling, I went across the campus to the dank depths of the Rat and spent the next two hours with my feet on a chair, well off the soggy carpet, and a beer within easy reach, reading the rest of the submissions.

What could I possibly pick that wouldn't "outshine" PatPhang's (and now Ed's) masterpiece? Not the story about killer mechanical dolls, no siree. Not the lurid novella about the sexual side effects that faster-than-light travel had on a coed crew. Certainly not the strangely credible story about the alien origin of slide rules. I slapped the last manuscript down in frustration, knocked back the dregs of my third beer and stood up with a lurch. Ed could have his magazine. He could "edit" all he wanted. But he couldn't pretend that what he was doing was right, no matter how well it sold. If nothing else, PatPhang would have to be informed.

I understood what I had to do now. I groped my way across the dank carpet, through a pack of loud, inebriated frat boys, across the December campus, and even though it was two in the morning, I banged on Ed's door.

Of course he was still up. This time I thought he looked grateful for the interruption.

"What the hell do you want now?" he said.

"If you're gonna *change* his work," I said, holding myself up by the doorjamb, "we're gonna have to *tell* him before we publish any more of it."

Ed rubbed the stubble on his chin and thumbed the stacks of mimeo masters.

"We should go see 'im," I said. "Don't you wanna see what kinda guy he is, anyway?"

"Yeah," said Ed. "I guess I always have."

"Then let's go!" I grabbed his car keys off the dresser and threw them at him. "It's a long drive to Lake Oki—Oki—"

"Okichobi," said Ed, and reached for his coat.

Needless to say, I'd sobered up by dawn, but by then the Michigan state line was well behind us. So were at least three coffee joints. I looked down at the empty cardboard cup in my hands and began to regret everything.

"Feeling better?" said Ed.

The truth was, I would have like to have puked up everything I'd ever eaten. "Sure," I mumbled, and stared out the window at the miles of snow and rows of cut corn. "Do we even know where this lake is?"

Ed prodded a map on the bench seat between us and the leather upholstery creaked with the cold. Ed drove an old Ford and the car had no heat to speak of. As our bodies warmed the interior, the inside of the windshield would ice up with condensation. I knew this because I had studied physics. I rubbed my head, thinking about what my mother would say if she could see me at this moment. "You know," I said, "maybe this is a bad idea. We don't even have his address." PatPhang sent his work from a post office box.

"Come on," said Ed, his breath steaming against

the windshield. "How many Phangs can there be in the phone book? When we get to Okichobi, we'll look him up."

"What if he's not listed?" I said. "What if it's a pen name?"

Ed reached for the radio and turned it on. "Here," he said. "Find a station with girl music, huh?"

I could have socked him. We listened to country music, since that was all there was, and my mood got worse and worse. I felt like I hardly knew Ed anymore. Everything was the same as before—his hair, his eyes, his smile—but now I could see more of what was inside of him and I didn't like it. When we finally found the road to Lake Okichobi, I'd decided I could easily, *easily* live without my "equal partnership" in the *UNI-verse*.

We pulled over and stopped where the road to Lake Okichobi intersected the state highway at an agricultural right angle. The sign sticking out of the snowdrift said:

Orsinville 2 miles

Lake Okichobi 3 miles

Lemuria 16 miles

Snow whipped across the empty landscape in white gusts. We both eyed the nominally plowed dent that led to PatPhang.

"Well," said Ed, "We've come this far."

What I wanted to say was, *If we get stuck, we'll freeze to death before anyone finds us*. What I actually said was, "Yeah," because I knew that if we turned around and went back to UNI right now, we'd be fighting this same fight in a matter of days. It was better to get it over with, and I think Ed knew that.

He turned the car and maneuvered it into the icy crush that extended as far as the eye could see.

Two slow, slippery miles later, we came to Orsinville, which consisted of a gas station and a distant farmhouse. Ed and I both checked the gas gauge as we crunched past the station. We were at a quarter tank, but the place looked closed. It was about nine o'clock on a Saturday morning. We probably should have stopped and checked.

"Just another mile," said Ed. "We can make it."

The snow ahead was flat and featureless except for the waning dark stripe of the road as snow drifted and stuck to it. Orsinville disappeared behind us as Ed drove at a crawl. Lake Okichobi could have been a million miles away.

"Have you thought about what you're going to say to him?" I said.

"To who?" said Ed, leaning so far forward that his chin was almost on his knuckles. "Oh. Well, sure. I'm just going to say I thought the work needed to be solidified."

"And it needed texture."

"That, too."

"Did you bring the revisions?"

He didn't say anything, which, obviously, meant *no*.

Pretty soon we saw a forlorn green sign leaning at an angle in the wind, but pointing undeniably to the right. *Lake Okichobi.* Ed hit the brakes and nearly swerved into the snow banked up on either side of the road. We peered to the right, but instead of a road, there was only a pair of tire tracks wavering through the snow, plunging down the only slope in sight.

"If you take the car down there, we'll never get it out," I said.

Ed turned the car off and opened the door. Wind and sharp needles of snow blew in, cutting through my hangover, replacing it with an ache in my nostrils that reached all the way into my sinuses. We got out of the car and stood, shivering under the perfect winter-blue sky. The wind shoved my coat against my back and rushed around my ankles.

"It's cold as crap," said Ed.

I peered down the snowy hillside. At the bottom, it was easy to see the flat outline of a lake, covered with ice, then covered with snow. There were two buildings; a shack by the lake and a farmhouse at least half a mile away. The tire tracks led to the farmhouse. There was smoke blowing in an energetic plume from its chimney and we could almost smell the morning biscuits.

It wasn't the sort of place where we expected to find PatPhang.

Both of us turned our eyes to the shack by the lake. There was no hint of smoke from the stovepipe sticking out of the roof.

"You think he's home?" said Ed.

"He'd better be." I pulled my coat tight and started down one of the tire tracks. Ed hurried after me, leaving the car right where it was, as though he was scared of being left behind. In retrospect, I think he actually was. The two of us had absolutely no way of knowing that this was where PatPhang lived, and yet we were both certain that this was it. At the time, nothing about the place made my hair stand up on the back of my neck the way the memories of it do now. Maybe I was just too cold and hung over to know how scared I should have been.

I heard Ed mutter something behind me, crunching along in the iced-over track. "What?"

"I didn't say anything."

We were walking single file. I twisted to look at him over my shoulder, and as I did, I heard the mutter again. It was low and resonant, and not Ed's voice. I thought it was the wind, but as soon as we'd dropped below the rise where the car was, the wind had mellowed to a stiff, freezing breeze.

"Did you hear that?" I said.

He made a peculiar motion with his lips, as though he had heard, but didn't want to say so. He looked very pale and thin in the hard light of morning. The circles under his eyes were like thumbprints, the color of charcoal.

The noise came again, almost articulate.

I stopped in my tracks. We were about halfway between the car and PatPhang's house. Ed stood close enough to press against me. I realized, somewhat dully, that he was really frightened. The wind buffeted around us making soft "whumps," but underneath that sound was the noise, like another voice, so deep and profound, I could have sworn it was right underneath my feet. We listened as it groaned and murmured, almost words but mostly tone, expressive and awful.

"What the hell is that?" whispered Ed. His fingers clutched my sleeve.

"It's nothing," I said, because to admit it *was* something meant admitting we'd exposed ourselves to too many scary stories in our editorial pursuits, and were primed to run like rabbits. "It's the, uh, temperature variation in the snow. Where the sun hits it. When it starts melting, it makes that noise."

What did I know? It sounded as good as anything I'd ever heard Prof. Thorsen shout about. Ed nodded as though it made perfect sense. He seemed to regain a little of his composure and let go of my sleeve. "Okay," he said, "come on."

This time he took the lead. The noise underneath the snow persisted, showing no sign of going away now that it'd been explained. We turned off the tire tracks and began slogging through knee-deep snow. I expected the noise to get louder as we got closer to PatPhang's shack. It didn't, but about twenty feet from the front door, the snow thinned enough to show brown mats of rotten grass underneath.

"Maybe he *is* home," said Ed under his breath. "He shoveled his walk."

It didn't look shoveled. It looked like the snow had melted into the ground. I stopped. "Does it feel warmer to you?"

Both of us were thinking about all that bizarre, patently fake crap about giant primeval worms and ancient cities under the Earth's crust.

Ed took a big breath. If he'd turned tail and run, I

would never have thought less of him. "There is no way any of that stuff's true," he said.

"He's just a nut with a great imagination," I whispered. My ears were freezing, but my feet were starting to feel warm. "And he's a lousy writer. He *needs* editing."

Ed nodded quickly. "And that's what we're going to tell him. Right?"

I swallowed. "Right."

Underneath us, the very ground groaned its objection. I could feel it through the soles of my shoes. Ed grabbed my hand and yanked me forward until we were standing on the cracked concrete slab of Pat-Phang's front steps.

Ed rapped on the door, still gripping my hand. "Mister Phang? Mister Phang! It's Ed Plummer from *UNI-verse* magazine."

The ground creaked. I swear the house shook. We waited like two people on the edge of a crumbling cliff, calculating the moment when it would be too late to leave. The door had a window, frosted over on the outside, streaked with dirt on the inside. Ed scratched at the frost and peered in.

"Can you see anything?"

"There's just a chair and a table and a typewriter."

"Let me see." I pushed him out of the way and stood on my tiptoes. On the other side of the door, the shack was a single, dingy room. No wallpaper or paint, no rug, not even a stove or a sink that I could see. And Ed was right. In the middle of the room was a wooden table and a chair, and a typewriter. There wasn't even any paper, only an air of desertion and terrible spookiness. But there was one other thing.

"What's that stain on the floor?" I said.

Ed breathed over my shoulder, fogging the glass. "What stain?"

The ground shuddered and wind ripped around the side of the house with a human shriek. I rubbed at the glass as the proverbial cliff prepared to give way and release us into the stateless space we could just see on the other side of the door. And it wasn't a stain, I realized, it was a hole in the floor of the miserable house. And there was something in the hole. I could see the top of a head—a coarsely hairy head—and a pair of eyes watching from floor level.

For a second, I was terrified. Then I realized it was PatPhang, sitting in his hole, eavesdropping on the underworld. For just a moment I was certain that what I was seeing was simply Lake Okichobi's local lunatic, huddled in his empty shack. Up the hill, his family was probably waiting for him to come home when he got too cold, with hot biscuits in a warm kitchen. For a heartbeat, it all made perfect, mostly ordinary, sense.

"He's *watching* us!" I rapped hard on the door. "We can see you!" I shouted. "Come out of there! We need to talk about your book!"

And then the head came up a little. I heard Ed catch his breath. It wasn't just a hairy head. The rest of the face was hairy, too. And it wasn't a human face. It looked a *lot* like Ed's gorilla-creature on *UNI-verse*'s most recent cover.

I freely admit, I screamed. Screamed just like that

buxom cover girl. My only comfort is that Ed screamed too. The two of us bolted like bunnies, making huge, athletic leaps through the snow. We scrambled up the hill along the icy track and sprinted to the car. The only truly positive thing that happened that day was that despite being low on gas and frozen to its mechanical core, the car obediently started.

We didn't say anything until we stopped at the gas station in Orsinville.

The owner, an older man, with teeth stained from chewing tobacco, gave us a funny look as we paid for gas, coffee, a box of donuts, and all the Slim Jims he had on the counter. "Thought I saw you headin' up the road about an hour back. You lost?"

"Uh," said Ed, still visibly shivering, "we were looking for someone in Lake Okichobi."

"That where you been?" said the owner. "You find 'em?"

I shook my head.

"Guess you heard the noises, though."

Ed looked up sharply from his coffee.

"Caves all through that part of the county," said the owner. "Wind blows through 'em and makes the darnedest sound."

"Darnedest," I echoed.

"Lose cattle and dogs in 'em all the time," said the owner. "Sometimes kids, too. Who was you looking for, anyway?"

"PatPhang," said Ed. "Ever heard of him?"

"Can't say that I have."

* * *

We drove home in what turned out to be one of the worst blizzards of the winter, and by the time we got back to the campus, we were too worn out to talk about anything. The next time I saw Ed, it was well after the end of Christmas break. Needless to say, our next issue of the magazine was on indefinite hold. I'd gone home for the holidays, and hadn't seen him in weeks. We ran into each other at the Rat. He bought me a beer and sat in silence while I made patterns in the condensation on the glass, trying not to think about PatPhang's window. I hadn't told anyone about our trip to Lake Okichobi, not even my mother.

"I have something for you," said Ed finally. He took a piece of paper out of his pocket and laid it on the bar. It was a check for two hundred and fifty dollars, made out to me.

"What's this?" I said.

He cleared his throat. "It's half of my advance from Deuce publications."

"For what?" I said, but as soon as I said it, I knew what he'd done. "You *sold* the *Hollow Earth* to *Deuce*?"

"They're going to publish it as a novel."

"But it's not even *yours*!"

"Most of it is," he said. "After we went to Michigan, he quit sending any more. I had to finish it." He rubbed his eyes. "It topped out at seven hundred pages. He only sent two hundred."

I just stared at him. I had no idea what to say. "What're you going to do if he finds out?"

"He won't," said Ed. "He's just a reclusive nut listening to the wind in the caves under his house. And even if he does find out, we never published any of that stuff in its original form. I rewrote it before it ever touched the mimeo machine. What he sent and what we printed doesn't match. Hardly at all."

I pushed the check back at him. "I don't want this."

He pushed it back, as though any evil consequences were going to be mine to bear as well. "You're an equal partner, Mister Cassidy."

"Stop calling me that," I said, and tore the check into pieces and dropped the pieces into his beer. I stood up to go. "If *anything* PatPhang wrote was true, Ed, do you know what's going to happen to you?"

He gave me a tired look. "It's just a crazy story. And it sells. They gave me a contract for three more books."

"Well," I said, scared for him, angry at him, amazed by his endless audacity. "Well, I hope it works out for you."

I didn't see Ed for a long time after that. He left UNI and began writing full time. I'd see his books in the stores once in a while. He had a steady, apparently growing, popularity.

So many people asked me what'd happened to *UNI-verse* that I decided to start the magazine again, and by my senior year, subscriptions were paying for more than half of my tuition. I stealthily changed majors without telling my mother and when I graduated, it was with a degree in publications and a minor in business administration. The magazine was so successful, that about a month before graduation, I got a letter from the editors at *Amazing* asking if I would be interested in freelance editorial work. Of course I said yes. Of course the letter was addressed to Mister Cassidy. It wasn't until I'd spent a year working for them through the mail that I went to their offices in person and introduced myself. They were surprised that I was a woman, and although they were civil about being fooled all this time, the look behind their eyes reminded me very much of myself, peering through the window of PatPhang's front door.

All My Children

by Leslie What

Leslie What has been a professional maskmaker, puppeteer, and tap dancer; Jell-O artist, psychiatric nurse, Campfire Youth Leader, humor columnist, medical writer, and manager of a low-income senior lunch site. She attributes her keen understanding of the male psyche to a marriage of twenty-something years, aided by helpful tips gleaned from raising a son. She won the 1999 Nebula Award for short fiction, and her work has appeared in literary and commercial magazines, anthologies, and other media. She has recently completed a novel.

WHEN I was eighteen, I earned fifty dollars for ejaculating into plastic bags. It seemed like easy money at the time. I was a varsity wrestling star, president of the local chapter of the National Honor Society, school valedictorian, and a certified stud. I was also, arguably, an idiot. An Aryan-looking recruiter had bribed me with cash, fed me grilled double-cheeseburgers, and let me watch real porn movies. He'd promised the whole thing was legit—was I supposed to say no? At the time, it seemed like no big deal.

Segue to the future, when it was a big deal because I'd recently been informed that I'd fathered some

10,000 children. This came as something of a shock—to me, my wife, and our sixteen-year-old twins (fraternal, neither of whom looked like me).

At the moment, my nuclear family and I were driving to the Rose Garden Arena, where my newly outed offspring were gathering for a reunion. It was not exactly a reunion, since none of us had ever met, but that was how they had billed it for TV. Officially, in the lawsuit, I was known as "The Donor," though my TV show was being called, "Life Without Father," which the producers thought had more appeal.

I was forty-nine, a surgeon in a thriving private practice, a Democrat with a house in the country, and a well-trained bulldog named Mr. Sniffles. I was a stocky blond guy with bifocals, a goatee, and a penchant for wearing tweed suits in public.

Circumstances had compelled me to forsake my tweed and get into something less comfortable. After suffering multiple fractures while skiing, I'd been immobilized inside a heavy plaster body cast that started at my neck and stretched to my waist and resembled a solid T-shirt. The plaster covered my shoulders but stopped above my elbows. It held out my upper arms to the sides scarecrow style, allowing my forearms to dangle loose. For this TV special, my wife Gina had draped a white dress shirt over my shoulders, and I wore new jersey pants with a drawstring waistband. A zipper was beyond my current capabilities.

I was feeling a little tense, maybe because I was propped up on the passenger side of the Suburban without a seat belt, maybe because my wife was in the back seat pretending to be asleep, maybe because my son was stoned and hiding behind earphones in the cargo hold, maybe because the only one in my family who was still talking to me was my daughter, who was doing ninety in a sixty-five-mile zone and lecturing me about child abandonment and its role in the development of criminal behavior. I'd taken two codeine tablets, but they were hardly touching the pain.

"Eighty percent of the women in jail were abused as children," my daughter Letty said. "And a lot of them grew up in single parent homes without a genetically related male to protect them."

"You're not blaming me for everyone who's ever been in prison," I said.

"It's not like he was around for us either," Henry Junior chimed in.

"True," Letty said.

I was tired of this complaint. "I'm a surgeon. It's a demanding job. I've been home every night except when I was on call," I said. "You have the luxury of a portable CD player because I worked to give it to you."

"Okay, so you're 'Father of the Year.'" Letty had inherited her mother's dark hair and sharp tongue, but none of my athletic prowess. She was tall and slender, a sophomore who hoped to become a sociologist. I couldn't have been prouder.

Henry was a bit more complicated. He had his Neanderthal ancestor's stoop, not to mention personal hygiene habits, and had no interest in anything academic; for the past few months, Henry's life had revolved around drugs and rap music. Lately, every time we tried to talk, we ended up yelling. Which didn't mean I loved him any less, just that I worried more.

"Slow down," I said to Letty.

She ignored me.

"I can't believe I have ten thousand siblings," Letty said. "What am I supposed to tell my friends?" She gave me buttocks eyes: a scrunched up angry expressed that showed how much she wanted to hit me.

"Look, I feel terrible," I said. How many times in one day was a man supposed to say he was sorry?

"I hate to be the saltshaker," said my wife Gina, coming out of her faux-coma, "but you're lucky *if* you only have ten thousand siblings. There could be millions, you know. Millions! Think about it."

Letty squealed, "Eueweeeuee! Do you *have* to remind me? Damn you, Father," she said, in her special teen sheep dialect that made it sound like "Faaahhhaahha-thur!"

I felt like I had lost leverage with the kids.

"Couldn't you have controlled yourself?" Letty asked.

"Well, no," I said. I was eighteen. "But I didn't know this would happen," I said. "I thought I was beating off for science."

"Oh, please," screamed Henry Junior. "Not in front of the children."

He was close to the age I had been when I'd fathered my first litter. This wasn't the kind of conversation I had expected to have about sex and responsibility. On the other hand, now it was sort of over and done, and maybe we could move on.

I saw the green sign that said, "Rose Garden Arena, next right," and tried to let Letty know to get over.

She screamed, "I know how to drive—you're the one who's a menace to society," so I shut up.

Letty cut through three lanes of traffic to squeeze between a Greyhound bus and a gasoline tanker. I went sliding across my seat. As my elbow hit the window, painful shock waves pulsed throughout my body. The combination of the codeine and teenage driving made my stomach vault and I felt like I was gonna be sick.

Letty made a hard right into the parking lot and almost ran down the guy directing traffic. She unrolled her window and dug through her pocket for the five bucks.

"Excuse me," I called past her to the boy in the orange vest. "We're supposed to have a place in 'Reserved Parking.' I don't think I should have to pay."

Letty glared at me and tried to shove a bill into the attendant's hands, but it was too late.

The boy's face lit up. "You're the guy!" he said. "You're the father!" He called over a few of his buddies and one asked for my autograph. "Does anyone have paper?" the first boy asked. Of course, nobody did, so he tore a parking voucher and turned it over and pointed to the blank spot and said, "There!" He thrust it through the open window, past Letty's nose.

If I tilted my body about forty-five degrees and wedged my head near the stick shift, I could just manage to scrawl illegibly with my right hand. "Sorry to ask this of you," I said to Letty, "but I need help."

Letty held the paper while I signed.

It seemed there were no end to the awkward moments.

Another guy in an orange vest let us through a wall of parking cones and we followed a marked lane to the VIP section near the main entrance. Letty pulled into a space marked by a huge plastic-covered sign that read, "Reserved for Henry Murkson and Family."

"Now are you satisfied?" Letty asked.

The press were waiting like car salesmen on a slow day and approached en masse.

"Why didn't you just let her pay the five bucks?" Gina screamed. Letty blared the horn and the press backed away.

"OHMYGOD!" said Letty. "I don't want to be on TV or in the paper! I can't tell you how much I hate you right now!"

"There's no need," I said, feeling the love.

"Could this be any more embarrassing?" Gina said. She opened the back door and pulled her coat over her head to run for the entrance. Henry followed from the cargo hold, his head down, and his arms shielding his face.

As Letty got out, she pressed the auto-lock behind her and ran off.

"Hey," I called. "Hey!" Nobody had opened my car door and I couldn't reach the handle on my own. "Hey!" I banged my head against the window, feeling useless. A few minutes later, a young woman in an orange vest tapped on the glass and waited patiently while I maneuvered my cast until I was able to press the release button.

She opened the door and I spilled out.

She was in her late twenties, very tall, slender, and pretty. She smiled, and I found myself smiling back, flirting just a little, even though I knew that from the front, with my cast on, I looked like a cartoon character flattened by a steam roller.

"Excuse me," I said. "My lawyer was supposed to meet me here, in the lot. Have you seen him?" Appearing on the show had been his idea, because he thought a guy in a cast would play sympathetically to the audience.

"Dad?" she said with a hopeful tone. She gave me a firm hug.

"Ouch," I answered.

Dad.

The cloudy sky swirled like vanilla soft-serve in a blue bowl; I pulled away and leaned against the side of the Suburban, lowered my head, and threw up.

The girl waited for me to finish before wiping my mouth with a crumpled tissue with pink lipstick marks in the center. She produced a bottle of water from the chest pocket of her vest and poured a little in my mouth.

The water was warm, but I drank it anyway. She gazed into my eyes as she dribbled water into my mouth. She gave me more than I wanted, and some dribbled down my chin.

She capped the water, and put it back in her pocket.

I burped. I'd just been bottle-fed by my new daughter.

Of course, a photographer from the AP caught the moment in a flash, but my daughter shooed everyone else away. She put one hand on my back to guide me toward the entrance.

"So you're one of them," I said. "Somehow, I thought I'd know." My feelings were complex. I tried to explain. "You're the first one I've met."

"Sorry," she said. "I should have introduced myself sooner."

"Life doesn't prepare you for these kinds of moments," I said, hoping to sound wise. "What's your name?"

"Heather," she said. "Don't laugh."

"Why should I laugh?"

"Everyone does," she said. "My parents are both women. Or maybe you don't remember the book *Heather Has Two Mommies*."

"Oh," I said, pretending not to be shocked. "Lesbians." My face got hot. "I hope you've had a pleasant life," I said. I wanted to reach inside my pocket for my billfold but couldn't do it. "I have money," I said. "I could give you some." I looked around for someone unrelated whom I'd feel comfortable asking to dig through my pockets.

"I'm okay," she said. "You don't need to give me money. I'm in college. This is just a part-time job. I really don't want anything from you. I just wanted to meet you. You know, say hello."

"I'm glad to meet you," I said, a line I'd practiced in preparation for these occasions. "I'm glad that you're okay." I couldn't help but be curious and blurted out, "Are you, you know, a lesbian, too?" I asked.

"It doesn't work that way," she said, and I could see that I'd offended her. "You have a lot of weird ideas about sexuality," she said. "But what do you expect from a guy who spilled his seed in a plastic bag?" She snatched her hand from my back and walked quickly away.

I understood that I was to follow her into the stadium. "Sorry," I yelled. "Sorry!" I was in no position to lecture anyone about alternate lifestyles. "I was just curious," I said, too late. I had poisoned the relationship. Luckily for me, I still had a chance with the other 9,999.

Without anyone to insulate me from them, newscasters and reporters swarmed and pelted me with questions.

"How's it feel to have so many children?"

"If the lawsuits prevail, how will you provide child support?"

"What does your wife think about all those other women?"

"No comment," I said, as my lawyer had directed. Where was he anyway?

"Do you have any favorites or do you treat them all equally?"

"No comment," I said. "No comment."

At last, I made it inside, where a security guard in a red jacket whisked me off to the underground tunnels. A guy in pleated slacks and a merino wool cardigan walked up and gave me an air handshake. "I'm Bill Burke, one of the promoters," he said. "Glad you were able to come. Nervous?"

"Well, sure," I said.

"That's understandable. Anyone would be. Now let's get you to makeup."

"Where's my family?" I asked, and Bill said, "They're in the stands, in a private skybox. You can join them later, during the halftime."

"There's a halftime?" I asked.

"For fifty bucks a ticket, we need to give them something," he said. "These kinds of 'Real TV' shows are never predictable. You need to have something fun in case reality is a dud."

A makeup gal powdered my face with a puff and someone from wardrobe, who introduced himself as "Jim, the propmaster," fretted over my white shirt and cast, shaking his head and saying, "This won't look good for the cameras! Too much glare. It could make his face go dark on screen."

"That might be okay," I said, but nobody believed that I was serious.

Jim brought out a red cape with black fringe and tied me into it.

"All I could find," he said.

The person I saw in the mirror looked like Zorro with unbelievably broad shoulders.

"That's a very manly look," said Jim. "You stud, you!" He gave me a playful punch on the chin.

Bill and Jim led me through the dark catacombs.

The tunnels shook a bit, as if there were cows stampeding above us.

"Sounds like a rough audience," said Bill. "Hope they don't eat you alive."

We walked up a flimsy staircase to backstage, and I peeked through a sliver in the curtain. On the grass field sat thousands and thousands of spectators in folding chairs—my children? Thousands more sat up in the stands. I felt dizzy.

Jim looked me over. "You're a little hard to mike," he said. "I think we'll have to go for the floor mike."

"Have you used a floor microphone before?" Bill asked.

I nodded.

"Just don't get too close."

"I know," I said.

Jim took over the explanation. "A lot of people, they think it's like a blow job, but it's not. Keep your distance," he said. "It's very sensitive! Okay, so that part's like a blow job. While we're talking blow jobs, there's one other thing—just remember, six inches. Stand *six inches* away and you'll be fine."

Bill rolled his eyes and said, "Showbiz people," and went to talk to the technician at the soundboard.

Onstage, the host warmed up the crowd with his Ed Sullivan impersonation. "Ladies and gentlemen," he said. "We're here for a rilly big shoe. Paternity with a capital 'P.' Sperm donor uber alles. The ultimate noncustodial deadbeat dad! Put your hands together and let's welcome your father, and a legend in donor circles, Dr. Henry Murkson!"

There were a lot of boos and hisses, but also whistles and applause, and in a while, the applause grew loud enough to mask the booing.

Jim made a few final adjustments to my cape and gave me a gentle push forward. "Go get 'em, tiger!" he said. "Grrrrr!"

I walked onstage and stood six inches away from the mike. "Hey, kids," I said. I looked at the faces of those sitting in the folding chairs and tried to figure out if anyone looked familiar. There were children, teenagers, young adults, and older people who must have been their parents. Then my mouth went dry and I started trembling, and the speech I'd practiced left me. I had stage fright for the biggest performance of my life.

The Ed Sullivan guy ran back to the mike and turned it off. He whispered, "Don't focus on any one face; just pretend you're looking at everyone."

I did as he suggested. It helped a little.

He flipped on the mike. "Well, okay, then. Let me ask you a few things. Your sperm was sold to thousands of well-to-do couples, who were told that they were purchasing a genetic legacy capable of producing Ivy League and Fortune 500 children, yet you claim you weren't informed about this at the time of donation?"

"I was never informed, no."

"But you signed a waiver."

"I might have signed something. I probably thought it was a form so I could be paid."

"Excuse me for sounding skeptical," said the Ed guy. "But didn't you ever think about what might happen to your sperm?"

"How many eighteen-year-old boys do?" I said.

"Any questions from the audience?"

Hands flew up like butterfly wings and ushers holding portable mikes flitted through the audience. I looked up into the stands and saw a row of glassed-in skyboxes atop center field. The faces were too far away to pinpoint, but maybe the kids were watching. This might be my best chance to explain myself.

The Ed guy said, "Let us know your first name, your age, and where you're from," and a young man in a wheelchair said, "Jeremy, fifteen, from Boca Raton, Florida. Are there any genetic flaws that it might help us to know about?"

I cleared my throat. I sensed he wanted to blame me for his condition. I wished I could have given him that. "Not that I'm aware of," I said. "Sorry."

Jim brought me out a glass of water and whispered, "You're doing great!"

"Next question," said the Ed guy.

"Shelina, thirty, from New Orleans," said a young black woman. "Do you want to have more of a role in our lives?"

"I'm not sure everyone would want that," I said.

"Another question," said the Ed guy.

"Renee, twenty, from Salt Lake City. If you lose the lawsuit, are you prepared to pay child support?"

"I don't think that I'll lose," I said. "It would be a terrible precedent for all donors. When you think about it, I'm a victim, too."

There was a wave of booing that made me lose my nerve.

"Liz, nineteen, from New York City. What's it like

to wake up one morning and find out you've got thousands of kids. Do you love us?"

I blanked, not remembering if the lawyer had told me to say yes or no to this question. "Could you repeat that?" I asked; the guy with the portable mike had already moved on. Too late, I recovered and said, "I love all my children," but my mike was dead and nobody heard me.

"Excuse us while we go to a commercial break," said the Ed guy.

Two armchairs were brought out onstage for the next segment I was introduced to a famous TV psychologist and famous TV lawyer who were regulars on the series. We made small talk while Jim brought out an extra chair and rearranged the furniture, leaving space to the side. He straightened my cape and fluffed the sides of my hair. "The camera loves you!" he said. "Just remember that!"

I whispered, "Have you seen my lawyer? He's supposed to be here!"

"He's a no-show," said Jim. "It happens. Sorry."

I tried to sit but couldn't fit in my chair. Jim ran off and returned immediately with a beanbag chair. He helped me down. We went live. The Ed guy introduced us all and asked the famous psychologist, "So what's the harm of having a turkey baster for a father?"

"Well, first of all, he's not the father, he's the donor," she said. "It's important to remember that being a father is sociological, not just biological."

"In an ideal situation," said the famous lawyer.

"But the point is, that in this case, none of the birth

mothers were misled as to the intent of the donor. They went to a clinic expecting to meet sperm and not man. None of the birth mothers held the expectation that this gentleman would help them change diapers, or play ball with the children. This was a financial transaction, not a societal one."

"Many of these innocent victims in the audience would disagree," said the famous lawyer.

The Ed guy brought out a woman named Audrey and introduced her as the mother of one of my children.

She shook the others' hands but just stared at me and said, "I thought you'd be taller."

The famous lawyer laughed and said, "You never get what you paid for, do you? I guess the lesson is *caveat emptor.*"

Audrey took the chair that had been meant for me. "And they said my kid would have blue eyes, but they turned out brown," she said. "At least I didn't pay as much as most of them. I bought the sperm on eBay." She pulled out her billfold to show a picture of her kid—my son—John. She flashed it my way.

He didn't look anything like me.

"I don't know what I'd do if you tried to take him from me," said Audrey.

"I don't want to take him from you," I said. The Ed guy ran over with the floor mike and told me to repeat what I had said. I shook my head. "I can't believe all this is happening," I said. "It doesn't seem real."

"Oh, it's real," said the TV lawyer. "The claimants have all had their DNA tested. But how about your family? How do you know that your children are really yours?"

"There's no need to test for that," I said. I looked up into the skyboxes and hoped Henry Junior was listening. "My children are mine," I said. "Case closed."

"You're so smug," said the TV lawyer. "I suppose you think that the other 10,000 are illegitimate?"

Audrey stood up and screamed, "Did you call my son a bastard?"

The three got in a fistfight, which I knew was staged because I saw Audrey slip a red capsule in her mouth a few seconds before the psychologist pretended to hit her in the chops. She spit blood over everything and for once I was happy to be wearing a red cape.

There was another commercial break and the TV psychologist and TV lawyer and Audrey all shook hands and left the stage. The next section featured four of my offspring: two girls and two boys.

"You're not—any of you—going to hit me?" I asked. I couldn't cower properly, because of my cast.

The four of them denied any bad intent.

We came back live. "If you've just joined us, we're here with the man who spawned 10,000 kids," said the Ed guy. "Let's talk with some of them now." He introduced us to Theodore, Jessica, Brittany, and Jared. None of them looked like me. With me in my beanbag chair and the kids in their armchairs, the perspective was wrong, and even the eleven-year-old seemed taller.

"What's it like growing up with a father who isn't your real father?" asked the Ed guy.

Young Theodore said, "My father is my real father," and if I could have moved my arms, I would have applauded.

Brittany said, "You always wonder who he is and why he abandoned you."

"I didn't abandon you," I said.

"But still, you always wonder," she answered.

Jared said, "It makes you think about how stuff you don't think matters, really does," and the Ed guy said, "That's deep, man."

Jessica said, "What I want to know is, was it worth the fifty dollars?"

"At the time, yes. Now, no," I said.

She looked as if she might cry. "I don't mean it like that," I said. "Your life has much more value than fifty dollars."

The Ed guy said, "Of course, if you divide up fifty by ten thousand . . ."

Jared said, "What will it be like for you when you meet your grandchildren?"

I gulped. Oh, God. Not another reunion.

"Do you ever think about us?" Jessica asked. "What we've gone through?"

This time I was quick enough to say, "Sure."

The Ed guy said to me, "Is there anything you'd like to ask your children?"

I felt on the defensive; the only thing I could think to ask was, "Are you glad that you're alive?" That must have been a good enough question, because we cut to a commercial.

And just like that, it was over. Jim helped me stand and led me from the stage. He whisked me through the underground to an elevator. "Wait!" I said. "What about my shirt?"

"Thanks for the reminder!" Jim said. He pulled off my cape and punched the button to close the elevator.

"My shirt!" I called. The elevator rose up and the door automatically opened at my skybox.

Letty stood by the window, drinking a soda. She was talking with a teenager who could have been her cousin but was probably her sister. The girl looked a little like me.

"Hey, Father," Letty said, noticing me. "Come here and meet Irene."

I walked close.

"Where's your cape?" Letty asked. "Superdad." She and Irene began to laugh.

I ignored that. "How do you do?" I said. "I'm Henry Murkson. Am I your father?"

"Eweeuuee! Gross!" said Letty. "This is Irene! My friend from school!"

Someone poked me on the shoulder. "But you're *my* father," said a young woman I hadn't noticed before. She was short and dark and didn't look anything like me.

"Oh, yeah, Father, this is my stepsister, Cecily," Letty said. "She's from Portland! Can you believe it! All these years we've lived so close and never known each other."

"I can't believe it," I said.

"It's probably a good thing. Cecily is, like, a genius. She got a full scholarship to Johns Hopkins. She's already invented an engine that runs on storm-water. I would have been jealous. You know, worried you'd compare us."

"Oh, like that ever happens," said Henry Junior. His eyes were cape red and I couldn't tell if he'd been crying or smoking. Probably smoking, because boys his age didn't cry.

"Hey, Henry," I said. "Want to introduce me to any of your brothers?"

"Why would I want to introduce any of them to *you?*" he asked, and stomped away.

I wished I knew how to make things right with him.

Gina sat at the private bar, nursing a martini. I joined her and asked, "Mind if I have a taste?"

"Get your own," she said, and signaled the bar-tender to pour me a drink.

He did, then slid the glass before me.

"Excuse me," I said. "May I have a straw?"

He set a couple of coffee stirrers in the glass and held them straight while I sucked up as much gin as I could get through the tubes.

"Sorry," he said, before I had finished. "I got other customers. You're on your own."

"Nice show," said Gina. "I hope you're proud."

I turned around to see Henry drinking a beer with one of the security guards.

Nothing in life had prepared me for raising teenagers.

"I don't know what to do about Henry Junior," I

said. "I feel like he's just fading away before my eyes."

"Can't you see how much you've hurt him?" Gina said.

"Yeah," I said. "I can. I just don't know what to do."

"Well, it's a little late to show concern now," Gina said. She tossed down her martini. "Maybe if you'd had more time to watch him win his soccer games. Or go to that spelling bee." She pounded her glass on the bar. "Another," she said.

"But now is all I have," I said.

Gina sputtered, "Well, isn't that just too bad?"

I felt a hand against my back—Jim's. "Hey, Doc," he said. "Found your shirt." He draped it over me.

"Thanks," I said.

He frowned and gave me a look of concern. "Something's wrong," he said. "I just know it. Buy me a drink and you can tell me all your troubles."

Why not? No one else was listening to me. I called over the bartender and Jim ordered a pink lady.

"I'm a failure as a father," I said. "My children hate me."

"They don't hate you," said Jim. "They just don't know how to talk to you about love. Give them a break! They're teenagers! People are idiots at that age, which you, out of everyone, ought to know. You have to make the first move. Go ahead. Be a man, you studly thing, you."

He made me laugh, but I knew he was right.

I got up from the bar and strode across to the far side of the box. I looked back, and Jim gave me the thumbs up. I don't know why, but that small gesture gave me courage.

"Come here, Henry," I said to my boy. Henry approached but refused to meet my glance.

"Son," I said. "I love you more than I can say. You're utterly unique to me. You're my boy—maybe not my only son, but the only one I love."

I wanted more than anything to hug him, to make things okay, like it used to be, back in the days when I was capable of hugging my children—just the one in each arm. "Can't you understand that you're the only son I need?" I said. "The only son I've ever needed?" My voice broke and my nose started to run. I felt overwhelmed by feelings I had no name for. "Come here," I said. "Please."

"Oh, go on and give your dad a hug," said Jim, sneaking up behind us. "He could die tomorrow and you'd regret this the rest of your life. That happened to me. I lost my dad when I was twenty. You don't know how many times I've since wished I'd been there to say good-bye."

Jim shoved Henry Junior forward until we were barely touching at the chest. I felt the warmth from his body penetrate my cast.

"Henry, I'm so sorry," I said. "For everything. Please," I begged him. "Forgive me."

"Dad," Henry said and leaned in against me.

"Kodak moment," said Jim.

We hugged, sort of, Henry Junior's arms flat at his sides, mine in a plaster straightjacket, the two of us incapable of reaching around to hold the other near.

What Goes Around

by Robyn Herrington

Robyn Herrington's been lucky enough to make three or four short fiction sales annually for the last few years. She's thrilled to be included in this anthology, in the company of such fine authors. She's asked, quite often, why she writes science fiction. The answer's easy, really—anything to escape thinking about the long, cold Canadian winters! But honestly, she loves a challenge, and science fiction offers her ample opportunity to challenge herself. She lives in Calgary, Alberta, and works at the University of Calgary as an editor and graphic designer. She's been married to her very understanding husband Bruce for "a good number of years."

I LIKE bars that are loud. Smoky. Darker than people usually find comfortable. And this is the kind of bar I like, lit by a few bioluminescent bugs in cages, air thick enough to taste. Legal and illegal substances gray the air, and the room's full of cops turning blind eyes. Good mix of humans and nonhumans, all morphed into a multitongued, nondescript, writhing mass. Makes me think of Donna and her peculiar, disgusting likes. Palpable body heat, living energy—and a healthy dose of loathing, directed right at me.

That's good.

Someone finally notices me, and table after table is morbidly silenced by a creeping muteness. Soon, the whole place is catacomb quiet.

Ryan snakes his way through the crowd, face screwed into a ball of barely constrained anger. He's furious.

And that's good, too.

"Why the fuck're you here?" he drawls.

Now I smile. Ryan, with his near-perfect record and near-perfect manner, has a death grip on his beer. He never swears like that unless he's closer to being hammered than not.

"Came to give my regards to Jim." I raise my hands like a cornered perp. "Don't want any trouble, Officer."

"It's your fault Jim got fired!"

Jim steps up before I can answer. Jim is—*was*—the cop with the most perfect record in the precinct, the man I was sent to destroy. Destroying perfect records are a pain—they take a lot of time and resources—but the payoffs are worth it. When my employer's happy, I'm happy . . . and my bank account's a whole lot fatter, too.

Jim stares at me, grim-faced, dark eyes set in stone. A vein stands out on his temple, a slim bulge bathed in a sheen of sweat. "I'd like it better if you weren't here," he says. "We'd *all* like it better."

I give a loose shrug. "If that's what you want. It's your going away party. Who am I to spoil it?"

Ryan slams his beer on table nearest him. The bottle teeters in a lazy circle and tips, spilling liquid gold onto the sticky wooden floor. Real beer, not synthetic. What a waste. "Spoil it? You bastard! You did this to him—we all know it."

"I didn't." I'm always surprised at how sincere I sound when I lie. Shouldn't be, considering how often I do it. "How could I?"

Ryan's finger launches itself at my face. I don't flinch. Don't even blink. Won't give him the satisfaction. "I don't know," Ryan says, "but you're gonna pay. Jimmy was a good cop, the best. You ruined his career."

Ah, yes. The "You ruined his/her/my career" line. Isn't the first time I'd heard it. Won't be the last. There's still a few cops that my employer wants to be rid of, and it's a point of personal pride for me to count how many outstanding careers I've sent into the proverbial dumpster. Whether the ruination comes slowly—as it had in the poor, sad case of Jimmy Matheson—or quickly, it doesn't matter. The ruination always comes.

Ryan's face twists into a snarl that makes him look more alien than man. "Get out."

"I'll go," I say, loudly enough to satisfy the whole bar. Jimmmy gets a half-assed salute. "Good luck, eh?"

Ryan grabs me by the arm. Hard. "Can I show you out?"

I smile at him again. "Sure," I say. "It's a long way up those stairs. I might get mugged."

Ryan hesitates, eyes and cheek muscles twitching. He figures I'm up to something. He's right, of course, but too dumb to follow his own instincts.

On the street, away from prying eyes, I turn on him. His booze-dulled senses aren't fast enough to stop my forearm from blocking his throat and shoving him up against the wall. Ryan makes a funny choking noise, claws at my face. One well-placed meeting of knuckles and nose puts him in a more polite frame of mind, though the idiot still fumbles uselessly with my jacket.

"Listen up, you block-headed sonovabitch," I say to him. "You'll never prove I was involved."

Ryan spits blood on the sidewalk. "Doesn't mean you weren't."

I nod. "That's right." My own blood starts to pound, threatening to kick off my communications implant. I take a deep breath—don't need the automated distress signal going off when it's not necessary—then decide to throw Ryan a bone, wondering if he'll jump like a good little doggie. "But let's say I did do it. What're you gonna do?"

Ryan's eyes bulge, so I ease up on his neck a bit. Can't talk if he can't breathe. "You won't get away with this."

God bless the indignation of the almost-righteous. "You're married, right?" I ask, imagining Ryan's face paling in the blue light seeping from the bar's "Open" sign. "Got two little girls, right? Be too bad if something happened to them."

Ryan's face turns hard. "You bastard!" he says. "I'll get you. Somehow, I'll make you'll pay." Blah, blah, blah. I shove Ryan back down the stairs, toward the bar's door, then dust him from my hands and straighten my silk jacket. "Yeah. I've heard that one before."

I've been on one force or another for fifteen years, always getting the move-on before things get too ugly—before circumstances get too difficult to explain. Leave clean—that's the way my employer likes it.

He hired me because I'm genetically predisposed to survive the body transfers necessary to get the jobs done, and because I'm the best. If I wasn't, I wouldn't have the network I have, wouldn't have the snitches—from this world and the other ones—wouldn't be able to alter evidence so well.

And I wouldn't be able to skim from the boss as expertly as I do. Wouldn't have the house in Miami, the condo on Deneb and a nice little getaway, deep near the heart of Io—all under different names, of course. I'm not an idiot.

I keep waiting for someone, somewhere, somehow, to nail my ass to the floor. Jimmy came as close as anyone had in a good long while. Actually gave me a week or two of worry, but then everything fell into place. For me.

For him, it just all went to hell.

Time to move on. Different precinct, different name, different body, maybe a different world. Same job: destroy those holier-than-thou cops that murdered my employer's son.

Been screwing the tech since this job started, making sure I always get a new body I'll really enjoy. Now Donna wants a relationship. I just want the next bag of bones I end up in to be hale, hearty, and handsome. Donna's not bad in bed, but she's got some fascination with freaks and bug-eyed monsters. Been trying to get me to this one traveling carnival, but I could care less. Lately, she's been trying to tell me about some problem of hers, but can't get up enough guts to spit it out. I pretend to listen, regurgitate the right words. Gotta keep the help happy. Usually, though, it's a waste of breath.

Can't help but grin about good old Ryan. His reaction is icing on the cake. The almost-righteous make life so damn interesting.

The noise is like a crack in my bones.

When the hell did my shirt get a red smear on it?

A second crack, a second smear. Shit. I touch my chest, and my hand comes away slick. Glistening.

It burns. Itburnsitburnsitburns, and my legs drop out from under me. I fall against the stone wall of a hacker's shop, then curl into the shadows, hugging the peeling paint of the door.

Brain and body scream.

Can't see straight.

One blink. The street's turning this way and that. Another blink. Ryan's there, staring down at me, his eyes white and wild.

Jesus, look at him sweat.

"So," Ryan's mouth pretzels up at one corner. "How's that? You bastard, threatening Maureen and the girls." He levels a gun at my forehead. Sonovabitch is wearing gloves. Nice leather. Probably Italian. Definitely illegal. And the gun. It's my gun.

Ryan grins when he sees I recognize the piece. "Thought I was too drunk to do anything, didn't you?" He twists the gun around to look at it. It shakes in his hand. "No one uses projectiles anymore." Then he points it back at me. "Bet it hurts like hell."

And I can't help it—I laugh. A thick warmth dribbles down my chin. Blood. Under normal circumstances, that isn't good—but these aren't normal circumstances. "You stupid prick. You can't hurt me."

Ryan laughs drunkenly. "Looks like I did!"

My implant's already sending a mayday to my employer, putting the contingency plan into motion. A rapid transfer. Donna worked on the tech stuff said rapid transfers aren't ideal, but they're better than nothing. I slap at Ryan's face with my bloody hand. "This is nothing. A scratch. Won't stop me."

"You don't think so?" Ryan cocks the gun.

"You have no idea who you're dealing with." Sounds hokey, even as I'm saying it, but I'm blood-loss dizzy.

Wish I understood how they got me from one body to the next. I can shift evidence, alter records without leaving so much as a skin cell behind, no problem. Transferring bodies, though . . . genetic tags, data-stream traveling, prionic homing beacons planted to facilitate me moving on. That's all I know.

"You can't kill me," I tell Ryan. "You'll never kill me. And I promise you, I'll be back." I start coughing and spit up—feels like part of a lung. "If it takes a dozen lifetimes, I'll get you."

"Yeah?" Ryan's hand is steady now, his eyes narrowed and focused. "You go ahead and give it your best shot."

* * *

My dead body isn't a pretty sight. Two holes in the chest, through and through from the back, and one large hole in the middle of my forehead, right above my nose. Brain matter spatters the door, leaving a chunky trail where my body slides to the concrete.

This lack-of-body crap feels like hell. Surprised I can see, but I'm still connected to my implant. New jacket's blown to hell and . . .

. . . somewhere over the city, looking at arteries clogged with miniature cars, buses, trucks . . .

. . . in the sewers, dripping and slick with the shit of nearly a million people . . .

. . . an alley town of blue and green dumpsters, a ramshackle box village, forty-gallon drum fires. Minds aching, confused . . .

All those doctors and technicians. All their brilliant equipment. All those damned hours spent screwing Donna, and those equally damned hours sucking up to my equally damned employer.

Son of a bitch, somebody help me!

I need to blink, but can't. It's annoying, an itch I can't reach. It's dark. Head feels like it's filled with lice. On the inside.

Can't lift my arms. What the hell? Take a breath Danny-boy, take your time. A new body's always hard to get used to, and this was one bitch of a transfer.

Something's on my head. Prickly. Sticky. Oh, God—dirty wool. It smells like shit. Strands of greasy hair on my cheek. Oh, this just gets better and better.

At least I got a body again.

"Where am I?" The words form in my head just fine, but come out as a guttural mew.

"So. You're awake."

I don't know the voice. The next words spring up right inside my skull. "How'd you like the trip, Dan?"

It's Donna.

"What did you do?" My words go right into her mind.

"Something special. Show time's in a few minutes." A hand reaches up and pulls the filthy hat from my head. "Gotta get up. Time to get us dressed."

"Us?"

"You'll see."

Someone snaps the light on, and I do see. And I scream.

"Hey, Lou, easy," the guy says. "Lenny, talk to him."

"Lou's not feelin' too good," I hear Lenny—Donna—say.

The guy nods once, looking at me. "You're okay to go on, right?"

"We're good," Donna says. The guy gives me one last look like he doesn't believe what Donna says, then closes the door.

I'm still screaming, but no one's listening.

"Don't like the new body?" Donna says.

"You bitch! You . . ."

"Who's screwed who now, Dan?"

"Danny-boy," I answer. Got used to that name. It suited me.

Donna lifts up a shirt. Blue silk. Some sequins on

the shoulders. "Good enough." She slips one neck over my head, tugs it into place, then slips the other neck over hers. Donna admires us in the mirror, and I can't make my eyelids close enough to block the image.

One body. One and a half heads. Donna—Lenny—he's a bit of a Frankenstein, but otherwise not bad. But me. Shrunken, misshapen, eyes bulging and off-set, skin sliding down to a slack jaw. A set of teeth sprout from the side of my cheek.

"What the fuck did you do?"

Donna laughs her pretty girl laugh, so absurd when I see a massive, freakish body.

"You're a piece of work," she says. "Screwing me and the boss at the same time."

"What?"

"I found out you were skimming. The boss was unimpressed."

"I was putting money aside for us," I say. Thinking quick is only one of my talents.

"Bull."

I want to say more, but the guy comes back. He holds the door open and says, "Hey, lookin' good, Lenny. It's time."

Donna walks us down a dark hallway. I can hear dull thunder coming from the other end, and as we get closer it changes to "Lenny and Lou! Lenny and Lou!"

The guy pauses by the swinging folds of a purple velvet curtain. "Full house tonight, boys," he said, pushing his hands between the material. "Give 'em what they want."

And we do. Donna struts about the stage, growls at the audience, thumps her chest. Then she sings, dances—does some work with a hat and a cane, tells a few jokes. And me?

I drool.

The room's wall-to-wall people, all screaming. Laughing. The front row's filled with guys that could've been me. Pointing. Spitting. Howling.

An eternity of shame.

When it's over, we go back to our room.

"Have fun?" Donna asks me.

"Bitch!" is all I can think of to say.

Donna peels the shirt from us and shrugs awkwardly into a rough cotton. My—*our*—chest hurts, heart hammering so hard I think my head's going to explode.

"Why?"

Donna laughs again. "I was dying," she says. "Couldn't manage to say it before, but I can now." And she stops, comb paused above Lenny's greasy, stringy hair. She turns Lenny's face from side to side, and makes the hair part a little more to the left. "Those prionic beacons cost a lot, and the boss was reluctant to let me shoot a couple into Lenny and Lou. But when I told him you were skimming, and told him what I wanted to do, he was all for it. It actually made him smile."

"But . . . why?"

Donna shrugs. "I have—had—an incurable disease. The boss wouldn't let me body-shift. Then I gave him a good reason, and you gave me a couple of 'em. Hate. Revenge. Two of the best reasons there are, Danny-boy."

My innards shrivel into a cold little ball. "I didn't treat you that bad!"

"You were a prick!" she says. "Thought you were better than everyone else. Now, you're not even better than Lenny."

"So that's it?" I ask. "You're done? Happy?"

She sits us up and faces the mirror. We're a fat, blotchy slug of an abomination. She pokes me in my lowest eye.

"Feel that?"

My answer well and truly indicates that I did.

"I'd pretty much resigned myself to death," Donna says. "Made peace with my gods. Made sure my sister was taken care of." Donna's new face smiles, a lopsided, fleshy-lipped sort of thing. "Hey, did I mention that I helped the boss find your hidden accounts? Well, me and Warren in Records. Warren got your apartment on Deneb, and me—well, my sister—got your Miami property. Nice guy, our boss. Just don't piss him off."

"What now?" I ask. "This is it? Sharing a set of beacons, chatting back and forth, dancing for the idiots who'll pay the money?"

Donna was quiet for a time. I could feel her brain grinding in the head next to mine. "Maybe."

Hope. I dove on it. "Whatever you want, you can have. Money—I bet I still got some the boss didn't find."

"Yeah," Donna says, "I bet you do."

"So?"

"So nothing. This is what I want. I've been a fan of Lenny and Lou for years. Lenny and Lou—they're famous. They get good food, a nice place to sleep, decent quarters when they travel. I always wanted to be a star. It's better than dying."

"What about me?"

"You?" Donna says, out loud. She cackles a spittle-filled laugh. "The link between us'll fade out. We got a few hours left, maybe. Then you're on your own, Danny-boy."

At least I don't have to sleep when she does, and my thoughts are still my own.

And I have been thinking. She thinks she's won, but she won't get the better of me. No one has, and no one ever will. I'm going to bide my time, wait until that bitch believes I've come to terms with what she's done to me. Then, I'll kill myself. One swift slash, right down the jugular, and she can watch her life drain onto the floor in a sticky puddle, through me. Hell, if I do it while she's sleeping, she won't even know.

But where would be the fun in that?

Donna stirs. "What are you thinking, Danny-boy?"

"Nothing that concerns you."

"The link'll be gone, soon," she says. "You figured it out, yet?"

"What?"

"You," Donna giggles. "Me. Lenny and Lou. Lenny's always been the boss, and now, that means me. Bet you'd like to take a swing at me, right?" She sits us up then puts one sausage finger on her chin. "Go on. Give it your best shot. Right here."

"I don't see . . ."

"Humor me."

The idea of smacking her upside the head is as appealing as hell, so as appealing as hell, so I . . .

. . . do nothing. I wan't to, but I can't. I *can't*!

"I got the lion's share of control in this body," Donna says, pinching my nose between her thumb and forefinger. "I make us eat, move, speak—I even make us piss. All you get to do for yourself is breathe and sleep."

And I thought the detached, numb feeling I had was because of the rapid shift. I figured it would go away, and then I'd be able to . . . I figured . . . oh, *shit!*

Then Donna grins so broadly her face should split wide open and says, "Whatever goes around, Danny-boy . . ."

Thumping the Weaver

by Susan R. Matthews

Susan R. Matthews' fiction is informed by her military background and her professional experience as an officer, a janitor, an auditor, and an accountant. The more things change, the more they remain the same—stories and situations found in histories of early China are uncannily resonant with the realities of the modern political world; so that the synthesis of Chinese legalism with the constitutional separation of powers that forms the basis for her Jurisdiction stories has acquired resonance that transcends its original framework. She and her partner Maggie have been keeping house for nearly twenty-five years, and live in Seattle. She is the author of seven novels to date—including five in the Jurisdiction universe. "Thumping the Weaver" is her first appearance in print with a short story.

IT wasn't my idea, but after twenty years of thumping Daff, I had no other skills worth mentioning. A female weaver. Who ever heard of a thing like that? Bad enough for a man to have to be a weaver. For a woman I could only imagine it would be that much more disgusting.

"She works in power generation," the town-speaker said. "The windmills. You can find her there. If she isn't a weaver, she's the next worst thing, so if we can't find a thumper soon, we won't be able to keep her. Can't afford the conflict."

I knew what she was saying. Looking out from the tiny landing field, I could see well enough that there wasn't much of a settlement, but at least it was there. When the Jurisdiction's Bench had sold us to our enemies, those who could had fled to Gonebeyond, and the rest had mostly died. Well, been killed, but there's no sense insisting on the word. Dead's dead.

"Daff used to say that there had to be weavers so long as there were Nurail." I almost didn't bother missing Daff anymore. I'd been thumping him since I'd been sixteen. He'd been my life, but I was still breathing and he wasn't, so I had to do something. "I'll go have a look. Can't hurt. I guess."

The town-speaker nodded her head. "I'll send someone out with a ration tag. There's bunking for five out there, plenty of room. If it works out, we'll all be grateful to you."

If it didn't, I'd be on my way. That went without saying. The station really didn't need another unskilled laborer. It would be a place to stay for a shortish while, though, maybe, I thought. What did I have to lose?

I stopped in the doorway of the dock-master's office and looked out past the admin plat up to the power generation station, on the ridge behind what passed for a manufactory. Once people made it out to Gonebeyond, they stayed here—there was no going back—so there were no spare parts for ship's maintenance but what could either be salvaged or done up almost by hand in small lots, in places like Halliburton Station.

The ship that had brought me here was loading and would leave soon. It was up to me to decide where to go next and how to get there. I was going to be at Halliburton one way or the other till the next ship came; common sense, really, to try to find a way to make myself useful.

So I went up to the windmills, to see the girl. The door to the power plant was unsecured—no sense in locking anything, was there?—and nobody came when I called, so I went in.

Found her in the mechanism of one off-lined vane about a mile into the transfer corridor, hanging her tail across the rotor-housing and singing to herself. I knew thc tune well enough, it was the one about the dog with a black eye-patch, an old herder's tune.

I wasn't sure if she'd heard me coming, and since she had a heavy lever in her hand by the sounds of the clanging, I didn't want to startle her. I don't know the words to "Patch-eyed Dog," Daff had never traded for it; but there was "Overgrazed Lee Slope," the scan was the same and it was from the same general class even if a song about a favorite herding dog's heroic accomplishments didn't seem much like one about the adverse consequences of failure to successfully negotiate a shared grazing field arrangement across mutually dependent communities.

I gave her "Overgrazed Lee Slope" as I came near.

She stopped pounding, but she didn't move to pull her head and shoulders out of the rotor housing, not right away. She was as flat as a boy behind, almost. Eating is on the thin side in Gonebeyond, generally speaking, but a handful of grain eaten under sovereign skies has nourishment you just can't get from subsidy grain, that goes beyond the physical. People were healthy enough, and that included the residents of this station. Just not very comfortably padded.

I stopped at the end of the fifth stanza, because I was right there. Waited. After a moment she pulled out of the box so I could look at her; sharp-faced, thin-lipped, cold-eyed. A problem. Ugly. Well, not attractive, but I don't know if I've ever seen a handsome weaver. It's part of the joke the gods play on them to give them so much raw seductive power and then make them something you'd look at in the morning and wonder "What was I thinking?"

She might have been wondering, but she didn't say anything. Up to me, I decided. "You're Kerai? I'm Parmer. Just landed at airfield. Town-speaker said I could come work in windmills for a while till the next ship comes through."

Her eyes widened into a feral glare at the word "town-speaker," and suspicion flared in her muddy brown eyes. Sharpened them. Almost familiar, that effect.

"Did she? Did she warn you? I'm a troublemaker, and nobody will talk to me. Didn't like you, or she wouldn't have sent you here."

Suspicious, hostile, resentful, and combative. But I'd lived with that for twenty years. You get used to it. And when a weaver is in a good mood, there's no better company, I promise you that. Makes up for almost everything, with extra on top.

So I thought about things for a moment while she waited for a response, glaring at me. I decided to risk a little. Not a lot. Not everything at once.

"Actually, she said you were a weaver."

She shot pure fury at me like spitting in my face, but I'd thumped for a weaver before. I could read her.

"Making the mock at you, you poor stripped stop-chock, telling you that. When everybody knows."

But it was aching fear, behind the venom. Poor rag. She was terrified and all alone, as well as ugly and abrasive. That's a bad combination. Beautiful can get away with fear and generally find sympathetic company. Ugly and ill-spoken can sort well enough, as long as it comes with a sense of security for tempering. It could be, I thought. Very weaverlike of her to be ugly face and feeling, if she was a weaver.

"I don't know about that. I just want to work off my ration-tag. You can set me to work or I can just make something up and pretend at it, your choice."

She put away a little of the hostility and a little of the pain with it. Not too much of either, but enough to make a start. "As if you can get anything started. In a month, you'll be out of here on the next transport, won't you? But you can degrease vane bearings. That'll earn your rations. Come on."

I followed her because she didn't bother to stop and wait and see if I was coming. "I don't know," I said. "I might like it here. I've never met a female weaver."

She ignored me.

Fine. It was only until the next transport came. She'd been right about that.

If I didn't have a job that only I could do inside of two weeks, I'd be on the next transport out, farther out, deeper into Gonebeyond, with as little thought of what to do with my Daff-less life than I'd had since they took him away from me. No loss; no gain.

It was good to feel needed again, even if only as a degreaser. The vane bearings were in a disgusting condition, but they probably hadn't been able to get anybody out to work with her for a while. Anybody with any other place to go would go there, and not just because degreasing is filthy work. She was a bitter, angry, acerbic sort, but I'd lived with Daff for twenty years. Compared to Daff at his prime, this young piss pot was still very much in development. The acid hardly etched my mood at all.

"Why did the town-speaker say you were a weaver?"

Three days in. Mid-meal had come out from the communal kitchen, and Kerai was apparently hungry enough to sit down in the common room and eat right away, instead of taking her food and going. If she was that hungry, she wouldn't get offended and leave if I asked her some impertinent questions; because that would have been a defeat, then, and weavers never accepted defeat. It's just not in them. That's why they need thumpers, to accept defeat for them and carry them off when the time comes; apart from the other things, of course.

She scowled at her biscuit. "Because that's what I

am. And I don't care if you've never heard of a female weaver. It wasn't my idea."

It never was. Weavers all tended to fall into the same weave, in a sense, normal children with normal lives but then they'll get sick or have some sort of a terrible accident or something before they start to smell like men instead of boys. Then the normal child that their family thought they'd had goes away and never comes back, and they find themselves with a weaver in their midst like a misfortune. It's a curse, you know. *I hope your family comes down with weavers.*

"Well, come on, tell me." I wanted to know. I knew she could tell that I wasn't making fun of her, because that's one of the worst things about being a weaver, you can't pretend about other peoples' feelings. Or if she did think I was making fun of her, she wasn't a weaver.

Unless maybe she just wanted to talk. "I was twelve," she said, brooding over her biscuit. "The winter cough was hard that year. It was before we had to leave home."

The Bench had put the hammer down on the Nurail seven, eight years ago; by six years ago Nurail in Jurisdiction space were slaves or dead. That made her maybe eighteen, maybe older. If I hadn't spent all that time thumping Daff, I might have gotten married, and then I might have had children her age. It was a frightening thought.

"And I got the winter cough. But I didn't lose it. Three years. And I couldn't stand to be inside. Went wandering through the city in all weather."

Not a herding family, then, but she'd been singing

"Patch-eyed Dog" to herself. It meant nothing. Lots of people know "Patch-eyed Dog." "Your family let you?"

Girls that age weren't safe in cities. Not even ugly girls. She just grimaced. "For a while they tried to pen me in. But they stopped caring. It was easier after a while, I guess."

It actually sounded more and more weaverish as she went along. But people knew how weavers happened, there was a pattern, weavers were expected to behave weaverishly. She still could be making it all up, or have decided that a weaver would be a good thing to be if she couldn't be beautiful and pleasant. It would be a good way to be special—a female weaver, think of it—except for the fact that nobody with a basic serving of sense would ever actually want to be a weaver.

"Yeah, but the weaving," I prompted her, because she'd fallen into a sort of an abstracted state, chewing on the corner of her biscuit. Gnawing on the corner of her biscuit. It was stale biscuit, but it was mid-meal. By suppertime it would be staler yet.

"My brother got married." Her voice had flattened out. "My family had to let me come to the party, I got cleaned up and everything. Somebody started to sing about increase of trade, but it sounded pretty cheerless to me. I thought I'd show my appreciation for the party, and all. But her family didn't know who I was, they laughed at me, so I decided to have some fun. And then it came out all wrong."

I could understand that, all too well.

Young weaver. Anxious, and upset, and suffering,

and the bride's family made fun of her, so she made fun of the bride's family. If they'd been lucky, it had been something that they could all patch up afterward. When a weaver started making fun, people were lucky if they got away with just hurt feelings, and no scars.

"It wasn't my fault," she added, but there wasn't much protest left to her voice. It was just habit. She'd been trying to explain for so long that she'd lost any expectation that she'd be believed, I supposed. Except that I believed her. It was too perfect. And she sounded sincere.

"And then they got you a thumper." It would be the next logical step, but there was the problem, of course. She was a girl. There's no such thing as a female weaver. Certainly not any such thing as a thumper for a female weaver, or a female weaver-thumper. We were breaking new ground here.

She shook her head. "My brother took against me. The rest of my family, too. I came away with some tanners, they wouldn't let me come back, ever."

"It must have been a lot of fun." I was impressed. "Your song, I mean." Because, usually, it takes more than one such incident before a family realizes it has to get rid of its diseased child. That was when they knew they'd got a weaver, though.

"What's it to you," she said, and pushed away from the table in the common room to take her biscuit and go back to doing whatever it was she was working on with the vanes. "You don't know. You don't believe me. Nobody does. Not even when it happens, again."

She sounded more sad than snarling to me, though.

She was still ugly.

But I was beginning to think that she might actually be a weaver after all.

So the next time there was common-meeting in the port she and I walked down the hill together, or not exactly together because she wasn't having anything to do with me and I didn't blame her. So far as she knew, I was still planning on being gone the next chance I had; my degreasing wouldn't last me forever and I hadn't found anything more permanent to do.

The station was hoping I would thump her. I could tell that the moment we walked into the commons hall. Nurail need weavers. Halliburton would make do with a female weaver if there weren't any others to be had. Nobody there was looking forward to having to send her away from the station because they'd all been sent away from their own lives already and knew it wasn't any fun. So they were looking to me to save the situation for them.

Maybe they were even really worried about Kerai, even though she was unpleasant. Somebody gave me a glass of beer, which was unexpected but appreciated, and I sat down by the door to listen to the meeting and get a sense of what was going on. Habit, sitting by the door. Thumpers need to be able to get their weavers out of crowds in a decent hurry when the occasion calls for it.

There was the crops report and the inventories,

traffic and trends; it'd been a good year for what grain would grow out here and there would be beer for the fallow season. Not much of a surplus, but Halliburton Station sounded like a developing place to me. A nice place to stay for people with a place. Not like me. I wondered if I couldn't find a niche after all, but it all depended on Kerai, so I just sat and waited as the party started and then the music and the singing.

She kept apart from me, and everybody else too. People would speak to her, she hadn't made herself that unwelcome yet, but it was clearly on the edge. If she'd weave, they'd forgive her almost anything; and on about the middle of the evening when the talk-song people were done and the silence fell and the people turned around and looked at her, Kerai started singing.

She didn't have a very good voice for a weaver, but it isn't the voice people are hearing when a weaver sings, it's the feeling that's there. She had to have been feeling pretty good; she gave them a "Fattened Grains" that almost gave me the shivers, and I've heard "Fattened Grains" so many times before I could almost have woven one myself. She had the turns right, making it a song for Halliburton, making people feel good, confident, secure. Fattened grains. Peace and prosperity.

Running right into "Sorry-I-left," which was a good choice, people like to have a chance to cry a little once they're feeling safe enough to think about their sorrows, but "Sorry-I-left" was one that Daff used to do—and he did it very well. Almost always got him whatever girl or woman or boy or man he wanted at the time, which was always a different one, Daff not being of a constant temperament, but "Sorry-I-left" will tear your heart out if you've lost your "Sorry-I-left" for good and all, and I had. They'd taken him away. He was a weaver. They didn't bother to take me with him, they didn't care about me one way or the other; without Daff, I was just another disposable Nurail after all, and Daff was dangerous to the Bench because he could weave.

You see? She got me.

She had me right where she wanted me, and she rolled every stone she had down on top of my head and buried me in misery. I couldn't handle it. I missed Daff. Twenty years. What's a thumper without the weaver he thumps for?

There was no question in my mind, not any longer. Kerai was a weaver, even if she was the wrong sex. Her "Sorry-I-left" explained it all so clearly. The only person who had ever cared about me or who I'd ever had to care for had been tortured to death, alone. I hadn't raised a hand to protect him, and what possible reason did I have for even living, anymore?

Which meant that if I couldn't get out from underneath her "Sorry-I-left," I was going to hang myself by morning, and it meant nothing to her, it was just a weave and that was what she did. I hadn't told her. She didn't need to be told. She was a weaver. She knew.

I had to leave. It was good that I was sitting by the door.

I barely made it out of there in time. I went back

up to the power generation plant, but I couldn't afford to sit still. I wanted to die. I had to walk. I walked. And after a few hours I heard noise from the commons hall that carried all the way up to the power generation plant and remembered, suddenly, that I was a thumper, and that Halliburton Station needed me. I ran back down the hillside and burst into the common room to see if I was in time to prevent a riot.

She was standing in the corner of the commons hall, barricaded in behind a pile of chairs and a table on its side, singing her weave. It was as solid a "Misplaced Chance" as I've ever heard. This was a problem, because nobody with even as little sense as a weaver does "Misplaced Chance" unless there's a war on; but she was loving it. It had her. If she'd been a man, it would have had her by the gollies, but she wasn't, so I'm not sure what it had her by—but it had her.

She was into it so strong and true that people were set off against each other; there was pushing and swearing already, and the pulling of knives just about next. "Misplaced Chance" will do that to people. It does wronged outrage better than anything, and when people are filled with wronged outrage, they'll push the nearest person, who is also filled with wronged outrage, and in the absence of an external target you can just guess how it goes.

She needed thumping.

At least she needed to be shut up, for the community's sake, so I wrestled my way through the crowd—feeling her "Misplaced Chance" myself—and scrambled over the barricade to grab her.

" 'Six-month-Curds,' " I said. "Now. Or else."

Even "Six-month-Curds" might not have done it, by that point, but it was the best chance I had. She wasn't having any of it. She was full of the weave and flying on it; weavers get drunk on their own weaving, there's no talking to a weaver in spate; you just have to thump them, and I needed to thump her good and true and quickly.

I couldn't thump her.

She was a girl. A woman. Women weren't thumped. I couldn't thump her. She couldn't thump back. I was bigger than she was, and a man besides, and men don't hit women, they just don't. Not unless they want a "Puling Jack" with their name on it forever and ever after, they don't.

She knew what was going on in my mind because she was in spate, and it made her furious with me, which put even more energy into her "Misplaced Chance" because she was betrayed and disappointed. If I believed she was a weaver, I would be thumping her. Wasn't she giving me all the proof I needed? Why didn't I thump her? Because she was a woman? No. Because I didn't really believe she was a weaver.

I could hardly stand it. I grabbed her by the arms, not like I'd thump Daff but like I'd wanted to shake him, and I shook her. " 'Six-month Curds,' you snip, or you'll be sorry, I'll make you sorry, you listen to me, now."

Behind me in the common room somebody

screamed; I could almost smell the blood. This was not going well. I shook Kerai, I had to get her attention, but I was out of practice and too full of "Misplaced Chance" myself, and I knocked her head against the wall. I hadn't meant to. But it shut her up. She went limp and unconscious, and I kicked the barricade away and carried her out of the hall. When I was as far away from the common room as I could carry her I dumped her on the ground.

She'd come to herself by then.

"You hit me," she said.

And I hadn't, but I'd wanted to, so I didn't argue.

"That's what thumpers are for," I said. "To thump the weavers when they get off on the wrong weave. What were you thinking? What did these people ever to do you to deserve 'Misplaced Chance'?"

She started to cry and reached for me, but you have to understand, it wasn't feeling her fault for having done the "Misplaced Chance," it was something entirely different. Nobody had ever thumped her. Nobody had really believed she was a weaver, not even seeing what she could do. It was as close to recognition of the thing that had happened to her as anybody had come, and it took her by surprise.

She put her arms around me and clung to me and cried, and I wanted to cry, too, because I was still thinking about Daff. But she wouldn't have understood it. So I took her back up to the power generation station and took off her shoes and put her to bed. If she'd been Daff, there would have been more to it, but she wasn't, there wasn't, and mind your own business.

In the morning I went down to see the town-speaker, and found her where you'd expect to in the dock-master's office. "How did it go last night?" I asked.

She didn't look entirely happy. "If you hadn't come back, it would have gotten ugly. We got off easy that time. Why did you leave?"

I couldn't tell her about Daff. Thumpers grew layers of protective insulation, they had to, or else they'd never be able to thump their weavers. I didn't have much protection against Kerai. She'd surprised me.

So I lied. "I can't thump her," I said. "She's a girl." Daff hadn't been much bigger than Kerai, maybe, but he'd been a man, and he'd had muscle. Not to mention native spite and hostility. Daff had been almost more than I could handle, even knowing as he had that I had only his own best interest at heart. Kerai was nothing like that. I'd knocked her head against the wall by accident. I was just lucky that I hadn't hurt her.

The town-speaker didn't look unsympathetic, but it was clear all the same that she didn't want to hear this. "I can understand your position," she said. No, she hadn't even thought about it until just now, though to give her credit she smelled the full ripeness of the problem as soon as she had the fruit in hand. "But it's a trade-off. Somebody's got to deal with Kerai or we'll have to lose her. We can't afford her. It's thump her or she's gone."

The next ship wasn't due in for another few weeks anyway. It was going to be much easier to lie about it and wait the time out than stand to my claim and spend the next few weeks arguing with people. I didn't have the energy. Daff was dead. Most of me with him.

"Well, I'll do what I can." That wasn't even so much of a lie. It was true. I'd do what I could to get through the next few weeks, because I wasn't about to take a job of hitting women. That was for Bench torturers to do. I wasn't one.

I went back to the power generation station. Kerai had woken up with a headache, from having her head banged against the wall; the doctor had told her to lie down for a day or two, so I did the maintenance myself. It was much better than degreasing. Kerai and I didn't talk; I think she was embarrassed, mostly, but she was also afraid that I'd go back on thumping her and she wouldn't really be a weaver after all. It was going to be hard. But what else could I do? No, I wasn't going to hit her. I'd only hit her by accident as it was.

Once we'd started not-talking after the night in the common room it was easy to go on not-talking, because being taken for a real weaver at last didn't change her personality much and she was still ugly. So we went on as we had begun, but time kept on as well, and it got to be the night to go down for common-meeting again too soon. I went with a sense of regret in my heart. After tonight they'd know that I wasn't going to thump for them, and then I'd be out of here on the next ship, and they'd probably send Kerai with me just for spite. I wasn't looking forward to it.

It wasn't my idea, but Kerai kept close to me this time, and people brought me beer again which didn't make me feel any better about what I was going to do. She was feeling pretty happy about things. When she started off on "Peacock Feather," everybody else was happy, too, and there's no harm in the "Gaily Wrapped" either. But Kerai was starting to feel too good. She had a lot of resentment to work off, years of suffering the weaves without even so much as an acknowledgment to help her bear up. She wanted to let people know how she felt. She put herself into "Own Country," and people started to get restless.

Nobody likes to be called thoughtless or unkind. She was making them uncomfortable, but she either wasn't seeing it or she wasn't caring. The weave was using her for a channel and she was beginning to hit flood tide. You could get to "Seek-the-Pass" from "Own Country" if you had enough of the weave in you; and unfortunately she did.

It was going to be worse than it had ever been, because once you were firmly into "Seek-the-Pass," it was almost impossible to avoid dropping down into "Vengeance is Mine," and once that happened there would be killing. I've only ever heard "Vengeance is Mine" twice in my entire life and both times I was lucky to escape with most of my skin in one piece. Daff at least had had the benefit of learning from other weavers, he knew better than to go into that weave, even when he was deepest in spate. Usually. Kerai didn't know. I could hear her voice getting round and pregnant, looking forward to "Vengeance is Mine," sharpening the knives in the words and setting the detonation charges. I couldn't let it happen.

I had to do something.

I couldn't thump her. I couldn't. I'd hurt her. Men didn't hit women. Just not. I could see into the future—I'd been thumping for Daff long enough, I knew, I could see this place littered with debris and bodies. It would take weeks to sort everything out. "Vengeance is Mine" can poison a well forever.

But she was at the bridge.

Her voice put its foot forward; she was on her way. The rest of the people didn't know, not yet, but I could hear "Vengeance" coming, and I struck my fist as hard as I could down on the tabletop in pure hopeless frustration.

She jumped. She hadn't been looking at me. She heard the sound, she jumped, she almost lost her footing, she only caught the thread of her weave the moment before it would have dropped into the river. Frowning at me, she struggled with the song, and fought it back into the track she meant to take it on.

I had an idea.

Twenty years, with Daff.

"Vengeance is Mine" I'd only heard the twice, but if you crumbled the top line in places and put some gravel underneath its feet, you could end up with something that was a lot more like "Fresh Pigs" than any "Vengeance." And "Fresh Pigs" is very popular, everybody likes "Fresh Pigs," all of the little piglets. Very appealing. Did Kerai know "Fresh Pigs"? She almost had to.

I waited for my moment, and I hit the table again,

as hard as I could. Kerai nearly dropped her road to "Vengeance" all over again. I gave her five steps so that I could catch the train in my mind, and hit the table two times, three times; anybody who could hear would recognize the thread. "Fresh Pigs."

She staggered under the impact and went on, but I had the thread myself now, not of "Vengeance" but of "Pigs," and I hit "Fresh Pigs" out on the table without mercy. She couldn't carry it in the face of "Fresh Pigs." You can't put "Fresh Pigs" together with "Vengeance" and not drop one or the other, and in the face of "Fresh Pigs," "Vengeance is Mine" starts to look a little silly.

"Fresh Pigs" was getting easier moment by moment. Kerai had turned around to glare at me full-face, trying to keep to "Vengeance" and losing it note by note. I could read her mind, I was a thumper. *What are you doing.* She could read mine; she was a weaver. *I'm thumping you, of course.*

We struggled together for a good long verse, but I won.

I thumped her from "Vengeance" to "Fresh Pigs," she lost it, she couldn't resist it, the weave had her and the weave wanted to talk about "Fresh Pigs." I could hear Daff singing, in my mind. It didn't hurt to hear him. He'd given me the way to do this. It was going to work out after all.

We went on throughout the evening just like that, and when I thought there was real danger of her sliding from "Sheep-shearing" into "Seven Staves," I thumped her into "Black-bread-grass" instead and she went without complaining, and the people embraced her as their weaver with tears of relief. There's nothing like a weaver in a good mood. Nothing.

The next ship came and went. I wasn't on it.

Daff is dead, but I've found a whole new way to thump the weaver, and I get better at it every day.

Maxwell's Law

by Adrienne Gormley

Adrienne Gormley has lived and worked in Silicon Valley for more years than she cares to contemplate. She enjoys playing with computers and other techno-toys. Her short fiction has previously appeared in the anthologies *Alternate Tyrants* and *Out of Avalon*. "Maxwell's Law" is her third sale.

"HEY, Damon." I stopped and waited, wondering what Harry was going to pull this time. When he joined me, I turned and leaned on the file cabinet next to the sergeant's desk. I studied Harry, his round face, the idiot smirk that told me he thought he was going to be funny.

"What?" I checked my watch. "Make it quick."

Harry shrugged as he took a swig of coffee, wrinkled his nose, and swallowed. "Must have sat on the burner for hours. God, this stuff is awful." I didn't ask him why he drank it. Harry was a cop and drank coffee to keep awake, period.

He looked at me slant-wise. "I hear you're in for a commendation on that 594 out on Pico. Not bad for a screwup."

"You call a hostage situation malicious mischief?"

Oddly, Harry flinched. "Just joking. Hey, man, you okay? I mean, your eyes—they're almost glowing."

Oh, shit. I didn't need that showing. "If I were as much a screw-up as you tell everybody I am, Harry, I'd have been thrown off the force years ago." I turned away.

"How'd you manage to make a decent bust, Murph?" he asked.

I froze. Turned back. I didn't give a damn if my eyes were shooting off fireworks. "If you ever call me that again, Harry, I will report you to for harassment." I tapped my name tag. "It's Maxwell, not Murphy."

Harry spread his hands and grinned weakly. "Hey, it's just a nickname, Damon. Why the hassle?"

"The Imp of the Perverse?" My ears burned. "Half the damned squad calls me that, at least the ones that I don't know well. I've put up with hearing it behind my back, but I'll be damned if I'll let anybody call me that to my face."

This time I did leave, stepping aside only as the watch commander from the previous shift stepped through the door.

Grumbling, I jammed my hat on my head and headed for the squad car. While I was opening the door, Jilly trotted up on the other side. I caught her wink as we got into the car. One thing I could say for Jilly Abrams, she never called me Murph.

I turned the key and fastened my belt. Jilly ran the radio check and told Dispatch we were rolling.

"It's about time you told him off," she said curtly, once we were westbound. "Idiot is always cracking jokes about different people, all the time. You're not his only victim."

I glanced over at the venom in her voice. "What's he done to you that I don't know about?" She frowned but said nothing. When I stopped at a red light, I said, "If it's that bad, you can get him on a sexual harassment charge."

"No. It isn't that." She sighed. "He calls me 'Tank.' "

Huh. Typical. The light turned green, and I watched the traffic as we turned onto Vermont. Jilly reached for her thermos and opened it. She handed me a cup and poured one for herself.

"Thanks." I slowed to cruise with the late afternoon traffic, while watching storefronts for anything unusual.

After a moment, Jilly said, "On one thing he's right, Damon." I saw her looking at my hands; I loosened my grip on the wheel. "Nothing nasty, but you do tend to have a string of off-the-wall mixups from time to time."

Of course. "Just not consistently," I said, "which is what he keeps implying with his barbs. And you know that the commendation for snagging that idiot holding that TV crew hostage isn't the only one I've gotten." I waited for her to finish her coffee. "You've shared in four, so you know it's no fluke."

Jilly tossed her head, checked her bun to make sure it was in place, and chuckled deep in her throat. "You know, Damon, you're right." She flipped a salute. "Up yours, Harry."

Two hours and ten traffic stops later, we stopped at a coffee shop for a break. "Thank God for onboard computers," Jilly said. She peered at me over her coffee. "How did you keep up when you had to do all your reports by hand?"

With my back to the wall, I scanned customers as they entered. "Filled out the absolute minimum at the time, then finished filling them out back at the barn." I finished off my eggs and toast. "We put in lots of uncredited overtime doing paperwork." I stood when the waitress brought Jilly's refilled thermos. "Let's hit the pavement."

As I steered the squad car out of the parking lot, a motorcycle whizzed past. "Going fifty at least." I hit the siren and began pursuit.

Jilly grabbed the radio. "This is Baker-seven."

The Dispatcher replied, "Baker-seven, go ahead."

"Currently in pursuit, southbound on Western, approaching Slauson," Jilly rattled off. "Motorcycle, late model, Kawasaki, green, speed estimated at least fifty." She paused as the squad car closed on the bike. "California plate, one Dog Edward three five eight three. Over."

I felt like we were on a roller coaster as I swerved the car in and out of traffic as we followed. The biker made a sudden U-turn against a red light, and cross traffic came screeching to a halt in a jumble that looked like Pick-up Stix. Lights flashing, siren wailing, I steered the car over the center island and hit the gas. Jilly was still on the radio.

"Baker-seven," the dispatcher said, "plate was reported as stolen in Santa Monica. Registered to a '78 Harley-Davidson."

"Ten-four." As we gained on the bike, I heard Enrico, our sergeant, and another car announce they were on their way. I made a note of their twenties; I could see Jilly did, too, from her nod. *Good.* If it worked, we'd form a pincer and stop the bike. I put more pressure on the gas, alternately watching traffic and bike. *Getting there—just a few yards—*

A pedestrian stepped into the street. I hit the brakes. I steered into the skid and prayed that the idiot would *move!* When the tires squealed, the guy screamed and froze. We ended up against a pole, the motorcycle was gone with the wind, and the idiot we'd almost hit shook his fist at us one finger at a time.

Two days later, Jilly and I stood on the grass berm in front of the USC stadium and mourned the passing of the radiator as coolant drained out of it and down the grass to the sidewalk. While July radioed for a tow, I turned to track the squeal of tires from the light green SUV we'd been chasing as it came screaming back down the street, scattering other vehicles in its wake. Too much traffic; too many people. No way could I put a shot through his tire without endangering the public. *Damn.*

"This is the second car we've trashed this week," Jilly said. "Well, Damon, at least we're keeping the mechanics busy."

I glared at the mute patrol car and muttered Kepler's Laws of Motion, just to relieve stress. I could feel my temperature rising again, and no way could I let it take over. Was this new string of incidents going to be marked by front-end damage to squad cars—or something else?

Strings of incidents? That took me back to my first string, back in my rookie days. Those'd all revolved around fast food robberies. Then I stopped at Mickey D's on the way home after a long, frustrating day, too tired to even nuke something from the freezer, when I saw this guy in front of me with a pistol in the back of his pants. Maybe he thought it was hidden, but his Rams jacket had bunched up over it, and I saw the grip. So I dropped a friendly hand around his wrist, flashed my badge, had the cashier call 911, and cuffed and read him his rights before the on-duty squad showed. Concealed weapon charge—and a stolen car.

Then there was the string of incidents where my old partner and I kept missing, by scant minutes, a series of car thefts on Crenshaw, got chewed out by our superiors, and a few days later made a vehicle stop—for expired tags, for God's sake—and ended up netting not only stolen tags but a stolen vehicle and a key link to breaking a major auto theft ring.

This time our quarry was a speeding SUV, with tires so big it couldn't be street legal. What would cause the next accident? I puffed out my cheeks, exhaled—my temperature was down—and sat down to log the report while Jilly kept watch for our tow.

"Kepler? Planetary motion?" Jilly asked. I stared at her; she grinned. "I took physics and astronomy in junior college, before I went into the academy. With your last name, though, I'd figure you'd go more for Maxwell's Kinetic Theory of Gases, including his theoretical demon who separates hot and cold molecules."

The next day, Jilly held out her hand. "I'll drive."

Fine with me. I hoped having Jilly at the wheel would make a difference. Jilly steered the black-and-white onto Pico westbound. A bang, the car lurched, and I nearly choked on my burrito. I saw buildings swing past, then hold steady. I looked to see what hit us. A green van. Then I remembered the SUV—green—and the motorcycle, also green. *Hmm.*

Jilly hit the gas and we wobbled. I heard a scraping noise, then we settled to the right. "Stop!" I looked out the window and saw that the fender was bent enough to cut into the tire. "Damnit! Damnit all to hell and gone!"

"Temper, temper," Jilly said. "Radio, Damon."

"I don't fucking believe this!" I picked up to call in.

Then I saw Jilly staring after the Chrysler. "You know what, Damon? Every vehicle has been green." She turned to me. "Why green, for God's sake? And why us?"

"Hell if I know." I finished the call and racked the radio. "Maybe they're doing it because I refused to let Harry call me 'Murph' any more."

Jilly chuckled. "That makes about as much sense as anything, doesn't it?" she asked. When she clapped me on the shoulder, I unwound a bit and settled back to wait for the tow.

"The Chrysler and the van are the most serious so far," I told her the next day, "because they're hit and run. Plus, with the partial plate we got off the

Chrysler, they managed to get a make on it. The plates belong to a '93 Rabbit."

"Both stolen," Jilly said. She handed me the keys. "You drive. When I drive, the cars hit us. When you drive, they don't—we just hit something else instead. I need a change." She climbed into the right-side seat and buckled in. "It'll be interesting to see how this one ends."

I snorted. *Right. Car damaged beyond repair, both of us in the hospital. I can hardly wait. Especially if the folks in white coats try to x-ray me.*

We decided to pick up an early lunch at a place we both knew and liked called Bob's Deli. While I parked the car on the side street, Jilly radioed in our 10-7 and location, then got out of the car. Jilly started out ahead while I made sure the car was locked; it just wouldn't do to have a squad car stolen. Not in this neighborhood.

Jilly's hand appeared on my wrist. "Unlock it," she said. *Huh?* "Get the shotgun. One of us has to go in the back."

"Jilly—"

"There's a brand new Mustang convertible parked in front, Damon," she said. "Metal flake green. It's wearing plates that were issued in '92."

I felt a chill, a pleasant change from the burn I felt when I was angry. This was one of those things I liked about being a cop, why I became one this time around. I got the shotgun and clipped on my radio, checked it to make sure it was working. *The uncertainty of the job.* I walked to the back of the mall. *The random movements that somehow tend to keep the entire system in equilibrium.* I slipped behind the strip mall and in moments was at Bob's delivery entrance.

In my ear I heard Jilly say, "I need a make. California plates." She read off the number. Mustang convertible, green, brand new." I knocked on the delivery door and waited for someone to open it. Dispatch confirmed Jilly's guess; "—issued to a '92 Honda Accord."

I knocked on the door again. A moment later, it opened a crack; Bob's wife looked out. She took one look at me and flinched, but she let me in. I still listened to the constant drone in my ear.

"You have a customer who's driving what is probably a stolen car. It has stolen plates. Tell me about him. Or her."

Mrs. Bob hunkered her shoulders and glanced toward the door to the front of the store. "My husband's out there with them. There are two of them. They came in together."

"Wait." I moved to the door and glanced through the streaked window into the front. Two men, one white, one black, looking over the options. I backed away.

"This is Baker-seven." Once I got the confirm, I said, "We have two possibles, according to the owner's wife. The owner is in front with them." I paused for confirmation, then continued. "Number one is a white male adult, twenty-five to thirty, five-ten to six feet, brown hair, jeans, and red plaid work shirt. Two is a black male adult, same age range, six-three or -four, black hair, jeans, Raiders T-shirt."

"We need to avoid a hostage situation," Sergeant Enrico responded.

I looked at Mrs. Bob. "Can you get Bob to come into the back? You need a fake real reason." She winced, but nodded and went to the door, while I hunkered down where I couldn't be seen.

Enrico continued droning instructions in my ear. "Once he's out of the front, can you get in there unseen?" I confirmed.

I kept my ear tuned to the radio. "Baker-one, requesting any backup at Bob's Deli on Crenshaw." Enrico again.

"Baker-nine, currently at Sixth and San Pedro, en route to assist on Crenshaw." Good old Harry and his partner Rajid. Harry might be an asshole, but in the end he was a brother cop.

I spoke softly into the throat mike. "So far, no action. We're waiting until Baker-one arrives on scene." I took another peek through the window. "One of the two men keeps looking out the front window at the Mustang."

The dispatcher came on again. "The plates were reported stolen in Simi Valley yesterday."

Enrico said, "Baker-nine, proceed Code Two to the Crenshaw destination." Then his radio clicked off. Lights but no sirens, so they wouldn't warn the perps in advance. I waited, nerves tingling, for Jilly to make her entrance. When I tasted blood, I knew I'd bitten my lip. *Teeth are too sharp, Maxwell.*

"Vehicle matching the description stolen from Pico Ford at approximately oh-seven-fifteen yesterday."

I heard Enrico announce his arrival. Scant moments later, Enrico said, "In place, below window level." *Finally.*

I nodded to Mrs. Bob. She stuck her head through the door and said, "Bob? There's a problem with the freezer door. It won't close." I heard Bob muttering, but he came into the back.

"Out the back door, both of you," I said, pointing. To Mrs. Bob, I said, "You explain." I didn't bother to watch them stumble away. I waited until both men had their backs turned, then slipped through the door, and elbow-walked so they couldn't see me. I lay prone by the gate to the public part of the store. My temples itched. *Not now.*

Finally Jilly walked casually in the front door, helmet hanging from her Sam Browne. "Hey, Bob!" she called. "Damon and I are in a hurry so—Bob?" She turned to the two men and shrugged her shoulders. "Either of you seen Bob?"

The white man fidgeted, glanced at Jilly, and shook his head. "I think he went in back to fix something," the guy said.

"Huh." July strode toward the counter. I watched the two men as they watched her. They were antsy, all right. In fact, the white guy was sweating. Jilly kept glancing at the meat counter, and I wondered why. Then I mentally kicked myself; she could see their reflections.

Jilly slipped behind the counter, stuck her head through the door to the storage area and called, "Bob? You okay?" Then she shrugged and let the door close. "Guess I'll have to get my lunch somewhere else today, huh?"

"Baker-seven and all units in the vicinity." Dispatch said clearly in my ear. "Description of thieves from a saleswoman at Pico Ford." She read the descriptions.

My face got warm, but not angry warm. *Hot damn. A match.*

Jilly could see me, I knew, so I nodded once. She nodded back and leaned on the counter. "Nice wheels," she said to the two men. "I've been thinking of getting one like it for myself." She nodded toward the street. "How much did it cost?" I waited while she unsnapped her holster, all still below counter level.

The white guy's chin dropped. "Uh—uh—"

Jilly grinned. "So where'd you buy it? Not the one I've been drooling over at Pico Ford! I even love the window tint."

The white guy broke and ran for the door.

"Freeze! Both of you!" I slammed the gate open, the shotgun aimed at the black guy. Jilly had her pistol pointed at the white one.

"What the hell!" the white guy said. He moved toward me, snarling. Jilly's pistol followed him and he froze.

I waited until Enrico appeared in the shop window, his own shotgun leveled. Then I stood.

The black man blustered; street bravado. "Why you hassling us? We're just in here getting stuff for a party, man."

I nodded toward the Mustang. "Where'd you get the plates?"

The black man sneered. "From DMV, same as everybody."

"Indirectly, of course," I replied. "Those plates belong to a '92 Honda that lives in Simi Valley."

"Shit!" The white man lurched toward Jilly.

Jilly snarled. "Stop or I'll shoot!" He turned and threw the door open—and came to a tottering halt, hands lifting into the air, staring down the barrel of the Enrico's weapon.

"I wasn't going nowhere," he said. "Honest, Officer."

While I covered her, Jilly got the white man spread and frisked. She found his ID and tossed it over, and I rattled off the vitals to the dispatcher. Then she cuffed the guy.

When I gestured with the shotgun, the black man shook his head and raised his hands. "Aw, man, I don't believe it!"

We made sure they heard and understood the Miranda, then watched Enrico haul them away, and settled down to log our reports while we waited for the tow truck. We had excellent sandwiches to eat as we worked; Bob piled on lots of extras.

"At least this time the tow's not for *us*, " Jilly said with a grin. She slapped the roof of the car. "Back to work, partner."

I grinned back. "Back to work it is." I opened the door, then paused. "I wonder what will go wrong next?"

"Who knows?" Jilly asked as she settled in the passenger seat. Once the car was moving, she went on. "One of these days, Damon, you're going to have to find a better use for this talent of yours. Street patrol doesn't quite cut it."

* * *

Two weeks later, when I checked my mail after we got off shift, I cornered Jilly in the squad room. "Guess what?"

"What?" She leaned against the wall, her arms folded.

"I took your advice." I grinned and handed her the paper.

"You're transferring to auto detail? Plainclothes?" I nodded. "Lucky man. Think things will go better for you there?"

"Hope so," I said. "When they checked my record, they decided auto detail was where I belonged. Enrico told them that I have a special touch when it comes to hot cars and thieves."

Jilly nodded; she knew my record from all those long conversations on patrol. Then she caught me fidgeting and lifted an eyebrow.

"Okay. Remember Harry calling me Murph, for the Imp of the Perverse, and I objected?" She nodded. "Well—" I hesitated, not sure how she'd take it—"—um, it's, ah, too close to the truth. The counterbalance comes from the busts that we—me and whatever partner—make at the end of a string of incidents."

She folded the transfer paperwork and tapped my shoulder with it. "'Splain."

"Every bleeding bust was serendipitous," I told her. I sat down; she dropped next to me. "Like me happening to be in line right behind the fast food robber. Like we decided to have lunch at the deli where the green car thieves were looking for a meal."

Jilly frowned and rubbed her chin. "Ah. Serendipity being the balancing force for Murphy's Law, I take it. But how will this work out in auto detail?"

I hesitated, then said, "Look again, especially my name."

"Huh?" Then Jilly took out the form and looked at it again. "Maxwell, comma, Damon C." she recited. "What's so special abou—shit." Her eyes opened wide and she dropped to sit on a chair against the wall with her head hanging.

"Jilly?" Now what was wrong? She lifted her head, tears streaming running from her eyes. She was laughing.

"So Maxwell's Demon is more than a theoretical construct?" she asked. I nodded. "No wonder you flinched when I brought up Clerk Maxwell. So why are you showing me?"

Shrug. "I guess I got tired of keeping it a secret," I told her. "You won't hold it against me?" She shook her head.

"Police work must be quite different from keeping hot and cold molecules separated—oh, wait a minute. I guess it isn't. What's the difference between molecules and cars, besides size?"

I shrugged and studied my hands.

"One thing still puzzles me, Damon. If you only let hot molecules go through the trapdoor, how did the cold ones get back to the other side? Because if I remember right, the demon let only one kind of molecule through the trapdoor."

I grinned at her. "There were two of us," I said.

Diving After Reflected Woman

by Terry McGarry

In her past lives, Terry McGarry has been a bartender on Wall Street, an English major at Princeton, a street trader in Ireland, a senior copy editor at *The New Yorker*, and a SFWA officer. Her novel *Illumination* will be followed by *The Binder's Road* and *Triad*. She's the author of more than three dozen short stories and an award-winning poetry chapbook. An SF copy editor and Irish musician, she lives in New York.

MY mind was far away as I turned the camera to follow the agitated pacing of the white youth in the other room. This confession was unnecessary icing. They had already identified the killer by the teeth marks on the body.

As I half-watched perpetrator William Harrison, twenty-four, of Bed-Stuy, reenacting his rape and strangling of an eighty-three-year-old woman in Greenpoint—and half didn't watch the fingers curved into talons, the rictus of orgasmic cruelty and pain, the pelvic thrusts so hard they shook the kid from his chair and set the disgusted cops scrambling—I thought about where I would go for lunch, how much cash I had on me, which drugstore might have a sale on the shaving cream I liked.

Anything to avoid engaging the scene before me, anything to avoid thinking of my mother, my sister. So when the door opened behind me and my colleague said my name—no tap on the shoulder, which might startle me into jerking the camera—my clipped "Yeah, Ron?" did not carry half the relief I felt at the distraction.

Ron Teller glanced at the posturing youth on the other side of the mirror. "Jeez, you've landed some doozies lately, Taino."

"You're not kidding." I zoomed to a wide shot so that I wouldn't have to follow the perp's erratic movements. Prosecutors preferred a dramatic recording if they could get it, but this kid was a one-man road show—no artfulness required. "What's up?"

"Thought you should know that Rezak lost."

I swore. Steve Rezak had killed two teenagers who had attacked him and his daughter in the DeKalb Avenue subway station, and left a third with a paralyzed arm. He'd had a box cutter, they'd had switchblades; he'd been faster and angrier. I had burned his statement. He hadn't gone to jail, but the third kid and the families of the other two had sued him.

"That's it," I said. "He'll lose the house, the construction business, the money for his daughter's education. Whatever's left, anyway, after the lawyers."

"Just goes to show, maybe you shouldn't fight back. They'll get you in the end even if you win."

I shook my head. "His daughter's alive" was all I said. I said it so softly I didn't think Teller heard me.

"Anyway, that's not why I'm here. I'm supposed to take over for you here and send you down to H. The Jay Doe the A.D.A. wanted you to cover has just agreed to a confession. I'm sorry, Tai; I think it's gonna be a bad one."

I moved away from the camera and gestured for Ron to take over. "*Mierda*, man, it can't be much worse than this."

"You gotta stop being so good at your job," Teller said, his eye to the viewfinder. "Lend me some of that talent of yours. Or go into movies, where you should be."

I laughed bitterly, spread my arms wide. "And give up all this?"

I left the AV cubicle and walked down the gray corridor of the Kings County Courthouse, my Nikes whispering on the stained and scarred linoleum floor.

I was good, and I knew it; my only consolation was that I was good because I was good, not because I was a voyeur, like McKennie, or because I got my rocks off on vicarious criminal experiences, like Wenkler.

And Teller was bad, and he knew it, because he was none of the above. He didn't give prosecutors jury-swaying theatrical presentations. He didn't keep a pot by his chair to throw up into anymore when he worked. He didn't get too close to the perps. He was afraid that the sickness in them would come through the camera, inject itself needlelike into his eyes, and ooze into his soul. Teller was the one who should have gone into films, if he could, or commercials—any business but this.

But a job was a job. It beat robbing banks.

I opened the steel door to AV Cubicle H and found my supervisor and the assistant district attorney waiting. The interrogation room on the other side of the glass was empty.

"No perp yet?" I said. "Ronny said this was urgent."

My supervisor stood up. "They'll bring her in now."

"Her?" I always felt butterflies before a session, but my stomach churned this time. *God, not a ped, not a child-killer.*

"That's all we can tell you right now," the assistant D.A. said. "This has to be good. I don't want you to feel manipulated, but we need genuine reactions from the camera on this one, nothing prearranged. Think you can handle it?"

"I'd rather not," I said, surprising myself. I had never turned down an assignment, but this one felt wrong.

"There's a bonus in it, Taino," the supervisor said, his tone implying that there would be a sanction if I said no.

"How about Wenkler? This sounds like his thing."

The supe shook his head. "No, and you know why. Or you will."

Because I wasn't supposed to enjoy this. I was supposed to be horrified and project that horror into the jury. *Hijo de puta.* But I said, "Whatever. Let's get it over with."

Both men nodded and left the cubicle, left me focusing the camera on a stark, empty room with a metal table and folding chair like the one I sat in, cold and uncomfortable. Maybe the SuperSave would have that brand of shampoo that had disappeared off the shelves for two weeks. I hoped the company hadn't stopped making it.

The perp was escorted in by a policewoman and seated at the table. I began with a wide shot, fingering the filter pad to pick up the deep blue of the officer's slacks; then I moved in on the seated perp, and the officer's legs walked out of the field. I adjusted the color again: the perp was pale, her straight mousy hair hanging lank on her shoulders, and I filtered in a bit of green and moved my other hand to the remote room-lighting controls to soften the glare. She had round, china-blue eyes that looked unerringly into the camera. When I met their gaze through the lens, unprepared, accidentally, I felt pierced, and had to force my head to stay at the viewfinder. One of my eyelids took up its annoying tic.

As the officer droned out the docket number and charges for the record, I studied the perp's face. It was long, the planes of the cheeks rising smoothly to be cut off by the dark sockets of the eyes. Makeup would slide right off the translucent skin, the thin, pale lips, the heavy lids. It was a face that a premillennium flower child should have worn, or an exercise girl at a racetrack, or an amateur poet—except for the beige hints of old bruises, and an ugly new one, a purplish smudge over her right eyebrow. I cursed myself for already being drawn in, and zoomed out a bit so that the perspective over the blue shoulder of the officer would suggest the opening of an interview, a technique I had often used to good effect.

"The accused has signed Form 8037-D confirming that she is willingly offering her statement for the record," the officer recited.

The blue eyes didn't waver from the camera's lens, though the camera wasn't visible from the interrogation room. A weird shudder went through me, like I'd just stepped into an icy sea up to the waist. The lips opened to speak.

"I have been properly Jensen-Mirandized," the perp said, her voice a steady alto, "I agree to the recording of this session, and I have requested that the lawyer assigned to my case not be present. Nobody has coerced me into making this statement."

She blinked a couple of times, as if collecting herself, and so did I, involuntarily. Toothpaste, I thought, zooming in past the shoulder to a head-and-torso shot as the confession began; I wanted to change toothpaste brands, maybe to one of those baking-soda kinds that scrubbed your teeth really, really clean.

"My name was originally Ginny Alward. I have changed it several times, as I have changed my residence; when I'm done, I will furnish a list of all but one of those names and cities.

"I'm here on grievous-assault charges. They are not valid—I have assaulted no one, and have in fact only been assaulted myself—but I want to start from the beginning, and I can only hope that my story will not be edited for viewing by a jury. I don't care if I'm indicted or not, but I would like to be heard.

"On August 19th, 1999, I was raped. It's on the records; it happened here in Brooklyn, where my parents and I were living at the time. I reported it, but the rapist was never apprehended by the police, although I did see him twice in the same neighborhood and I did alert the authorities. They made some effort to catch him, but they were too short-staffed. He is on the records now, too. I believe he died of loss of blood on the way to Methodist Hospital, late in the summer of 2004."

That was four months ago; it had taken them that long to apprehend her. I edged the camera in a bit closer, trying not to focus my own eyes on her face now; I had done victims' statements for a while, and couldn't stand it. Distance from a crime was possible for me only from one side. When I recorded the people it happened to, that was when the anger came. Maybe that was it, I found myself thinking, for the first time; maybe that was what made me good at this. It was my revenge. Despite all my touted impassivity, what I was really doing was "getting" them, playing an active role in society's retribution. . . .

"I was walking to the subway at about seven-thirty in the morning, on my way to a summer job in Manhattan to make money for school. I was studying anthropology. A man came out from an alleyway, with a knife. He raped me, and when he was done, he wiped off what he'd done, with the knife."

I panned in close enough to pick up the sweat that had dewed her upper lip, but my hands were shaking, so I left the camera there and poured some water for myself from the half-empty pitcher on the table. This was supposed to be a perp, not a goddamned victim.

Errands, I thought. There had to be more errands. But I couldn't come up with any.

"Someone who'd been watching from an apartment window called an ambulance, so I didn't bleed to death. I wasn't surprised that they never caught him. My parents sold the house and we all moved to another town.

"I got my degree in school, a B.A. in anthro. I was writing a paper on the Native American trickster mythology when the news had an item about new techniques in body alteration. I sold my car, took cash advances on my credit cards. I went to a body specialist in yet another city with my idea. The specialist figured out a way to do it.

"And then I went out. I went out and walked around. For two years."

Dios. Her eyes gleamed with a cold, crystalline light; her face was radiant, somehow, though the expression had not changed.

Maybe the radiance was in my own eyes.

I put down the water, returned to the viewfinder, and went in even closer, so only her face showed on the screen. In the back of my mind, connections were being made to articles I had read, newsnet stories from other parts of the country, tabloid reports of male mutilations . . . it was beginning to make sense to me, a complete and perfect sense that stopped my shaking, made me forget the water, the room, everything but her and the camera.

"It didn't matter where. I just walked, every day, twice a day. I moved jobs and apartments a lot. I ended up back east, where it all began. It was an accident that one of the men who attacked me during that time was the original rapist. I didn't go looking for him; I didn't walk down that street. It was in the subway station I had been heading for. That made me feel less stupid about having walked down that street in the first place; funny how all the big emotions can be numbed out, but self-recrimination remains. That's gone now, too."

My camera could see through her poker face now. I knew that was a kind of penetration. At the same time, my legs squeezed involuntarily together, and I had to force my hand to stay on the camera controls instead of dropping down to protect my groin.

"It's a very old concept, nothing new; just applied mythology.

With the help of the body specialist and an iris of razors, I made that mythology real. Consider it my dissertation in anthropology—which is, of course, the study of man."

I was about to zoom back, to take in the room again, to remind the viewer that the world outside this narrative existed. Then she smiled. The smile filled the camera, a curve of lips to reveal perfect, perfectly white teeth, and I was drawn in to that smile, pulling the camera with me until the glistening white seemed to burn the lens.

"They've improved the tech since I had it done," she said, articulating very precisely. "Now you can have the implant and have consensual sex safely, too. I feel better knowing that." She paused, the only pause she had made for dramatic effect in the whole matter-of-fact narrative. Then she said, "Don't you?"

I withdrew as the smile closed slowly down, the face shrinking to allow the body back into the picture, the body shrinking back into its seat across the table from the straight blue line of the police officer's shoulder.

"That's the end of my statement."

If her lawyer was any good, if she could set up a train of logic that relied on self-defense and the fact that there was no crime in body alterations—yet—the woman might be cleared. What could they get her on? Carrying a concealed weapon?

But they would get her, somehow. They wouldn't permit this. A system that could break the back of a man who saved his five-year-old daughter's life would not permit anyone this kind of power. They would twist it, and they would suppress it.

She should have gone to the six-o'clock news.

I was angry. I was pissed at her for putting this on me.

And maybe I didn't want it to get out either. Christ, for the sake of men everywhere, this couldn't get out. My sister could take care of herself. My finger twitched on the skipback dial. Just go back three minutes, record the end of the interview over the middle, poof, no usable record. She'd never make it to trial. She'd disappear. Her body specialist would disappear. Her story would disappear.

I had done that once. That was why it had to be me burning this statement. Because I could be trusted to do it again.

I never forced it on a woman who didn't want it. Never. Except that one time, but I was drinking then,

I'm not sure what happened. And there are times when no means yes, that's such a load of crap, that no is no. How can you tell anyway? No one ever really understands what women want. Sometimes maybe you make a mistake. What if you could lose your dick for that? What kind of a world would it be if some woman could cut off my dick for just making a mistake?

The officer repeated the pertinent data. I followed with the camera as the subject was escorted to the door. A voice in my head was saying *stop, we're done here.* My finger was spasming over the skipback dial. There were only a few seconds left to make a plausible recording error.

I kept the camera on her as the door opened.

Just as she was about to step through, she turned and looked at me again. She would see only a mirror; maybe that's what she was looking at. But I swear the eyes focused on me.

It was a challenge. I thought I was safe behind my mirrored-glass shield, but she looked right through it and she challenged me.

Maybe she hadn't had a chance to go the media. Or maybe she hadn't wanted to be a deterrent, maybe she had wanted revenge, as much revenge as she could get for as long as there were perps to get it on.

Or maybe she was some kind of martyr, going through hell again and again, offering herself up as a sacrifice for her gender. Maybe she was relieved that it was over, and ashamed to be relieved. I don't know. I never understood women. But she was challenging me to be bigger than that. To do the right thing. To see the big picture. To be bigger than my own dick.

That's what I saw, anyway. Different eyes see different things.

After they took her out, I let the camera linger on the closing door: I recorded the sound and sight of it clicking shut. Then I stopped the record and sat back.

I took the storage disk out of the machine and slipped in a blank for them to erase, or hide, or try to alter. My hand didn't tremble at all, even though I heard steps in the hall, the doorknob turning. I tucked the disk in an inner jacket pocket and let the hand drop away. Casually. As if its fall hadn't gestured in the end of my career.

"You all right?" It was my supervisor, with the assistant D.A. behind him. He took a look at me, then frowned at the A.D.A. "Damnit, maybe Teller was right. This must have been rough, if it messed up *this* guy. . . ."

I just smiled, thinking about an errand I had to run, guy I knew over at the network . . . and showing teeth.

Like this. See? Want a second to zoom in there, buddy?

Okay, never mind. I know the score.

That's the end of my statement.

Sweeps Week

by Mercedes Lackey

Mercedes Lackey has published numerous novels, including the best-selling *Heralds of Valdemar* series. She is also a professional lyricist and a licensed wild bird rehabilitator.

I SAT at my kitchen table, an amazing array of microelectronics spread out on the oiled butcher block in front of me. What I had there would have sent my bosses—both of them—into spasms.

What was most amazing was their size—microphones the size of a grain of sand, cameras no thicker than a human hair—in fact, the leads were bigger than the camera. I couldn't begin to understand half of what they did or how they did it, and—

Well, I'm a microelectronics engineer working on nanotech. These were beyond nanotech. So far beyond it that the rest of my team would have taken one look at them and shot themselves.

Of course, there's no way *we* could have come up with anything like these gadgets. No one on Earth could.

Huh. No wonder no one ever believes abductees when they say they've been implanted . . . without an electron microscope—*or* the knowledge that these *were* devices and they *did* things—they'd just look like the sort of random misplaced bits that show up all the time in human tissue. Old bits of gravel and glass from accidents as a child you don't even remember, a bit of tissue deciding it wants to be bone in the wrong place. And *that's* an implant—most of these were "just" nanotech bugs.

If I hadn't managed to hook one of these arrays up to a pocket TV receiver and seen the results myself, I would have thought they were stray hairs and bits of dust.

One of the devices, a triangular bit of something a quarter of the size of a pea, stained the oiled wood of the table beneath it a watered-down crimson. That was because I had just removed the thing from my wife's left sinus cavity, from directly behind her eye, and the crimson stain was her blood.

I'd gotten to it by splitting open her skull with a camping ax.

As I prodded the thing with a long needle, feeling as utterly detached from that reality as if I'd simply plucked the thing from inside a lamp, it occurred to me that it was probably the controlling device I'd suspected, rather than an observation device I'd *expected*. It also occurred to me that I was probably in shock, and this dispassionate detachment was a symptom of it. Well, I'd never killed a wife before. I'd never killed anyone before. Odd sensation knowing that Rita was *gone*, irrevocably, and I'd done it.

At least she hadn't known it was coming. I might be a straight-edge geek, but I'm not completely unaware of what goes on in so-called "popular culture."

A little careful cultivation of the slacker-hackers in software netted me a couple of roofies, the so-called date-rape drug, guaranteed to be tasteless and colorless, and put out the recipient within an hour. I intended to kill her, not hurt her. It wasn't *her* fault the aliens were using her. Too bad this wasn't a book; I'd have had some doctor friend who could have removed the thing without killing her, or figured out some way to shield her from it.

But I couldn't take the chance. This was self-defense. A man in my position, working on black-budget projects, *can't* take chances. No one was going to believe me without evidence; I couldn't collect the evidence without alerting the aliens. The moment I alerted the aliens, they'd move on me, probably using Rita. So I had to get rid of Rita, and with luck, collect an implant from her, too.

It had to be the aliens, of course. *I* have been working on black-budget milspec stuff for the last three years, and *I* have never heard of anything like this before.

I'd always thought aliens existed, in a kind of wistful, if-only manner, rather than a Roswell-Conspiracy True-Believer mode. Going where I've gone, seeing what I've seen, well, it makes that type look pretty damn funny. I've *been* to Groom Lake; no crashed saucers in sight, only some black-budget ops for a while, then just enough black-budget testing to keep the lunatics focused *there,* and not on the new testing base, deeper in the Range where civvies couldn't get near it.

But aliens being *out there,* somewhere—if I had a

religion, I suppose that must have been it. Aliens made more sense than angels to me, always had. Hell, that was why I was a science fiction fan—*real* science fiction, *Analog* stuff, with rivets and hard science, not movie guys in bathrobes beating each other with glowing sticks and pseudo-Zen mysticism.

That was how I'd met Rita, at a convention, where I'd been on a nanotech panel. Couldn't tell a tenth of what I knew, of course, but my bosses liked me to do it. Partly smoke and mirrors to throw the clueless off, partly to find out what the private sector was up to, partly the theory of "hide in plain sight."

Now I know she'd been trolling for a husband, and had switched her targeting system from the software nerd she'd been sizing up to me once she realized that I was probably making a better and more stable living than some support dude at a dot-com. Then, I'd just been convinced she was my soulmate, and delirious that she had been so pleased about removing that inconvenient virginity of mine . . . with a wedding in the offing, of course. TANSTAFL; I wasn't *that* naive. I knew what I was getting into as far as what she wanted out of it.

Well, blind infatuation on my part, blind ambition on hers. And if lately we've been more like roommates than husband and wife, well, at least she was a roommate who cleaned and did the shopping, and managed to microwave a decent dinner for me every night, which was a damn sight better than every other roommate I'd ever had, most of whom were slobs, slackers, or both. And she didn't tell me to shut up when I talked real SF, and ridiculed Sturgeon's

Ninety Percent. In fact, up until I'd figured out what she was, or rather, what she'd become, I'd been looking forward to spending the next couple of evenings watching TV with her. It was sweeps week, and even the science shows had some of their best programming for the year on. We'd do an MST3K on movies, though she made me keep my opinions on *Trek* to myself. She had a thing for Picard, I guess.

When had the aliens taken her over? I hadn't noticed any obvious changes, just gradual ones. She stopped talking much; the cat took a sudden dislike to her, and the next day it was gone. Her meals had never been gourmet, but they took on a rhythmic sameness, on a seven-day cycle. All of that could just have been boredom, and the fact that the cat never was quite right, more than half feral. Hell, maybe the cat was their first control, maybe she replaced the cat.

Then I found the first of the eavesdropping devices, a couple of weeks ago. . . .

I'm not sure why I was so certain of what it was. I just *knew,* that was all. I looked around, found more—but left them alone. I didn't want the aliens to know I was on to them.

Instead, I "accidentally" broke one, the first one I'd found, hidden in a plexiglass sculpture I'd bought at a con just before I'd met Rita. In fact, if I hadn't *known* every millimeter of that sculpture better than I knew my own face, I'd never have spotted it. Then I set myself up a little spy device of my own, with bits from work, and waited.

What had I been waiting for? An alien to come teleporting in to fix it? Maybe I had; maybe I'd expected to be able to grab the thing and knock it out or something, just like out of one of those damn movies I made fun of. Well, what I got was Rita, in the middle of the night, fiddling with it in the dark, and in the morning the device was back and better camouflaged than before.

Right. That was when I knew that I was going to have to get rid of Rita before I tackled collecting the rest of the gadgets, or as many of them as I could find. Because I didn't know *why* they were spying on me, but I had to assume it was for no good reason, and my first loyalty had to be to my bosses and my species. *Maybe* they were benevolent, but I couldn't take that chance. You get paranoid in this job, but—well, you know what they say, just because you're paranoid, that doesn't mean they *aren't* out to get you. So, good-bye Rita. Hell, if they were benevolent, why were they *using* her? I'd've been open to direct contact; after watching me, they had to know that.

Well, now I had what no one else had ever had; proof. In a little while, I'd call my boss—the military one—and have him come over. With a squad. Show him this stuff and what it could do, then show him Rita in the bedroom, explain what had happened, and why I'd done what I'd done.

The last thing they'd want was for me to get into the hands of the civvies. I figured they'd probably make me vanish into a top-secret lab, but that had always been a risk when I started doing milspec, anyway. You get too good a breakthrough, well, guess what, you become a national asset, and Uncle owns you. It says so on the contract you sign. Given the circumstances—they'd make it look like I did Rita, then ran; most of the setup was already in place. So far as the world would be concerned, I'd just be one more of those guys the neighbors always talked about on the news after the body was found: "Nice enough guy, quiet, didn't bother anyone, got along great with his wife, never thought he'd do anything like *this*. . . ."

Better get it over with. I reached for the kitchen phone and picked it up.

There was no dial tone.

Now, the first thing was, I got mad. It wasn't the first time the phone had been cut off, it was Rita's one bad habit, she stuck bills away and forgot to pay them. So I thought, had Rita gotten so obsessed with programming the VCR to catch everything this week that she'd forgotten to pay the damn bill *again?* But then a movement barely glimpsed out of the corner of my eye made me freeze.

The alien strolled into the kitchen as if he owned the place.

It was a Gray, one of the tall ones, maybe seven feet. I knew most of the UFOlogy designations, you kind of picked that sort of thing up by osmosis in SF circles.

It just looked at me, tall and skinny, smooth gray skin, glittery, big black eyes. *It's no use trying your telephone, Richard.*

The voice was in my head—telepathy, of course.

That was when something in me broke, and I felt something I'd never felt before. Rage, pure, primal, unfocused rage.

I lunged at the frail-seeming creature, perfectly

prepared to send it where I'd just sent Rita. And I wasn't particularly concerned except over how much I hurt *it* in the process, because I *wanted* it to hurt. A lot.

The only problem was, I couldn't move. I tried to lunge, but nothing happened.

The thing's tiny, lipless mouth didn't move, but I got the impression of a smirk. *Really, you should have assumed we'd think of that. You may be intelligent and rational by the standards of your species, Richard, but to us, you're still a hairless ape. You would not believe the things I have to go through merely to make myself intelligible to you.*

I hadn't *wanted* to kill Rita; it had been a matter of pure self-preservation. But, oh, I *wanted* to kill this thing.

Yes, I know you do. How predictable. Do try to think instead of emote, will you, while I tidy up?

The alien moved to the table, and swept all of the tiny bits of electronics into one hand, including the pocket TV I'd hooked one of them up to, just to see if it had transmitted (it had). I more than half expected it to disintegrate them or something of the sort, but instead, it took them over to the sink, turned on the tap, and started the garbage disposal. A minute later, and that industrial-strength disposer had macerated the lot, and it was all somewhere in the sewer.

I groaned. I knew very well what *that* meant. The alien turned back to me, and all I could think of—besides the fact that I was doomed—was an anguished and unformed "Why?" Why me? What did they want? Why were they doing this to me, of all people?

Ah, questions. Again, the suggestion of a smirk. *Richard, your little species is so delightfully egocentric. When I think about your religions alone—*

The creature convulsed with silent laughter. *And the joke is so on you! We created you, you know. Not some invisible, omnipotent hairless ape in the sky. We did it. A snip in the genes here, an addition there—oh, you weren't the* best *candidates, but when our backs were turned for a few moments, a space-rock managed to send the best prospects into extinction, so we made do with you. You're coming along quite well as a species, actually. Much better than we expected.*

I'd gone from enraged to dazed. The *concept* wasn't foreign to me, after all, it had been used for almost half a century as a plot device. But the alien's tone was all *wrong,* somehow. A benevolent creator shouldn't sound so—cynically amused. And why *use* people like they'd used Rita?

It stared at me as those thoughts ran through my head and convulsed again.

Oh, Richard, Richard, this is utterly priceless! I haven't heard anything so funny in a century! Do you really think we made you out of the kindness of our hearts? Why? To help us populate the universe? To ease our cosmic loneliness?

But—if not that—

The alien's black, pupilless eyes glittered. *To* amuse *us, Richard. We have so little that can amuse us! We've been manipulating you ever since you first bashed each other with rocks and sticks!* We made and designed *you to bash each other with rocks and sticks!* It drew closer; I couldn't have moved now if I'd wanted to; it felt as if my brain was collapsing under an intolerable weight of despair. *How many of your fellow apes have lamented their condition, and wondered how a benevolent God could allow war, accident, terror, and disease to exist! And we, your "gods," created these conditions deliberately, Richard! We set them among you, and set you at each other's throats, all so we can watch and see what happens! It is our highest art form! From the simple domestic quarrel to world wars—some of us work in small dramas and some in large—we watch, we record, we laugh. You hairless apes and your pretentions, your little teacup tragedies, are the stuff of endless amusement and comedy for us.*

Amusement. The human race and its struggles were—a sitcom?

A sitcom. Trust an ape to come up with a ridiculous designation for such an advanced art form as this that we have produced. But I suppose it's the only analogy that you would understand. More of a sneer than a smirk this time. *And now it's time to bring in the fourth act—at least for the episode that* you *are in. Oh, I worked long and hard on this one, Richard. I thought you would* never *find the first device. I nearly wept when it seemed you wouldn't realize that Rita was controlled. Though you* did *give me a truly delightful surprise when you killed her; when that plays, it's going to be a sensation. I truly thought that all you'd do would be to drug her. Hilarious!*

The eyes were as hard and shiny as polished obsidian, and as heartless. *And the fact that now you have been told the truth makes the episode all the funnier. If you'd only drugged her, we'd have had this little talk, I'd have cleaned up all the evidence, and left you here. It would have been good—watching you try and decide whether to tell anyway, without proof. It would have been funny, seeing how long it took your rigid little psyche to fracture. But now! Oh, this is going to be choice!*

Of course it was right. No one would ever believe me. My own bosses wouldn't save me, I wasn't *that* important to the team. I could run, but I didn't know anything about being a fugitive, and anyway, how was I supposed to get cash to keep myself alive on the run?

I was going straight to death row. I couldn't even claim temporary insanity, *everything* I'd done pointed to premeditation—I'd *bought* the roofies, I'd drugged her, I got the camping ax. . . . Hell, I'd have to hire Johnny Cochran to get out of something like this.

The alien's head rose a little. *What a charming thought! Perhaps we'll arrange that, as well,* the creature said. *We'll have to see how the ratings for this episode go. But now—* It cocked its head to the side, and in the distance, I heard the faint wail of a siren. The alien walked slowly toward the kitchen door. *Yes, I believe that our current episode is coming to an end. Good-bye for now, Richard. And feel honored for being chosen. After all—*

The alien turned back for just a moment, its big eyes glittering balefully at me—*this* is *sweeps week.*

A Good Idea at the Time

by Karen E. Taylor

Karen E. Taylor is best known as the author of *The Vampire Legacy* series, including the novels *Blood Secrets, The Vampire Vivienne,* and the upcoming *Resurrection*. A Bram Stoker Award Nominee for Short Fiction, she resides in Maryland with her husband and two sons.

I STUDIED him as he walked down the street. A likely suspect, I thought, clad in a suit and tie and carrying an expensive briefcase, but with a confused look in his eyes, as if he had lost something very important, something crucial to his life. He was right, of course, he had. They all had. But I was the only man alive who knew that for sure.

As he neared, I straightened my clothes and considered my approach. "Excuse me, sir," I said, respectfully—the ones in suits always appreciated respect. "May I speak with you for a moment? It is a matter of some importance to me. And may be of interest to you."

While he appraised me, I thought of what he must be seeing: an older man, mid to late sixties, dressed normally if shabbily, with a corpulent look that hinted of a not so perfect past. The eyes were sad, but clear, with no trace of possible violence or drugs. In short, I did not look like a mugger or a bum.

He gave me a wary nod.

"For the modest price of a beer and a hamburger, I'll tell you a good story. Yes, I know, it's a line you hear every day in this part of town, but surely you can tell from the way I speak that I'm not one of your usual street scum. I am a highly educated, some might say overeducated, scientist. Once renowned for my discovery of time travel."

This line usually grabbed them or lost them.

"Time travel?" he mused, "I don't remember reading about that in the papers. But you're right, it could be interesting."

Got him. Odd, it usually took more than that, I'd had the whole spiel prepared. Some of my best lines were in that spiel. I was especially fond of: this story also involves the fall of a great mind, a great career and a great civilization. Certainly, good sir, you must agree that is worth the cost of lunch and a beer or two?

As a scientist, though, I'd learned economy of effort. Why waste the words if I already had him hooked?

We entered a bar about a block away. They knew me here, always kept the best booth open for me. I figured it was the least they could do.

"Did you know," I said to him, after we'd been seated and our orders had been taken, "this is the first bar I ever frequented, and the one I always come back to? No, how could you? Still, I've found that there's nothing like a comfortable, straightforward bar, one in which you can drink in silence or in companionship with others of your kind. Mankind, I mean. Notice there are no women in here? That is, to me, part of its charm."

He obliged me by looking around and nodded.

"Not that I don't like women, you understand," I continued, "but every so often a man needs to get away and relax. This sort of bar affords one that luxury."

"Yeah," he smiled, "I know exactly what you mean."

"Even the food here is basic, good food. None of your frills or fads. One of the city magazines voted this place the best hamburger for several years in a row. And they weren't lying. Just wait; you'll be able to see for yourself."

"Actually," he said, his voice slow and reasonable, "I've eaten here before myself. I may even have seen you once or twice, you certainly look familiar. Funny how that works, isn't it?" He paused, then held out his hand. "The name's John Jones. You?"

"Dr. William Jones."

He laughed. "Small world."

"Smaller than you think, Mr. Jones. But, in fact, it is quite a common name."

"True enough, Doctor. You did say 'Doctor,' didn't you?" He raised an eyebrow, staring pointedly at my clean, but ill-fitting, old clothes.

"Yes, I have earned the title of Doctor. It's part of the story, Mr. Jones, all part of the story. But," I saw the waiter approaching with our lunch, "let's eat first, shall we?"

The waiter set our plates down in front of us. "Can I get you anything else, Dr. Jones?"

"Another beer for me, Jim." I looked over at my companion. "You?"

"Sure," he said, "why the hell not?"

The waiter left to draw our beers; I held my plate up in front of my face, sniffed and gave a satisfied sigh. "Ah," I said to Mr. Jones, "look at this. Just the right amount of grease in these, don't you think? See that little pool of it? And then there's the good red meat, medium rare, with lettuce, tomatoes, a nice thick slab of red onion, smeared with real mayonnaise, and topped with a huge slice of melted cheese. They even toast the buns on the grill. A man's meal."

I took a huge bite; grease ran out of the side of my mouth and dribbled down my chin. Wiping it off with my napkin, I smiled. "Have you ever been a vegetarian, Mr. Jones? Do you know what it's like to go years, decades even, without ever getting something good to eat?"

"Can't say that I do, Dr. Jones. Why do you ask?"

I shook my head. "Let's finish these first and I'll tell you everything."

The two of us ate in relative silence, interrupted only by the solid sound of chewing.

"Nothing like this," I said before taking that last bite, "nothing else in the world."

He nodded. "Yeah, it's good."

I finished the burger, belched, and tapped my chest with my fist. "Pardon me. As much as I love the food, it always makes me burp. But this is a man's bar and no one cares. One is not ostracized for demonstrating basic human actions."

I drained my beer and motioned to Jim to bring another. When he brought it, I took another long drink, wiped my mouth with the back of my hand.

"Here, one is not ostracized for basic human actions," I repeated, "but it was not always this way. Or maybe it was. Time has become a difficult subject for me. Is it now? Is it then? I am the only one who remembers."

I paused. Dramatically. "You see, Mr. Jones, I remember the future."

He gave a little snort of disbelief.

I nodded. "Of course you don't believe me, what sane man would? I assure you, though, the story is true. The future I remember is a very clean place, sterile. There are no diseases, no wars, no dissension. Utopia, in other words. Men judge others based on their intellect, on their contribution to society. Children seek to further their education; one needs to coax them to play, to entice them away from their books and their studies.

On a normal day, I would awaken, shower, dress, enter the kitchen to a machine-prepared breakfast of nutrobars and energy drinks. My wife would smile at me, perhaps even kiss me on the cheek, her hair, skin, and figure perfectly suited to mine. The rooms of my house were immaculate, no clutter, no dropped crumbs or spilled drinks. Nothing to mar the beauty of the basic but comfortable furniture and the wide expanse of green grass and blue skies visible from the picture windows. The children would be busy with their studies and look up with smiling clean faces if I entered the room."

I grew quiet for a moment at that thought. But continued quickly so as not to lose his attention. "Yes, I have children, or I had them once. They have been swallowed up by another time stream."

I gave him a discerning look. "For all I know, Mr. Jones, you could be my son. In another time and another place."

"Somehow, I doubt that, Dr. Jones."

I chuckled. "Well, to be honest, so do I. But it adds a little bit to the story, I think. The elements of doubt and 'what if' are very important."

Mr. Jones looked at his watch. "About this story, Doctor? Are you going to tell it or not? I have a meeting soon."

I nodded sagely. "Yes, of course, everyone has meetings these days. But they will wait for you, I'm sure."

He gave a noncommittal grunt, but stayed in his seat and sipped on his beer.

"Now, we were talking about the future, I believe. It was a very nice place as I remember. I worked in a laboratory outside of Newark, New Jersey, as a young man. A very clean and lovely place. Or at least it once was or would be. I haven't been there since the future.

"I had everything then. A distinguished career, a loving wife, two daughters, and a son on the way. All of it carefully planned and neatly organized. But, when I looked around my gleaming office and my perfect home, I felt that something was missing.

Something elemental to the human experience. Disorder, chaos, grit, and grime."

"You lived in the utopian future and wanted grime?"

I sighed. "I didn't necessarily think that perfection was the preferred human condition. You see, I was also a historian. And I longed for something that had been lost along the way. Passion, savageness, raw emotion. We knew none of these. And I felt we were lacking because of it."

"So you developed a time machine to better study the past?"

I nodded and gave him the smile that at one time would have been reserved for an especially bright research assistant. "You're quick, Mr. Jones. I'll give you that. I did, indeed, develop a time machine to study the past. It took me years of research, years of experimentation. I could explain the process, but I doubt that you have enough time to hear it all. Or, if you'll pardon me, that you would even have the comprehension necessary for such an explanation. Suffice it to say, I succeeded in creating my machine. I studied the past with avid curiosity. Eventually, though, you can probably guess what happened."

"Watching wasn't enough?"

"Exactly." I beamed at him across the table. "I wanted to experience, wanted to jump right into the life I studied. One fateful morning I kissed my perfect wife and my perfect daughters good-bye and took the plunge."

I paused again, staring into my half-empty mug,

until Mr. Jones checked his watch and cleared his throat.

"I really must go soon," he insisted. "I'm already more than half an hour late."

"Trust me, Mr. Jones, you will be missing nothing of importance."

He laughed then. "And you know this, of course, because you are from the future."

"No, I know this because I know what this world is like. No one knows better than I."

"Because of your studies?" Jones lifted his mug to his lips.

"No, I know because I made this world what it is today."

He choked in mid-gulp, sputtered a bit, then swallowed hard. And began to laugh again. "Now, I suppose I'm to believe you're God?"

"Your belief doesn't matter, Mr. Jones. Shall I continue?"

"By all means. I want to know how this ends."

I finished the last of my beer. "As for me," I said softly, "I don't care about how the story ends, just that it does."

"Excuse me?"

"Nothing. Now, where was I? Oh, yes, I kissed my family good-bye and embarked on my first trip. The year I arrived was a deliberate choice—about forty years ago, your time. That decade was particularly rife with what I like to call critical patches. It was a time of change, a time of great experimentation. I felt I would fit right in with the society. Coincidentally or not, I ended up here. In this very establishment. It was here I had my very first taste of meat, alcohol, and the ambiance of a neighborhood bar. I became intoxicated with more than the beer. Still, on that trip, I did nothing but eat and drink."

A laugh behind me caused us both to jump. "He drank way too much, like now," Jim said, setting two more beers in front of us, "and then just walked off without paying his bill. Or so my dad used to tell me."

I gave Jones a sheepish grin. "I'd left the appropriate currency in my other pair of pants. Or something like that. I believe, though, that I was merely drunk on the life I'd found around me.

"It was inevitable that on my return to the future, I found myself dissatisfied. I craved the experiences I'd had in the past. Simple, basic experiences which I felt I deserved. Eating meals with my family became a chore. The healthy food I'd once loved became dry and tasteless, the energy drinks, dull, discussions with my wife and children became a duty rather than enjoyment. All I could think about were juicy burgers, the taste of an ice-cold beer, the ability to just sit and be silent or converse with others who had the same interests as I."

He looked around with a mock-surprised expression. "This is a time travelers' bar?"

"Now, Mr. Jones, please try to control your sarcastic tendencies. You know what I mean."

He shrugged. "Yeah, I do. Sorry. Go on."

"I would sneak away to the past every opportunity I'd get, merely to come here, to this bar. I would eat and drink and then return to the future, growing more discontented with every trip. My wife accused me of seeing another woman, my children felt that I was ignoring them. I grew careless at work and was threatened with termination. This establishment seemed to be the only place now or then that had people who really understood me, people who took me at face value, who allowed me to be the person that I was. I resented the time I spent in the future, began to hate my life there and long for the past, but I thought that my obligations precluded me from making more than small furtive trips.

"Until one night as I was sitting in the reading room of my perfect home, I had a revelation. One I felt was greater than the actual discovery of time travel. I could live both lives. Even with my invention, my thoughts had been foolishly limited by linear thinking. Ridiculous! Was not every second of time at my disposal? Weeks, months, years: they all belonged to me now. I could spend as much time as I wished and still return to the exact moment of departure.

" 'Yes!' I jumped up from my chair, startling my two daughters as they pored over their schoolwork. They stared at me with blank faces.

" 'Father?'

"I laughed. 'Nothing, Daughters, go back to your books. I must go to the lab.' "

"I brought nothing with me except a fairly large stack of currency appropriate to the times. I knew enough of future events to parlay this amount into a small fortune. And from then on I knew that the world belonged to me. I traveled, I talked, I ate and drank at every opportunity, meeting influential people I'd only read about, meeting seemingly unimportant people who would become the pivotal points of my future society. And then . . ."

My voice trailed off and I drained my beer.

"You got bored with it all?"

I gave a short laugh. "Not at all, Mr. Jones. Bored? How on Earth could I be bored? I lived like a king; I possessed everything I once dreamed of. Women flocked to me, and men as well. I owned mansions on both coasts and a castle or two in Europe, each fully stocked with the food and drink on which I thrived, each fully manned with a staff dedicated to my every need.

"I woke exhilarated every morning and went to sleep each night exhausted, but utterly pleased with the day's events. Now this, I thought, is truly Utopia. Full-blooded and meaningful, not thin and ethereal and lifeless like the life I'd left behind in the future."

"So what went wrong?"

I cocked an eyebrow at him. "You're an intelligent man, Mr. Jones. Surely you can figure it out."

He sat silent for a second, thinking. Then, "Aha! All of your interaction with the past began to affect the present."

I nodded. "And worse yet, it began to change the future. Suddenly, I no longer knew what was going to happen. The world became uncharted territory for me. I, the man who conquered time, had been trapped in a world that grew more and more incomprehensible with each passing day. I lost my fortune in disastrous stock ventures, saw each of my mansions sold off, one by one. The women abandoned me, the staff of dedicated employees went elsewhere. Gone was the exhilaration, the excitement. When I woke one morning, penniless and homeless, shivering in an alley, I knew that all I had left was the future I'd abandoned. Tail tucked between my legs, I returned."

Jim brought me another beer. I'd told this story so many times in here to so many different men, he knew exactly where I'd need the comfort. I drank, long gulps, like a drowning man gasping for air.

"And?" my companion prompted me. "And?"

I sighed. Drank. Sighed again. "And, Mr. Jones, there was no future. Not the one I'd left. No wife, no children, no perfect home, no perfect society.

"At first I thought that the machine had malfunctioned and returned me to an area of the past I had never visited. The streets were filled with rubble and trash and barely recognizable human remains. This could not be my time; gone were the trees and the broad expanses of grass. The sky hung, dark and sooty, over a landscape that felt right and wrong at the same time. Still, this place was of interest. I wondered when I had ended up.

I explored this new time. Words cannot express the horrors I witnessed there. Plagues, degenerative diseases, insanity. I held myself distant from it all, viewing it dispassionately, like the scientist I once was. For a time."

I stopped and looked him in the eye. "You see, I fought to hold onto the belief that this could not be my perfect future, fought to find the malfunction in the machine. But the evidence was there and could not be denied for long. A scrap of newspaper. A video report flashing on a screen. This, I realized, the enormity of the revelation stabbing in my gut, was my future. Our future.

"Wars had been fought while I'd celebrated in the past. Millions of people died in horrible ways while I was watching a baseball game and enjoying a beer."

I shook my head, wiping away a tear of rage and sadness. "Those sad people of the future. Sick, deformed, dying. They never knew what I had stolen from them. From their children. From the entire human race."

Giving a choked laugh, I grasped my mug. "Take all the tyrants of history, Mr. Jones, add them all up and multiply by the number of years we have occupied this Earth and still the total would not equal the enormous consequences of my actions. For what? And well you may ask." I picked up the mug, held it in the air. "For this!" I said and slammed it back down to the table, splashing beer over my hands. "And," I pointed to a tray of food being carried out to a waiting table, "for that sold out the future of the human race for nothing but a beer and a burger with the guys."

Jones stared at me, unsure whether to laugh or to cry. I knew exactly how he felt. It was all too absurd. Too ridiculous. And, unfortunately, too real.

"But," he said, his voice soft, "how does it end? What did you do?"

"I did the only thing possible. I brought myself back to the past, destroyed the machine so that no one else would be tempted to make the same mistakes that I did. Then I searched for a way to make things different.

"Every day, I tell this story to a different person, in the hopes that it will serve as a warning. In the hopes that they will believe enough to change the world."

"And?"

I shook my head. "Not yet, Mr. Jones, it hasn't happened yet. I fear it may never happen."

"So." He pushed back his chair, looked around, and motioned to the waiter. "I'll take the bill now, please." He paid and stood up, extending his hand. I shook it. *A good handshake,* I thought, *firm, strong.* He'd been a good choice. Maybe . . .

"It certainly has been interesting, Dr. Jones. Although I'm not sure I believe a single word, you promised a good story and you delivered."

"I'm glad you enjoyed it. It was an honor for me to tell it to you."

"So," he hesitated, "what will you do now?"

"What else can I do? I'll wait out my days here, telling the story over and over to anyone who'll listen, to anyone who'll pick up the tab." I winked at him. "They really are very good hamburgers."

He nodded and left.

Jim came over and cleared the empty beer mugs. I got up, went to the bathroom. All that beer. Afterward, I washed my hands and stared into the mirror. The tired eyes of an old man stared solidly back at me. "I'm not sure why you keep trying, old man, it never seems to do any good. So many of them and only one of you. This one, though, I have hopes for him. He felt right."

I nodded back at myself, pushed open the door and walked back down the hallway to the bar, pulling up a stool and staring vacantly at the widescreen TV.

"You okay?" Jim wiped the counter in front of me and set up another beer.

"Fine." When, of course, I was anything but.

"Was he the one?" Jim's voice contained a hint of laughter. He'd always been a skeptic, like his father before him.

"Maybe. We should know fairly soon. Or at least you will." I barked out a humorless laugh. "I probably won't know a thing."

"He seemed like a good man. What will happen to him?"

"To him?" I gave a small shrug. "Nothing, most likely. To his perception, there will be no difference. He was late for his meeting, we know that for a fact, and as a result, missed the chance to be introduced to Carol Smith. She will be on a plane now, going to Chicago, to meet her fiancé, the one she had once jilted for a man she just met. She will be happy and content, I hope, unaware of the life she missed. And Mr. Jones? I feel sure he will meet another woman who takes his fancy. They will marry and have children. Granted, not the same ones he might have had, if he had not taken time from his schedule to buy a crazy old coot a beer and a burger. And, after all, that was the point."

I stopped and sighed. "Things will not be quite the

same, you know. I can't promise that the future will be as bright as the one I lived in. But it will be different than the one I glimpsed and, more importantly, it will not be of my doing. Not entirely. Not like before."

I shook my head. "I did the best I could, Jim, to make amends. And I will never know if it sufficed. How could I? If I've done the job I set out to do, I won't have existed."

"What?" Jim looked over at me, alarmed. "What do you mean?"

"I liked Mr. Jones, didn't you? Although he is younger than I remember him, he is still a good man. With solid values. Grandma Carol always used to call him a solid man. Thank goodness Grandfather John always had a kind streak, a love for his fellow man, he was always the kind who would go out of his way to help another, even if all it meant was sharing a meal and listening. And he always did enjoy a good story."

I laughed at memories that had never existed, looking down at my hands resting on the counter. Were they not as solid as they had been before? Was it possible I could see the surface of the bar shimmering through the skin and bones?

"It's all true?" Jim joined me in looking at my hands. I could hear a trace of awe in his voice. I'd been telling the same story for years and he'd never believed until now.

"Yes, it's all true. I sold the birthright of man for a beer and some grilled meat between two pieces of roll."

"And now you're just going to fade away now? Because your grandfather never met your grandmother?"

"I certainly hope so. But before I go," I smiled at him, seeing my reflection waver slightly in the mirror, trying to calculate how much time I had left before present events caught up with the future and the past, rippling the world to a new configuration, "I think I'd like another hamburger, please. One for the road."

Jesus Freaks

by Jennifer Roberson

Jennifer Roberson has published twenty-two novels, fifteen of them in the fantasy genre. There she has been successful with the *Cheysuli* books and the *Sword-Dancer* series, which the author facetiously subtitles "Conan the Barbarian meets Gloris Steinem." The latter is told from the hero's point of view as his consciousness is raised—slowly, painfully, and sometimes under protest. She has also contributed short fiction to many anthologies, and has edited three herself. She lives in Northern Arizona with nine dogs, two cats, and an Anglo-Arab gelding.

"JESUS Christ!" she shrieked.

Ho-lee shit. It's not supposed to be like this.

She slapped one hand to her heart, buried somewhere beneath the synthetic—no, faux—tiguar coat she wore. "Jesus—" But she broke it off, scrabbled inside the glitterbag slung over a shoulder, and came up with something that looked like a cross between a handgun and one of those dollar-store phaser toys featured on an old '60s science fiction TV program Gabe had showed me. The original series.

Not a gun. Not a toy. Mike had called it a zap.

"Don't get zapped," he said. "It won't do any permanent damage, but the effects aren't pleasant."

I believed him. Mike knew about these things, since he worked in Medical. And besides, the shape I was in, I didn't feel much like dealing with anything that might scramble more of my circuits.

Meanwhile, this woman . . .

"Wait," I croaked, holding up a bare-palmed hand, my right one; the left was splayed against the ground to keep me upright. If I moved it, I'd fall over in a heap. *Okay, Gabe, where'd the scotty cough me up this time?*

She was just about the last thing I'd expected. Mike had done a pretty good job of bringing me up to speed from the last gig, but maybe Medical had passed me along too fast. I was wobbly from the scotty, which was frustratingly idiosyncratic, and distinctly disoriented. Everything I owned ached. Some of it was supposed to, to trigger the proper responses, but this time I felt like hell.

Except right now what bothered me most was the girl—no, the woman; I'd been briefed on old-style Women's Lib—gaping inelegantly.

I tried a harmless smile, but she wasn't buying. Shock altered to suspicion; she felt safe enough with the zap in her hand to challenge. "Where'd you come from, anyhow? You weren't here a minute ago—I checked my sweeper. I ain't stupid enough to walk into a dark alley without checking first. Light flashed green . . ." A quick toss of her head rid her eyes of the tangle of purple-dyed ringlets. "So how'd you get here?"

She wouldn't believe the truth; I didn't bother to explain. I just squinted painfully, trying to focus.

Gabe, you promised it would work the way it's supposed to. . . . The scotty had been debugged since the last time, but I've learned the hard way not to believe everything they tell you.

It was night, as usual. A dark alley. A dark, narrow, debris-strewn alley that reeked of Pop knew what (He is omniscient, after all; a knack I hadn't inherited), and most of it very dead, or the detritus of the dead. And it was wet, to top it off; not raining now, but the crumbling patchwork of decaying plasphalt was puddled with oily water. "'S okay—" I mumbled "—promise."

Wan moonlight illuminated her face. The skin underneath gold glitterstars and tiny CZs glued high on oblique cheekbones was a warm, smooth brown. A fine line of perspiration stippled her upper lip. The zap's nose—or mouth; or anal orifice—didn't waver. "Yeah. Right. I heard that before."

"Not from me." I gathered legs, aware of cramping, and thought about dragging myself upright with the wall's help. I could feel blood running down my side; more dribbled into my eyes. "Can I just—?"

An explosion of light cut me off. She squinted, thrust a hand skyward to block the flash, swore. "Those damn rockets—cops oughta shove 'em up their ass to see where their brains are, 'steada botherin' people like me . . . hey." The light died out slowly. She stretched her eyes wide to improve her dazzled vision. "They steal all your clothes? Or you just run like that?"

I wasn't running anywhere. My feet hurt too

much. "This is all they left me." It was all they ever left me.

She considered it. "That thing you're wearing, that diaper-thing . . . you look sorta like that guy I saw an old vid about once. Gander? Gondy? Something." She hitched a mostly-naked shoulder; meanwhile, the zap still stared me down. The light was nearly gone, leaving only an afterglare that painted the landscape of her face in angles of gray and black. CZs and glitterstars sparked fitfully. "Hey. You're bleeding."

"Shit happens." A lot. Too much. But that's the thing about a loop: you just keep replaying it. Mike and Gabe saw to it there were certain variations—so I wouldn't get bored, they explained—but the blood and pain was a constant. To keep me humble, they said.

A crock, if you ask me.

She'd dyed her ringlets purple, but the eyebrows were black. In bad light they formed a shelf across the shadowed sockets of dark eyes. "This ain't the way you usually run?"

I generally avoided running. Getting caught was part of the plan.

But she meant something else. "No."

"Hunh. Thought so." She edged a little closer, still gripping the zap. "Lemme see your wrist."

"My wrist?"

"Lemme see. Like this." She held up her left wrist, hand bent back, and displayed the mark. Looked like a brand, or a tattoo. I couldn't see the details. Just a blotch.

Dutifully I held up my left wrist and mimicked her, displaying the wound that was neither brand nor tattoo.

"Shit," she said, "they lazed you! Lazed out your number, didn't they? Those asshole Jesus Freaks . . ." She came forward, tucking the zap back into her glitterbag. Hostility toward me was banished, though she'd locked onto another target; well, I work fast when I have to. Not a lot of time. "All this shit about it being the Number of the Beast . . . they don't care lazing out the mark'll get us killed . . ." She bent, closing fingers around my arm. "Here. I'll give you a hand. We gotta stick together, people like you and me—who else'll give us a break?"

Everything was fuzzy. Medical *had* passed me along too fast—next time, I'd insist Mike give me extra shore leave before sending me out again.

"What else they do besides laze out your number?" she asked, levering me up with effort.

I grunted, bending over to catch my breath. "A few things here and there. They nailed me pretty good."

"Christ on the cross," she sighed. "They have their way, they'll run us all out of business. Asshole Jesus Freaks—whyn't they leave us alone? Some guy wants a good time, who're they to say no? Guy's got the card, he gets the ride . . . but those JFs think they can preach to everybody how we oughta live." She urged me forward. "Come on, it ain't too far. Can't stay out here—once a rocket goes up, the cops ain't far behind. And they'll bust you for no license. You don't want that—trust me! Ever since the chief got religious . . ." Her tone altered. "They do you pretty bad, huh?"

"I'll live." For a while. Long as it took, as always, before Mike and Gabe pulled me out.

"They laze your feet too, huh? Bastards. Lucky they didn't do your balls."

I swiped the back of my hand across my forehead, swabbing blood. "Yeah, well, some people might argue I don't have any, or was—am—too chicken to use them."

She grunted. "Don't put it past 'em, chico. Some of those JFs are pretty dedicated . . . they'd as soon laze off your balls as let you use 'em in Sin and Perversion." A pressure on my arm, turning me to the right. "Here. Up the stairs. Two flights; lifter's broken." She held her tattooed wrist up to a glowing sensor. "Don't know how much longer the Eye'll work—last week some JF fundie lazed off a guy's arm and lugged it to the nearest cribhouse, just to fool the Eye with the dead man's license number. Got the JF in, all right . . . luckily, they caught him before he could set off the bomb."

"Bomb?" I asked fuzzily.

"Yeah." The door slid open. She guided me through, made sure the door shut again behind us. "He said he was going to root out the nest of serpents."

"Shit," I muttered. "It's worse than we thought."

She aimed me toward the stairs. "Worse than who thought?"

I sagged elaborately. The decoy worked.

"Gotta climb," she muttered. "I can't carry you."

I wasn't that bad. Some of the disorientation was fading. But it wasn't wise to let her see it; not yet. I faked a few stumbles to make it look good, but did what I could to keep most of the weight off her. She was a tiny little thing.

"Here's the door." She flashed her wrist at another sensor, and the door ratcheted open. "Noisy SOB. Gotta get that fixed." Breathing heavily, she guided me through a small cube-shaped front room into the tinier cube beyond. "Think you can stay awake long enough for me to patch up those cuts?"

I mumbled an affirmative.

"Okay. Stay put. I'll clean you up, then let you crash. Chow's in the kitchen, through there . . . I'll be gone when you wake up."

I blinked owlishly, then collapsed onto the edge of the bed.

She grimaced a little, saying something about bloody prints on her floor and stains on her sheets, but she didn't seem to mean it. "Stay put." She was back before I could do much more than scrub blood out of one eye. She had a dish of water, cloth, a bottle of dark red liquid. "This is gonna hurt."

"Always does," I muttered.

She grimaced. "Happen a lot, huh? Those damn JFs . . ." She let it go, settling down to the task at hand. Carefully she sponged away blood, talking all the while. "They're like sharks, y'know. Once they smell the blood . . ." She peered again at my face, pushing matted hair aside. "Don't look like a knife did this."

"Didn't." The scent she wore was thick and

musky. She had used it liberally. Not that she needed it. Mike would say Pop had blessed her in the pheromone department.

"They crowned you good."

I grinned. "Yeah."

A purple ringlet dangled over one brown eye as she worked intently. She was hispania, or maybe afri/spania; I'd even heard the slang term afri/spic. "Don't look so bad, once the blood's wiped off—just some roundish scratches . . . they go all the way around?" I winced as she peeled hair from the back of my head. "This is weird . . ." She let the hair flop down, pushing her own tangled ringlets aside with the back of her tattooed wrist. "Then again, they were JFs . . . who's to say what they'll try on us, next? You were just damn lucky they left you in one piece . . ."

Well, very nearly. There were other cuts, and bruises; the stab wound in my side.

She dabbed the red liquid on each of the raw spots, grimacing as I hissed. "I know—stings like hell. I figure that means it's working . . . now, as for this cut in your side—" She broke it off, swearing. "Those damn jackals—they really tried to snuff you!"

I summoned a weak smile. "Too far from my heart to kill me."

"—deep," she murmured, touching gentle fingers to bruised flesh. "You need a Medic for this—but how in hell can we get one? No mark, no Medic . . . and those fucking Freaks'd be waiting outside the door for when the hospital kicked you out."

"So I guess that leaves you."

Residual anger blackened her eyes. "I'm no Medic—"

"You can patch me up."

"Have to." She hitched at the drooping CZ-studded strap of her top, hooking it absently over an otherwise bare shoulder. The matching stretchskirt she wore was nearly nonexistent, displaying lean legs sprinkled with CZs and glitterstars all the way down to steep gold heels. How do they walk in those things? "Just don't you go dying on me."

Dryly, I promised, "I'll do my best."

She flicked me a glance. Purple-dyed hair straggled down one cheek. "You think it's funny the JFs did this to you? You think it's funny they're doing this kinda thing to anyone who don't meet their standards?"

"No."

It mollified her, though her eyes still flashed. "They're screwing up everything, those Freaks. Tellin' people how to live, what to read, what to watch on the vid-plate . . ." But she let it go, kneeling to get a closer look at the stab wound. Then, chewing her tongue, she pressed the red-soaked cloth against my side. "Cuss all you want."

But I've never been a man for taking names in vain. Pop taught me manners. "What's your name?" I figured it would take my mind off the sting.

"Ria," she murmured, holding the pad still even as flesh twitched.

It hurt— "—what do you do, Ria?"

She snorted. "Whaddaya think, chico? You know that part of town."

"Actually, no."

She flashed me a glance under knitted brows. "Maybe you don't." A one-shouldered shrug freed the strap to droop again. "The JFs would call me the Whore of Babylon. Me, I call it a job." She pressed the cloth more firmly against my side. "Hold that. I'll get some tape and gauze, try to make up some butterflies, it probably needs stitching, but I never was Suzy Homemaker—you'll have to take what I got."

I wondered how long it had taken her to cultivate the vulgarity of her manner, her dress; the cheapness of her speech. She hadn't been born this way. Nobody was. Pop had been plain: people make themselves.

She went off to get supplies while I applied pressure to the wound in my side. I wanted to tell her it didn't really matter, that I wouldn't die from it, but one thing you can't do in this job is tell the truth, the whole truth, and nothing but the truth—unless you have to. I'd probably have to sooner rather than later, but to someone other than Ria.

She bandaged me, taped me, then dug jockeys, jeans, and a chambray shirt out of a closet.

"Brother's?" I asked dryly.

She snapped gum, grinning as she turned around. "You're cute, you know? Real wise guy, aren't ya?"

"Let he who is without sin . . ." I shrugged. "I just figure I shouldn't jump to conclusions."

"Why not? Everybody else does." She slanted me a bright glance, tossing ringlets out of her eyes. "When they ain't jumping me."

"Cute," I said, "real cute. Anybody ever tell you that?"

"Alla time." She dumped the clothes onto the bed. "I had a boyfriend once. A real boyfriend, not a baptist."

I blinked. "Baptist?"

"You know. A john."

I laughed, then caught my breath as my side protested. "Pretty good, Ria."

"I'm better than pretty good, chico . . . I'm damn fine." She cocked a hip and perched a hand upon it, baring the smooth length of her dusky throat. "Finer than you've ever known."

I laughed again, ruefully. "Without a doubt."

"So look, I gotta go out—gotta go to work, you know? So crash, eat—'cator's in the kitchen—shower . . . the vid-plate's in the other room, disks on the shelf." She shrugged. "Whatever you need."

"You seem pretty sure I'm harmless."

"Ain't you?" She snapped gum again. "I seen what the JFs done to you, chico—it takes a lot outta you . . ." She displayed her tattoo. "Besides, with no number, Dios wouldn't let you out of here if you trashed the place and tried to run."

I stared. "Dios?"

"Dios. God. Big Sister." She jerked a thumb toward the other room. "Mon-i-tor. By the door."

"Ah."

"I won't be back tonight; that is, if some baptist gets lucky."

"A Baptist might."

"Small 'b,'" she elucidated. "Capital 'B' means trouble."

"JF?"

"Most of 'em. 'Course now they've split into so many bits'n pieces it's hard to keep 'em all straight: Southern, Northern, Mason-Dixon, Manhattan . . ." Ria yanked up the glittering strap. "Where you been, you don't know this? The White House? Or did they laze your brain, too, damn 'em; I wouldn't be surprised."

It was far too easy. "I am a stranger in a strange land."

"Yeah. Ain't we all, with the JFs tryin' to run things." She picked up her glitterbag and threaded an arm through the strap. "Sleep tight." She flashed a grin. "Dream of me."

"Would—Dios—let me out of here if I needed to go somewhere?"

"Sure, so long's you don't have anything of mine stuffed into your pockets. Everything's chipped."

"What about these clothes?"

"Not mine, chico; different code. Dios won't squawk."

"Ah."

She frowned. "But where would you go?"

"Church."

"Church!" The gum nearly fell out of her neon-painted mouth. "Jesus Christ, you mean to slam-dance right in and get in somebody's face over what they did to you?"

I shrugged. "I usually turn the other cheek. Depending."

"Churches on every corner, mostly. Can't miss 'em. Mickey C's."

"What?"

"Mickey C's. MacChurch. They're everywhere." She scowled. "You after a special flavor?"

I grinned. "I'd like to go to the john."

She got it. "Huh." Gum popped in her mouth. "I'd have said you looked more Jewish."

"Don't judge a disk by its color."

"Never." Ria grinned. "But I can't pass up the purple ones." She flicked a ringlet dangling against a bare shoulder. "You like purple, chico grande?"

I jabbed a chin in the direction of the other room. "Dios doesn't discriminate, does—he? She? It?"

"It's pronouced shee-it." Beneath the glitterstars and CZs, her skin glowed dusky-rose. Well, I had pheromones, too. "Get it?"

"Hah," I said dutifully. "Yes, I like purple . . . I like all colors, all shapes, all sizes. It's how I'm programmed."

She froze. "You're not—? Christ, don't tell me you're a fucking cyboy. Damn it, chico . . ." Her eyes were huge. "Are you?"

"Would it matter? Are we not all one in the Eye of Dios?"

"Damn you—"

"Now, now. That's not polite. What if it stuck?"

"What if what stuck?"

"Damnation."

"Can't."

"How do you know?"

"Because if you're damned, you go to hell. And there ain't none."

"How do you know?"

"'Cause if there was one, I'd be in it. So would a lot of us. The Jesus Freaks would see to that; they damn us alla time." She scratched carefully at her cheek, deftly avoiding glitterstars and CZs. "You'd be there, too, I guess."

"Not a chance."

Ria laughed, good humor restored. "Snowball's?"

I pondered it. "If there is no hell, a snowball would not be at risk."

Ria squinted. "Kinda like the 'if a tree falls' question, ain't it?"

"Kinda."

"Well, they ain't solved that one yet either . . . and likely they never will. JFs don't much care for philosophy. They figure all the questions are answered. All you gotta do is look 'em up in that damn Book—" She waved at me violently. "Yeah, yeah, I know—we're back to hell already."

"Some, yes," I agreed mildly. "But the Doghouse isn't all that bad."

"Doghouse?"

It was my turn to grin. "Dog spelled backward . . ."

"Christ." She waved again, cutting me off. "I give up. I'm millering."

"Millering?"

"I'm outta here. Later." She was gone only briefly, then poked her head back around the doorjamb. Her expression was impish as she aimed a finger toward the monitor. "Vaya con Dios."

"Hey."

She turned back. "Yeah?"

"What's 'Ria' short for?"

She shrugged. "Old hispania name. A real mouthful, traditional-like, which I'm not. I cut it to Maria, then Ria." Her mouth twisted. "Something different."

"Ah." *Okay, Gabe. I owe you.* "Thanks for cleaning me up."

"Sure, no problemo." She hesitated. "If you go out . . . well, you comin' back here tonight?"

"Won't you be—busy?"

"Not here. This ain't my crib; it's home." Ria arched an eyebrow. "I let the baptist buy a cube."

"Then maybe I'll be back, if it's okay."

Something fizzed in her eyes. "I'll reprog Dios to let you in on your voiceprint. It's on file now. Just say your name at the door." She paused. "What is your name?"

Same as always. "J.C. Carpenter." I picked up the jeans. "Thanks again. I owe you."

Maria Magdalena shrugged. "So St. Peter can punch my ticket at the pearlies."

I waited until she was gone. Triggered the link. *Pete?*

Yeah?

She in?

Whaddaya think, chico grande?

I grinned. *Thanks, Pete.*

No problemo.

* * *

I slept off the scotty-lag overnight, showered, repatched my side, ate replicated bread and olives washed down with goat's milk. Ria wasn't home yet; some baptist had gotten lucky. I had Dios let me out, then went hunting the first Mickey C's I could find. It wasn't difficult; as Ria'd said, there was one on every corner. All I had to do was look for the golden crosses.

The vid-plate in the door glowed cool blue. White Scripture scrolled across it continuously in a multiplicity of languages; indeed, Pop's kids had been exceedingly fruitful. It was a real task to play shepherd now; too many far-flung sheep bleating in tongues.

"Yo," I said. "Dios?"

The screen blanked. No multilined Scripture, save for a single continuous crawl across the bottom, like a sports score. In hispania. Password time. I sighed. "Repent ye sinner?"

The crawl shifted mid-word to English.

New file. Try sporting events. "John 3:16?"

Nada.

"What's the deal?" I asked. "Little hard to minister to the masses if they can't get in the front door, don't you think?"

The crawl continued.

Scotty-lag's gone. Time to get into the swing of things and do the job I came for. I thought about Ria's instructions concerning Dios. "Voiceprint," I said. "Jesus Christ."

The screen blanked entirely. Then a muted, tasteful chime sounded from the invisible speaker, followed immediately by an equally muted, tasteful voice. "Praise His name, for only through the Son of God shall you discover Him."

Loosely translated from the original. "Praise the Lord," I murmured obediently, in fatuous self-flattery. The door hissed aside and tucked itself away into hidden pockets. I grinned irreverently. "All things shall come to he who believes."

As I crossed the threshold, the door whispered closed behind me. A man waited for me on the other side, hands folded together just below his waist. He wore a simple but well-tailored navy suit, a quiet synthsilk tie in muted burgundy-on-cream, a single modest ring, and a professional smile. "How may we serve you, my son?"

"Cut the crap," I said. "You don't look a thing like my Father, and you don't have the faintest idea how to serve Him. Just take me to the jerk who runs this joint."

His smile didn't slip; he was probably used to abuse. "This is a house of worship," he said quietly. "We seek no confrontation—"

"You seek confrontation all the time, my man. That's what videvangelists are all about: preaching the Word to he who doesn't give a rat's ass where he's going when he's dead." I got up into his face. "Does that compute?"

His mouth compressed only faintly. Blue eyes reflected no hostility, only a pinched kind of contempt. "Reverend Guy is very busy. Do you have an appointment?"

"He claims to know me very well," I told him. "Matter of fact, I hear he invokes my name a lot."

His face closed up. His mouth now was little more than a retentive seam. "I'm sorry—"

"So's Pop. He's mad as—well . . . let's just say he's not going to take it anymore." I flicked a nonexistent speck of dust off his immaculate lapel. "How about it? Do you take me to the reverend like a regular stand-up sort of guy, or do I perform a miracle and walk right through a wall?"

"I beg your pardon, sir—"

"Never mind." I stepped right by him and stared hard at the blank wall. "No voiceprint. No retinal scan. How about this?" I pressed the inside of my wrist against the smooth surface. The wall was Red Sea to my Moses and slid apart into pockets, displaying a handsomely appointed office lush with leather and living plants, not synthsilk. A massive desk stood paramount; on the faux brick wall behind it glowed three golden crosses. The office was empty, but I had no doubt some kind of Dios watched from somewhere.

"Sir!" Navy Suit's face was white. His hands trembled minutely. "Why didn't you say you had been blessed? You had only to tell me!"

I drew a blank. Gabe does the best he can, but he doesn't know everything—and Pop's too busy a lot of the time to explain the mysteries. "Blessed?"

His fingers touched the half inch of snowy cuff showing at his wrist. A gold cufflink glinted. "The Stigmata. So few of us have been privileged . . ."

"Oh." The light went on. "You mean I've been preapproved?"

"Sir." His expression was severe without quite bordering on blatant rudeness; I no longer fit into any of his preconceived slots, and it made him nervous. He wanted to throw me out, but no longer knew if he had the authority. "Forgive me if I don't respond to your levity, but we take matters of religion very seriously."

"You're forgiven . . ." Such a small matter when you know the trick. "Now, define 'religion.' "

He stared.

"Well?"

"Sir, there are many definitions."

"Tell me yours."

He was nonplussed, but did his best. Unctuously he began, "Religion is a system of belief . . . a code of ethics, a philosophy—"

I knew Mike and Gabe were listening through the link. They get a kick out of semantics. *Okay, guys, here we go.* "Philosophy? But I thought you shunned philosophers because they ask the kinds of questions that the Book doesn't answer—the Book being, I'm assuming, the Bible." He nodded; what other Book could there be? "So. How come you worship something you abhor?"

I was getting to him. "But we don't—"

"But if religion—in your own words—is a system for belief, a code of ethics—quantified, I presume, according to the dictates of a quorum—and yet is also a philosophy, how then can you deny that you worship that which you abhor?"

He breathed rapidly. He shot pristine cuffs once again with trembling fingers. "Sir—I think you should speak with Reverend Guy."

About time I got some service around here. "Please."

He gestured toward the office. "Through there. He will be with you in a moment."

"Thank you."

He stepped back hastily. The door/wall whispered closed between us, leaving me alone in the office.

Well, maybe not entirely alone. Yet another door slid open. "Number Three," I muttered as a man stepped through.

He moved purposefully to a position that put the desk between us, but he did not sit. "I'm Reverend Guy. How may I be of service?" Just the faintest suggestion of a drawl. Southern, then, or Mason-Dixon, according to Ria's labels. He wore an exquisitely tailored suit of charcoal-gray synthsilk, cream shirt, and a hand-painted, multihued tie. His white hair was thick and vigorous, brushed into stylish quiescence and lightly moussed. Good teeth—maybe his own; probably recapped—good smile. Sincere. Grooming was immaculate, and the diamond in the gold pinky ring was of tastefully moderate size.

"Tell me something," I said. "Is it a requirement for videvangelists to have big hair? I've never yet seen a bald Bakkerite."

His smile froze. Sincerity altered to wary suspicion. "Bakkerite?"

"Don't know the term?"

Suspicion was answered. His manner now was clipped, almost curt; he'd be asking his frontman how in the world I'd gained admittance. "Of course I know the term. It is an insult. We do not condone its use."

"Then how about Swaggart-stick?"

His nostrils pinched. "I think perhaps you should leave. James made a mistake in admitting you."

"James didn't have much choice." I lifted my right wrist and flashed him the wound. Then the left one. "He really had no choice—but then, he didn't know that. Now you do."

He didn't bat an eyelash. "Stigmata can be falsified."

"I imagine a Bakkerite would know that."

"If you expect me to accept that at face value—"

"Do you doubt the Lord, Reverend Guy?"

"I do not doubt that Jesus Christ will return one day—"

"He's heee-ere."

"—to relieve the world of its suffering—"

"And of those who mean to lead it astray. Even the elect. Remember your Revelations?" I placed my palms flat against the glossy surface of his desk and leaned on braced arms. "Depending on which version of the Bible you use . . . Pop only knows who's reinterpreted the latest translation for the hundredth-thousandth time." I turned and hitched one buttock up on the edge of his desk, swinging a bare foot idly. "You ever think about that? Translation? Interpretation?"

Reverend Guy was silent.

"Translation isn't an exact science, you know. Think about it. Translation has a huge margin for error; it has to, because it's solely dependent upon the skill and knowledge of the translator. And no matter how good your translator might be, he's human. He's mortal. He is flawed." I paused. He still maintained a silence bristling with outrage. "And when the text he's working with is a translation of a translation of a—well, you get my drift." I shrugged. "Your Book was written in a whole raft of languages long dead. It's a regular Babel, Reverend . . . and I find it unlikely—no, impossible—that any man on Earth, no matter how erudite, could literally translate what a whole series of men—no women, just men—with very different agendas wrote nearly twenty-two centuries ago."

Reverend Guy sat down with rigid grace. His expression had gotten stuck in I-have-to-listen-because-I-have-no-choice-but-I-don't-believe-a-word-of-it mode. Time for hardball. "Did you know King James was bisexual?"

The flesh of his throat darkened perceptibly. Slowly the wave of color crept up into his face. "We no longer use that version."

"Because you discovered the truth. Some historian 'outed' the king."

He worked hard to maintain an even tone. "There have been many versions since the King James—"

"The copyists who worked from bootleg translations—remember, back in James' time not many were permitted to own a printed Bible; maybe a means to maintain control?—were nothing but hired labor.

They worked for good old King Jim, who was the one who determined what stayed in, and what got thrown out." I shrugged. "The 'divine right of kings.' Except he wasn't. Divine. Neither are you."

He peeled his lips apart. "Why have you come?"

"Haven't you read your Bible lately?"

His face quivered. "Which version?"

I laughed. "Very good. But then most Bakkerites are pretty quick on their feet, or they'd all go to prison." I displayed my teeth; I'd had good dentistry, too. "I have come to set things to rights."

Congestion drained away. He was dead white and coldly furious. "If that is true—if for the sake of argument I accept your presumption—"

"Devil's advocate?"

"—and agree that you are whom you claim you are, why do you come to the house of God? WE do not need to be set to rights! THEY require it!"

"They?"

"Out there, in the streets." He gesticulated. "Everywhere. Sin runs rampant; have you not seen it? In our cyberbooks, on vid-plate, on the disks, in art, photography—even in our software! My dear Lord—"

"Thank you."

"—everywhere we walk we are accosted by sin! Whores ply the streets, children are suborned—"

"Rock music?"

"He comes in a bewildering array of guises: in art, in games—

"Who does?"

"The Antichrist."

"Oh. Him. Or—her." I grinned at his thunderstruck expression. "It is sexist to believe the Antichrist must be male."

"Sexism! Sexism! Do you see?" He rose up from his chair. "Women have shunned their true roles as helpmeets to put on the raiment of men—"

"Fig leaves were unisex."

Reverend Guy trembled with righteous indignation. "I will have you taken from this place. This is a house of God—"

"This is your house. You built it with the money you scammed out of innocents hoping to purchase peace." I shook my head. "Pop's never been here. There isn't room for Him here."

He was completely nonplussed. "Room?"

"Egos." I paused. "He's got one, you know. He'd have to. Not everyone can pull off Creation in only seven days."

"Six," he corrected mechanically. "On the seventh day he rested."

"Seven. He cheated. He forgot the crossopterygian. Had to make it from scratch and drop it in the soup."

He blinked twice. "Soup?"

"Primordial." Now the poor soul was really confused; being a chip-carrying Creationist, he'd neglected his science studies. "Remember what I said about interpretation? Well, Pop never meant everyone to assume he created man as man . . . I mean, with two legs, arms, eyes, ears, a nose, beer belly and repair-man butt. Let's face it, Adam and Eve weren't apes—"

His turn. "Thank you."

"—they were fish. Sort of. Pre-fish, maybe; it's a hard concept to get a handle on."

"This is outrageous." But he wasn't very convincing. By now he was fascinated, if still locked in denial.

"The truth is stranger than fiction," I agreed. "But truth is truth."

"I know the law." He drew himself up. "To be true, truth must be provably true in a court of law."

"So you want proof." I pointed toward a carafe sitting on his credenza. "Is that water?"

He didn't look. "Yes."

"Try again." I shrugged. "White Zin went out in the '80s. I made it a cab-shiraz. Arizona grapes, with California gone bye-bye."

He looked, then twitched his head back to me. His eyes now were like marbles, hard and cold and steely. "You have hacked the church computer and put a virus in the replicator software. You'll go to prison for this."

"Afraid I might find the proof I need to bring you up on charges?" I shook my head. "Not worth the effort. You'll answer to a Higher Authority."

"You are a clever man, but you cannot fool me."

"Never con a con man."

His right hand hovered near the front of his desk; computer controls, of course. "This has gone far enough. I shall have church security escort you off the premises."

"You want proof? I'll give you proof." I chewed

my bottom lip. "Do you watch old shows in the vid-plate?"

It was so inconsequential a question he answered immediately and without prevarication. "Of course. Old shows were cleaner, more wholesome."

"Not that old. No—there was a show on fifty years or so ago about this guy who went bopping around in time. Nice guy, with a holographic pal. Quantum something. Quantum Hop."

"Leap." Then he flushed, as if embarrassed to admit he knew the show.

"Hop, leap; who's to know?" I shrugged. "But they had this waiting room for the people who got taken out of their bodies when this guy hopped—leaped—in."

Reverend Guy stared. "What does this have to do with blasphemy?"

"Not much. I'm just trying to prepare you for the scotty."

"Scotty?"

I keyed the link. *Gabe?*

Here.

Ready for this guy?

Any time.

I smiled at him. "Vaya con Dios. I'll be waiting for you."

Gabe didn't keep the good reverend long. He never does. It's against the House rules to play too many body- or head-games; the scotty's a rough ride even for me. But by the time Reverend Guy was back, I'd settled into his chair with my feet up on his desk, leaving smudged heelprints all over the polished surface.

He wobbled a little on materialization, but steadied himself with a hand pressed against the front of the desk. I smiled. "We call it the Second Going, euphemistically speaking. Kind of appropriate, though."

Reverend Guy shuddered. "My God—"

"Everybody's." I drank wine, decided to go for a favorite instead and altered it to Scotch. Single malt, in fact, quite old, with nice peaty flavor that lovingly bathed my tongue—but never mind that. " 'A rose by any other name . . .' " I pointed to the chairs set discreetly aside for visitors. "Have a seat. Scotch? Or wine. Beer?"

"Nothing." He groped for the chair, pulled it up, collapsed into it. His mouth worked a few seconds before a voice emerged. "Why . . . why . . ."

"Somebody once told me that if you posed that question to a computer, you'd knock it into a loop and get it stuck there. My feeling was, if I were that computer, I'd come back with 'Because.' " I grinned. "Or 'Why ask why?' "

He swallowed heavily and tried again. "Why here?"

"My here isn't always here," I said. "Sometime's it's there. Or somewhere else entirely."

"I don't understand."

"It's not a Second Coming, Reverend. It's more like a twelfth, a twenty-first, a fifty-third . . . shoot, I've lost count. I just go where I'm needed."

"—Go?"

"Hop. Leap. Scotty. I'm just the meat, not the mind. I leave that stuff to Gabe and Mike."

"I met—" he paused; it was difficult. "—Gabe."

I grinned. "Gabe's a good guy. Got a great sense of humor."

"Gabriel."

"We're pretty informal." I sat up, pulling my feet off his desk. "What's this I hear about some nut trying to bomb a whorehouse?"

He reddened. "They are abominations."

"Bombs are, yes."

"Whores."

"They're women making a living. And all it is, really, is the law of supply and demand . . . if you want it to end, why not look at the men who seek out such carnal traffic?"

"The whores lure them."

"In some cases, I suppose. But I figure it's usually a guy looking for a good time. He'll take what he can get."

He swallowed visibly. "You condone prostitution?"

"It's the second oldest profession, Reverend. That goes a loooooong way back."

He was less condescending now—the scotty is pretty humbling all on its own, and then there's Gabe—but remained intransigent on the subject of women. "It should not be permitted."

"Who says?"

"The Bible says—"

"Which version? Whose translation? Good ol' King James?" I grinned as he winced. "Only one man can say what is and is not permitted—and I don't notice the streets are gridlocked due to a massive influx of salt pillars."

"A low-sodium diet is better for you."

I blinked. "Is that a joke? Did you make a joke?"

He passed a hand over his face. "This is—quite unbelievable."

"I hear they call you Jesus Freaks."

Silence. But confirmation pinched his eyes.

"Not much better than Bakkerite or Swaggartstick, is it? Socks you right in the gut, doesn't it?"

"We are trying to make the world a better place."

"By trying to force the world to live by your rules?"

"We live our lives according to the Word of God."

Good humor evaporated; well, I'm not perfect. Just forgiven. "You live your lives according to the will of whatever man—or woman—is articulate, imaginative, smart, and charismatic enough to assume the mantle of leadership."

Two livid spots of color burned high on his cheeks. "You could say that very thing about Jesus Christ himself. Yourself."

I applauded softly. "Bravo. So is the man deafened by his own tumult eventually restored."

His color faded again as he acknowledged my observation. "But—I—" He plucked his glossy synthsilk handkerchief from his breast pocket and blotted his upper lip. "I have questioned—"

"You're supposed to question. Pop gave you a brain."

"But . . ." He blinked three times in rapid succession. "I must never question. We must follow the Word of God."

"Or the word of Reverend Guy."

Desperation was setting in. "I am an instrument of my God!"

"Really? You're going to stick to that after where you've just been?"

His face matched his suit. "You cannot expect me to renounce my faith—"

"Ah. Faith. That's a different story. Faith is a whole different kettle of fish."

"Crossopterygians?"

I applauded again; he really was loosening up. That's half the battle; men and women like this guy are so anal-retentive. "Faith and religion are not synonymous. In fact, I view them as oxymorons."

"I don't understand."

"Religion is a ritual. People trust ritual. It's easy. It keeps them from having to think for themselves." I shrugged. "Smoke and mirrors. Mumbo jumbo. Sleight of hand. Dog-and-pony show. Just a few definitions of organized religion."

"But—faith is—"

"—entirely different. Faith is belief. Faith is a pure and unquestioning belief in God . . . whatever his Name or Guise might be. Pop likes masquerades." I studied my Scotch. "Ritual is power. The individual who conducts the ritual is the instrument of that power. If he—or she—is clever enough, the people forget the instrument is nothing more than that, and begin to put their faith in the human vessel instead of in the—entity—for whom the ritual is performed." I looked through the glass and saw his face warped by curvature. "You and people like you are fucking up the world."

He recoiled. "I will not have that word spoken in the house of God."

"He invented it."

"It is filth."

"It's ugly. It's meant to be. It's meant to shock. But it's overused, and now it means nothing except to those people who are truly offended." I wasn't smiling now. "You offend me. You are abomination. In the name of my Father—in my name!—you try to remake the world and everyone in it by dictating how they should live." I had his full attention now. "There are Christians in the world who believe as strongly, but in their own quiet way. These poor people are getting tarred by the same brush. Some of them are hesitant to admit they were born again because you've made it a dirty word." I shook my head. "Face it, Reverend—you and JFs like you are giving the rest of us a bad name."

"But you dictate how people should live! The Bible—"

"—is a book. Do you believe everything you read?"

He was trembling again. He was a con man, perhaps, but the most dangerous kind; he truly believed what he was doing was for the common good. He lived the party line. "I must believe. I must put my trust in God."

"It's a great how-to manual," I said quietly; no more need for bombast or fancy semantics. "There's a lot of good stuff in there. But it's kind of like an instruction booklet in a foreign language: you can make out enough of the words to get the gist of it, but there's always a part left over." I smiled and set down the glass. "Pop quit on you once. He hit the delete key, except for one small file called Noah. He swore never to do it again. But things were getting more and more screwed up . . . so he sent me. Again. And again. As many times as it takes."

"Different times?"

"Different times, different places, different races. I've got a trunkful of passports."

"Why . . ." His feet were flat on the floor. He smoothed damp palms down his trousered thighs. "Why come to me? Why not to the president?"

"Presidents come and go. Bakkerites usually have greater longevity." I stood up. "It only takes one man. One woman. That's all."

He was alarmed. "There is too much to do . . . one man couldn't possibly do it all!"

"I only had thirty-three years," I reminded him. "And we didn't have vid-plates, or the 'net, or any of the conveniences you take for granted. All I had was myself, and a certain knack for the language." I grinned. "You know—the parables."

He stared back in incomprehension.

I elucidated. "Communication is a two-way street. People hear, and people learn, if the language—if the imagery—jibes with their frame of reference. You know. Fiery chariots, the great red dragon with ten horns and seven heads, and all like that; it's easy to remember. Vivid imagery is the best way to plant an idea."

He nodded slowly. "I think—I think I'm beginning to understand."

"Look," I said, "let the kids play their fantasy games. Let the people read their cyberbooks, sing their songs, paint what comes into their heads. They're telling stories . . . painting parables . . . exploring the greatest gift Pop ever gave to mankind." I tapped my head. "Imagination. Creativity. The people of this country have fought long and hard for the freedom to simply be. Don't strip that away from them."

His hands were trembling. "I meant well."

"You all mean well. All you fundie Jesus Freaks."

He had the grace to wince. "I'm sorry."

"You've told me. Now tell the guy in the navy suit. Tell your congregation. Post it on the vid-plate on your door. Get it out on the nets."

"They won't listen."

"One day at a time, chico."

He swallowed heavily. "What happens now?"

"To me? I leave. I've got two days, still—it's always three days until they scotty me out of wherever I am. Stuck in the loop, I guess you'd say."

His handkerchief was crumpled. He dried his hands, then stuffed it into a trouser pocket as he rose. "Tomorrow is Sunday. Will you come to the service?"

"We'll be there."

"We? Oh—you mean Gabe."

"No. Pretty little chica name of Ria."

It shocked him. "You're with a woman?"

"Don't worry," I said, "it's strictly platonic." I walked around his desk and clapped him on the shoulder. "Keep the faith, guy. I'm millering."

On the street again I blinked into brilliant sunshine. One of Pop's best days.

I keyed the link. *Gabe?*

Yeah?

A day or two extra?

You know the rules, J.C. Just two.

She's a great girl, Gabe.

She is every time, J.C. And every time the answer's the same.

Yeah. I know. I glanced back at the vid-plate. The Scriptures were gone, replaced with a notice that said the screen was temporarily out of service and would be reprogrammed soon. *Gabe?*

Still here, J.C.

Tell Pop I think it'll work.

I think He knows, J.C.

Millering, I said. Gabe shut down the link.